MISSION OF DESIRE

Visit us at www.boldstrokesbooks.com

MISSION
OF DESIRE

by
Terri Richards

2012

ISBN 13: 978-1-60282-662-5

This Trade Paperback Original Is Published By
Bold Strokes Books, Inc.
P.O. Box 249
Valley Falls, NY 12185

First Edition: May 2012

Credits
Editor: Greg Herren and Stacia Seaman
Production Design: Stacia Seaman
Cover Design by Sheri (graphicartist2020@hotmail.com)

Acknowledgments

Thank you, Radclyffe, for the opportunity to become a member of the BSB family.

Thank you, Greg Herren, for your gentle approach to editing and lending your incredible talents to this story.

And much appreciation to Sheri, who created the cover artwork. You read my mind.

For Coram, circa 1986

CHAPTER ONE

Nicole glanced at her watch again. Was this bus ever going to move? According to the schedule posted outside the ticket office, they were supposed to have left Nairobi at noon. The departure time was also boldly stamped in English, as well as several other exotic languages on her ticket, but it didn't appear that anyone from the bus company was the least bit concerned about their delay.

She cast a weary gaze out one of the cracked windows. Two men wearing blue vests emblazoned with the company's bright red logo playfully kicked a soccer ball back and forth, laughing. Though she'd been sitting here for over an hour breathing in hot, stale air that reeked of unwashed bodies, she was reluctant to search out another means of transport. She'd read one too many articles on the Internet about the dangers of wandering alone in Kenya's capital. Even in broad daylight, the city's smoggy, gridlocked streets were said to be teeming with savvy pickpockets and con men. Becoming a statistic wasn't part of her travel plans.

She lowered her head onto the back of the torn vinyl seat, fanning her face with an advertisement for an expedition into the Serengeti, and smiled. Despite the heat, the funky smells, and severe case of jet lag, Nicole had never felt more alive. For the first time in her twenty-two years, she was traveling beyond the boundaries set by her mother years ago.

Finally.

She could still hear her mother's emotional outburst when she'd announced her plans to volunteer as a teacher in Kenya over the summer.

"Oh, Nicole, must you try my sanity so?" her mother had moaned, wringing her hands and shaking her graying head. "Have you even looked at yourself lately? A pretty young American girl traveling all alone is a prime target for kidnapping and who knows what! Like it or not, you can't blend into the background like you used to anymore. And why of all the places in the world—Africa? Who do you think are, Angelina Jolie?"

"I'm not planning on adopting any kids while I'm there, Mom," she'd responded to her mother's melodrama with restraint. "I'm just going to go teach a few and come home. *Alone*," she'd added.

When one of her language professors informed her she could earn credits toward her graduate degree if she taught English over the summer to children in a developing country, she knew the time had come to sate her long-suppressed wanderlust. Not only could she use the experience as research for her graduate thesis, the program provided her with the perfect excuse to escape from her monotonous life in Maryland for six splendid weeks.

"That part of the world is uncivilized and barbaric." Her mother had waved her hand dismissively, repeating the clichéd query she always posed whenever Nicole dared entertain the idea of venturing somewhere she didn't approve, as if the simple inquiry was all the rationale needed to end the discussion immediately: "Do you remember what happened to your father?"

Nicole banished those memories before they could even take shape inside her head. She was leaving that baggage back in America. This was a new chapter in her life.

After taking a long swig from the bottle of water she'd purchased outside of customs, she reached for her canvas bag and pulled out the itinerary the nonprofit teaching organization had e-mailed her last week. A wave of renewed excitement trickled down along the insides of her belly. She'd be staying overnight at a hostel in the city of Nanyuki, just north of the equator. After breakfast, each volunteer would be assigned a village where they would spend the next six weeks teaching tribal orphans basic English grammar and vocabulary.

"Kuna mtu hapa?"

A big, black shape stood in the aisle, its stance expectant, almost threatening.

"Kuna mtu hapa?" the soft voice repeated in what Nicole guessed must be Swahili. It was a language she couldn't speak. Besides English, she'd only studied French and Arabic. Whether or not she would actually be understood in either language in the real world remained to be seen. There was a big difference between conjugating verbs in front of a class of twenty-year-olds from the suburbs and actually talking to someone in their native language.

She looked up. The wide shapeless form was completely cloaked in an enveloping black burka. She tried to make out the image of a face through the dark, gauzy shroud, but the woman was now looking down, her demeanor suddenly deferential.

Nicole was aghast.

Of course she'd seen pictures of women dressed in the concealing garment in the news and in textbooks, but seeing someone actually wearing the oppressive robe in person was even more disturbing. Sadly, it reminded Nicole how females were still viewed in some religious cultures. If a woman revealed her face, or simply exposed her arms, she could be accused of being a seductress. And if convicted, she faced the possibility of being stoned to death.

"She want to know if she can sit with you!" an old man with skin the color of warm caramel snapped impatiently from across the aisle, jolting Nicole from her thoughts. "Stupid Western boy!" he added under his breath.

Boy? Chagrined, Nicole looked down and assessed her own version of a burka while sliding over to make room for the religious woman's girth.

Perhaps it had been all of her mother's chiding admonishments about traveling alone in a third world country known for terrorist attacks, drug trafficking, and violent political protests. As soon as her plane landed, she'd run to the nearest restroom to tuck most of her unruly shoulder-length chestnut hair up under a baseball cap and hide her wide, tilting brown eyes behind a pair of men's dark sunglasses she'd purchased at one of the airport's overpriced gift shops. Hoping to conceal her curves, she'd changed into a large, loose-fitting olive-green hoodie.

Pulling the bill of her ball cap low over her flushed cheeks, she turned to face the street. She should be pleased her disguise worked, but the old man's unintentional insult wrought a flash of remembered pain.

Nicole had spent most of her life being compared to her older sister and had invariably come up short. Having big boobs and long blond hair, Liz had been the proverbial bombshell since she'd turned fourteen, whereas Nicole spent those agonizing teenage years as a shy, geeky nerd hiding in the shadows, hoping no one would notice her.

Throughout her adolescence, the physical differences between her and Liz had always caused her uncertainty and angst, but something astonishing had happened to her appearance over the past few years. Though she still wouldn't dare compare herself to her sister, she was quite satisfied with some of her body's transformations.

A belated growth spurt when she was seventeen not only added three inches to her plump, pubescent five-foot-four frame but also purged the ten pounds of unflattering baby fat that had been clinging to it since the seventh grade. Not long after, her face suddenly stopped breaking out. Even her eyes took on a deeper mahogany hue and her hair a healthier shine.

"A late bloomer," her mother had gushed approvingly when Nicole donned her first and only dress for college orientation. Although grateful to whatever magical hormone her ovaries finally started secreting, Nicole had yet to shake her shyness or overcome her inability to stand up for herself. Sadly, telling her mother she was going to Kenya had been her second boldest move to date. The first had been moving out of the house and into an off-campus apartment with Danielle last year.

"Dis bus goin' to Nanyuki! All aboard for Nanyuki!"

Finally, someone from the bus company clambered on board to drive them to Nanyuki. He was a very tall black man wearing the same blue vest as the other men kicking the soccer ball. He didn't appear to be the least bit apologetic about being so late. Rather, he stood grinning at all the passengers as if he were waiting for applause before turning and fiddling with the ignition and clutch. After several false starts, the rickety vehicle's engine churned to life, releasing a bone-jarring blast from the exhaust.

Public transit in this part of East Africa consisted mostly of *matatus*, Swahili slang for *taxi*. Someone from school had warned her against employing one, as the minibuses tended to be little more than rusting heaps of soldered metal resurrected for use from junkyards. She was glad she hadn't. Downtown was filled with the brightly painted jitneys zigzagging recklessly through the midday traffic, passengers tightly crammed together alongside crates of chickens and random farm animals, rap music blaring loudly from open windows.

Nairobi's modest skyline gradually receded into the distance as the bus sped through the city. Here and there, she would catch sight of little shelters made from scraps of corrugated tin or see dirty children scurrying over piles of rubbish while gaunt, ragged-looking men mingled amongst the traffic selling wares such as potato peelers and socks. She knew most of these horrifying conditions could be blamed on Kenya's educational system. Only recently had the government begun providing free schooling to its citizens, and the illiteracy rate was still high, especially amongst young children in rural villages like the one she was heading toward. Most of the kids were orphans, their parents killed by HIV and AIDS. The nonprofit teaching organization's core belief was that literacy could not only provide information on how HIV/AIDS is transmitted but also start a process of questioning that could lead to changes in attitudes and behavior. She was going to find out firsthand if their efforts could make a difference.

"Murang'a! Murang'a! Murang'a!"

An hour into the trip, the driver sang out their first stop in a rich, melodious accent before turning off the highway of rutted asphalt onto a narrow track of dark red dirt. The urban blight of the city had slowly given way to rolling hills of rich, fertile farmland ripe with acres of tea plants as Mount Kenya materialized on the horizon. There were no other cars or people about and no township in sight. Nicole discreetly unfurled the small map she'd torn from the pages of her tour book. They still had at least another two hours of travel time before reaching Nanyuki. She wished she'd had the foresight to remove her camera from her duffel bag before allowing it to be stowed in the luggage rack atop the roof. The raw beauty of the land was breathtaking.

She was admiring the splendor of a dense thicket of fruitless mango trees when something peculiar amidst the lush greenery growing along the side of the road caught her eye—two dark figures on motorcycles, both identically dressed in black leather gear and matching helmets with tinted face shields. Something about their presence in this impoverished region of the country just didn't fit. And why did the other passengers on board seem to choose that very moment to stop talking to one another? A needling apprehension prickled her nape. For the next mile, all was unnaturally quiet, so quiet Nicole could hear the high-pitched whine of the motorcycles accelerating as they raced to catch up with the bus. A cloud of rusty earth billowed up from beneath their tires as they roared past, coating all the windows with a fine layer of brown dust. Her view was blurred but Nicole could still make out what was happening. The motorcycles had slowed, pulling parallel with the bus driver's window. The riders were now gesturing frantically but with authority, pointing to the side of the road with their gloved fingers.

"Look like we have us a hijacking!" the bus driver shouted in calm, halting English as if such an encounter was a fairly common occurrence. Ignoring the bandits' wordless demands, he jerked the bus sharply to the right.

Whack!

Nicole was slammed against the aluminum framing encasing the dirty window glass. Hard. Her teeth rattled inside her head. If she lived to see morning, there would be a black-and-blue mark where her shoulder and the metal had collided. Another jerk, this time to the left, sent her crashing into the bulk of the burka-wearing woman. It registered somewhere in the back of her terrified brain that something was awry; there were no soft, squashy rolls of padded flesh beneath the Muslim woman's voluminous garment to cushion her tumble. Before she could waste another second contemplating the incongruity, she gripped the bottom of the vinyl seat with knuckles that were now a bright bone-white, struggling in vain to keep her balance as the bus bounced and heaved. Her heart was now in her throat, her thoughts as scattered as the pieces of luggage falling from the roof. In some weird way, she was comforted by the fact that this sort of thing seemed to be routine to the bus driver. But what should she do if the hijackers wanted something other than the few hundred American dollars she had in her wallet?

Instinctively, she reached for her cell phone to call 911, but came up empty-handed. She'd been fairly certain that if she'd taken her mobile with her, her neurotic mother would have been calling twenty times a day to check on her. The bill would have been horrendous.

A few years back, she'd purchased a can of Mace and a pocketknife for the rare nights when she had to walk the campus parking lot alone. The Mace had long ago been lost, but it had become her habit to carry the blade with her wherever she went. With a less than steady hand, she searched every pouch in her canvas bag for the tiny weapon's hard nylon sheath, her heart pounding wildly against her rib cage. To her dismay, her fevered groping turned up little more than a few dimes and pennies, sticks of gum, lip gloss, and a slip of paper detailing her seating assignment on the connection from Brussels. She recalled placing the knife inside her checked duffel bag so that it wouldn't be confiscated by airport security. So fatigued from traveling halfway around the world, she'd forgotten to collect it when they'd landed.

The bus sped up. Faster. Then it slowed down. Nicole could see bus driver's reflection in the mirror above the steering wheel. He was grinning, apparently enjoying the game of cat and mouse. Once more he turned the wheel to the left and again to the right until one of the motorcycle riders pointed a gun into the sky and fired.

"Oh shit!" Nicole cursed out loud, causing the cloaked shape sitting next to her to turn her way. A pair of intelligent, blue eyes framed by inky black lashes stared out at her from the only opening in the dark hood, but before Nicole could ponder the incongruity, the bus driver slammed his foot down on the brakes, causing the rear end of the vehicle to careen forward. They skidded across the dust and dirt for almost a full minute before finally coming to rest dangling precariously over a small embankment overlooking a deep ravine. The eerie silence that followed was swiftly invaded by the approaching drone of the motorcycles. The noxious odor of diesel and burning rubber turned her stomach.

As she always did when stressed or scared, Nicole reached for the necklace her father had given her when she was a little girl. She tugged nervously at the long silver chain.

"Let's go, Nicole! Hurry!"

Nicole slowly lifted her head, dazed.

"We don't have a lot of time! Get up!"

The woman in the flowing black robe and mask towered over her and was shouting her name. Nicole watched as the burka was yanked off and cast away. It sailed through the air like a parachute, landing in a balled heap in the middle of the aisle.

She gaped in open-mouthed confusion. A tall, exceptionally fit and slender twenty-something female with a blond ponytail curling around a Kevlar-vested shoulder stood before her, looking cool and calm, despite the situation.

"What the—?" Words failed her.

"I'm with the United States government. I'll explain later. Right now we have maybe thirty seconds to get you the hell out of here."

The woman withdrew a small firearm from the inside of her bulletproof vest and proceeded to fire several shots from one of the broken windows in the direction of the motorcycles. The frightened passengers huddled low in their seats, whispering amongst each other.

"That should stall them for a minute," she boldly proclaimed before lifting a shapely, jean-clad leg and kicking open the latch that sealed the emergency exit door at the back of the coach. "Let's go!"

"What about them?" Nicole questioned with a wave of her arm, indicating the others aboard the bus. "We can't just leave them here to die!"

"They won't die unless we stay. The bad guys on the bikes are after *you*, not any of them. Now follow me! Quickly!"

Nicole hesitated. There was at least twelve feet of empty space between the rugged soles of her new hiking boots and the ground. The athletic woman jumped nimbly into the air and landed lithely on both feet.

"Hurry!"

Alarm and panic were giving way to reason and doubt. What

did she know about this situation other than what this mysterious woman was telling her? Why would anyone be after *her*? She was just a grad student on her way to a village in Kenya to teach for the summer.

"Damn it, Nicole Kennedy, do you want to be killed just like your father was? Jump! Now! They're coming!"

Nicole went weak in the knees. How did this woman know about her father?

"Jump now or you're going to be shot!"

Whether it was the hum of the advancing motorcycles or the frantic impatience in the government agent's tone, she finally jumped from the bus without preparing for the impact of her body hitting the ground.

Unlike her agile predecessor, there was very little grace in her awkward plummet and ungainly roll into a copse of prickly thorn bushes. Before she could take an inventory of her limbs, her arm was nearly yanked from its socket as she was pulled to her feet and then dragged down the ravine into the dark African wilderness before she could even lick the dirt from her lips.

They ran for nearly fifteen minutes without pause until she couldn't take another step.

"Wait, please," she pleaded, trying to catch her breath. "My—my sweatshirt's too long. It keeps getting caught around my legs."

Nicole was wearing a plain white V-necked T-shirt underneath the hoodie, and was grateful the fabric was so light. They were much closer now to the equator than back in Nairobi, and the temperature had risen. Adding to her discomfort, she had a severe stitch in her abdomen from running so fast. She jabbed the tips of her fingers under her rib cage in an attempt to impede the pain.

"Cramp?"

Nicole nodded her head reluctantly. The woman looked at some electronic gadget strapped around her narrow wrist, then back up toward the sky in the direction they'd been running from, then yet again back to her wrist.

"I suppose we can spare a minute."

"Who are you?" Nicole gasped out between breaths, still not able to get enough oxygen into her greedy lungs. Her mouth was dry and tiny grains of sand clung to her tongue.

"Kira Anthony," came the curt reply. She removed the Kevlar vest and held it out to Nicole. "Take off your hat and those ridiculous glasses and put this vest on." Her eyes returned to the device around her wrist. "We need to get moving."

"Sorry I'm slowing you down." Nicole bristled. Her hands were shaking and her heart had yet to find its normal rhythm. "It's been a while since I've been attacked by motorcyclists with AK-47s and chased across Africa. And what's with the body armor?"

"We'll be leaving the cover of the trees in a minute. Do I need to remind you one more time that they're after you, not me?"

Nicole wiped the sweat from her brow. "*Me?* What do I have to do with this?" she asked, obediently removing the baseball cap and sunglasses before grabbing the vest. "And how do you know about my father? How do I know *you* are who you *claim* to be?"

"No time for questions." Kira shook her head and looked toward the southern sky.

Nicole followed her focused blue stare. Flocks of disturbed birds fluttered in the skies above the tree line as whoever was following them on the ground below the concealing canopy of branches and leaves gained on them.

"Leave the sunglasses and sweatshirt. They can obviously follow our tracks, so leaving the garments behind won't cause us any harm. We have to go. *Now!*"

CHAPTER TWO

Nicole did her best to keep pace with Kira Anthony, but it was a losing struggle. The roots of the jungle trees grew close and thick and aggressively jutted up from the loose red dirt, making the course even more difficult to navigate for someone already weary from jet lag. The Kevlar vest was like wearing a wool sweater in July, and her feet ached. The new boots she had purchased for the trip weren't broken in enough for running, and she could tell her ankles were starting to blister and bleed. Every few dozen yards she would look back, fearing the motorcyclists were about to reach out and grab her—only to turn around and find Kira waiting for her up ahead with an expression on her face clearly conveying her annoyance.

At last, they came to a level plain of tall grasslands stretching out before them, but the physical ease of negotiating the flat terrain was overshadowed by the dread of feeling a bullet shatter her skull. Now out in the open, they were easy pickings for any marksman with a telescopic lens.

"We'll stop here."

"Here?" Nicole asked incredulously, her breathing labored. "Aren't we a bit conspicuous?"

Without answering, Kira simply squatted down onto her haunches, vanishing right before Nicole's very eyes into the waist-high, wheat-colored stalks. She started to follow, only to discover the blades of the plants were like razor blades against her bare arms. A tiny squeal of pain escaped her before she could stop it. Kira didn't seem to notice, flattening an area of reeds with the bottoms of her boots before leveraging her weight and bending down onto one knee. She readied her handgun, oblivious to the flying insects now swarming around them and the heat of the midday sun beating down. Nicole stared at the gun, fascinated by the sleek piece of black metal. She'd never been so close to a real one before—it was hard to believe something so small could be deadly. She noticed Kira's secure clasp of the gun's grip. Her fingers were long and feminine; their nails were void of any coating, just clean and rounded.

"From this spot, we can see them when they come out of the forest."

"Okay," she sighed. It felt great to sit, even with the bugs and heat. She wiped a layer of sweat from the back of her neck. "Back at the bus, you mentioned my father. What do you know about—"

"Shh!" Kira held a finger to her lips, her head cocking to one side.

"They can't possibly hear us, can they?" Nicole whispered.

"It's not them I'm concerned about at the moment. Did you forget we're in the middle of Africa? I thought I heard something." She paused to listen, this time curling a hand around her ear. "And it wasn't human."

Nicole pulled her knees up unto her chest, anxiously scouring the earth around her for something long, slithering, and venomous. She'd always had a fear of snakes but never had to worry about crossing paths with any back in the suburbs of Maryland. What if it wasn't a snake? What if it something else, like a lion or a leopard?

"We should go. Stay down and keep your head low."

Nicole obliged, happy to get away from the threat of a fanged snake. *What*, she wondered, *did I get myself mixed up in by getting on that stupid bus?*

Soon I'll be safe, she kept repeating to herself over and over. Surely her questions would be answered when they arrived wherever it was they were heading. She assumed it would be a small provincial town situated a bit beyond the crests of the green-terraced hills in the distance. She pictured herself limping into a police station, telling her outrageous story to someone in a uniform. Within minutes of reporting her ordeal, beret-wearing officers with epaulette-adorned shoulders would be standing at crisp attention, their radios filled with static and electronic chatter as they communicated back and forth with one another about the hijacking. Since she was American, some aged diplomat would probably be very concerned about the political ramifications of the incident, so he too would be hovering about to ensure that news of the attack was kept from reaching inquisitive reporters. Hearing of the threat to one of their volunteers, someone in authority from the teaching organization would probably come to collect her from the station and escort her safely to the hostel. Over the next few weeks, she'd be asked to recount the details of her wild escapade to the other volunteers over and over, and she'd laugh about how crazy her first trip abroad turned out to be.

They'd been walking hunched over for almost an hour when they came upon a copse of acacia trees. Kira stood to her full height. "Let's take a quick rest. I think we've lost 'em."

Nicole collapsed under the meager shade of the horizontal branches above her. Her shoulder blades throbbed from the tension and strain of the awkward crouch.

"Thank God. My back is killing me," she mumbled, rubbing her lower back with both hands. "And I'm dying of thirst."

"I suppose we didn't need to crouch the *entire* time." Kira wiped dried mud from her knees before taking a seat on the ground a few feet away. "As soon as we started moving we would've known if they'd seen us."

Nicole raised her eyebrows in question.

"The shifting of the grass on an otherwise windless day

would have been a dead giveaway—they would have started shooting at us." Kira shrugged indifferently before doing a series of arm and leg stretches. "But we'd have been hard to hit."

She can't be serious. Nicole fought her sudden urge to scream. "I imagine a dozen police officers are probably at the scene of the hijacking right now and here we are in the middle of freaking nowhere, lost, about to be dinner for some wild animal! Couldn't we have just walked back to the road and waited for help?"

"Calm down, Nicole. We're not lost," Kira responded matter-of-factly. "You're wasting energy, and you're going to need every ounce of it. Most creatures sense we're coming from a mile away. Believe it or not, most want to avoid us more than we want to avoid them. We stood more of a chance something would inadvertently bump into us if we sat quietly in the grass. You would have screamed, I presume rather loudly," she rolled her eyes, "announcing our exact location to our friends with the guns in that case. And yes, I suppose we could have retraced our steps back to the bus." She nodded her head and pushed a loose tendril of blond hair from her brow. "But it'll be dark soon. Many predators living here are nocturnal. They sleep during the day and begin foraging for food at twilight. With all the deforestation from logging, their food supply has dwindled significantly and they'll pretty much attack anything that moves—and we'd have been out there in the open on the road. But even if we had been lucky enough to have made it back to Muranga unscathed, there's still the little matter of the guys with the guns. You know, the ones on the motorcycles who knew exactly which bus you were traveling on and had planned the timing and location of their attack so you were in a remote area far from civilization. But I doubt you have anything to worry about." Her voice dripped with sarcasm. "I'm sure they probably just called it a day and are back home with their feet up on their ottomans enjoying a nice quiet night of television."

Overhead a huge bird soared through the cloudless blue sky,

its harsh squawking reminding Nicole just how far away from civilization she actually was. "But why me?"

"I was hoping you might be able to provide that."

Nicole stared at Kira. "Are you kidding?"

Kira's face remained sober. "Maybe because I'm American?"

"Think, Nicole." Kira's tone hardened. "What could they want from you?"

"I have no idea. The most subversive thing I've ever done is study politics and policy from used textbooks!"

"The same can't be said about your father."

A sickening dread rose up inside Nicole. "Why would you think this has anything to do with my father? He was just a geologist for a petroleum company. And he died over twelve years ago."

"He was killed in Yemen by a car bomb. You have to admit it's a highly unusual way for a man who studied rocks to die."

"How'd you know how he died?"

"We've been trying to figure out why you would be a target."

Nicole remembered her father's funeral, all the strangers dressed in black pouring in and out of her house, her mother's tearful cries, and her sister pointing to a small article buried low on the front page of the newspaper with the bold title emblazoned in her memory forever more: DEADLY CAR BOMB LEAVES ONE AMERICAN DEAD.

"He was just an American in the wrong place at the wrong time, that's all. He'd been researching a piece of land in Yemen his company wanted to purchase for oil production. He was on his way to the airport when his car exploded. We were told a radical anti-American group claimed responsibility." Nicole shrugged. "Not every terrorist victim is a specific target."

"Do you honestly believe some anonymous faction murdered your father for sport?"

Before Nicole could respond, a light began blinking on the

contraption Kira wore around her wrist. "We have to go." She stood up, repositioned the black nylon straps of her shoulder harness around her slender curves, then pulled them tighter. "We'll continue this discussion later."

"No way." Nicole remained perfectly still. "I'm not going any farther with you." Something wasn't quite right about this entire situation, but her brain wasn't functioning properly. The surge of adrenaline had ebbed, leaving her shaky and weak. She knew she was close to physical exhaustion and mental collapse. When she tried to sort out the chaotic jumble of thoughts racing around inside her head, nothing seemed to make sense. Answers remained elusive as she fought another wave of light-headedness. She was too tired and thirsty to think clearly.

"Do as you please." Kira stared at her. "You're not my prisoner. You can stay here and take your chances with the African wildlife or you can follow me. Fresh water and hot food is less than a thirty-minute hike from here."

Nicole took in the unfamiliar landscape and the impassive expression of the golden-haired, gun-toting stranger. *Maybe, just this once*, she sighed to herself while struggling to stand on her swollen and tender feet, *I should have listened to my mother.*

CHAPTER THREE

The rigorous march across the Kenyan countryside continued. Every muscle in her body ached and she was beginning to feel nauseous, but Nicole stifled her complaints. She wasn't going to give this blond female version of James Bond the satisfaction. And it wasn't like she was out of shape. She took pride in her health—eating right, running two to three miles almost every day, and lifting weights.

But Kira Anthony was a machine. Her workout routine would probably wear out an Olympic decathlete.

Nicole gave Kira a quick but discreet once-over. Despite what they'd already been through, Kira looked liked she'd just stepped out of a Secret Agent of the Month calendar. Her smooth, honey-blond hair was still securely fastened in a black barrette, not one single strand out of place despite the hasty removal of the burka, the death-defying jump from the bus, and the grueling trek through the wilds of Kenya. Her nose was small and straight, symmetrically positioned within the sun-warmed oval of her face. The planes of her cheekbones were slightly pronounced, conferring a shadowed definition to the fragile hollows beneath them, and her jawline was firm but feminine. She was pretty—almost *too* pretty, and this thought deepened that suspicion that had taken root in the back of her muddled brain.

"So you're a government agent?" she questioned Kira when

they'd reached the base of a rough hill scattered with jagged slabs of exposed rock.

"Nope," Kira replied.

Nicole's eyes widened as the response slowly sank in.

"My exact words were that I am with the United States government." Kira smiled and began scaling the craggy slope with athletic ease.

"You're kidding, right?" Nicole asked when she reached the top of the hill, which had been steeper than she'd thought. She was taking deep breaths through her nose, trying hard not to let the exertion show. "That could simply mean you work for the Internal Revenue Service! Or that you deliver the mail!"

Kira laughed out loud.

"We-e-e-l-l." Kira chose her words carefully. A smile still pulled at the corners of her mouth. "If it'll ease your mind, you *could* say I'm part of an organization similar in purpose to the Peace Corps."

"So let me get this right. Usually you're digging wells so people can have fresh water to drink?"

"At times, I've been called to dig a ditch or two," Kira replied, walking quickly toward a path leading toward towering camphor, pine, and eucalyptus trees. "Drinking water may not have been the objective, but my work was equally important."

"You're not doing a very good job today. I'm drier than the Sahara."

Another sunny smile curved Kira's lips, exposing an even, white set of teeth.

"Let's just say we deal with all matters pertaining to sustaining peace in this extremely volatile world."

Nicole eyed Kira's holster insinuatingly. "And a gun helps achieve world peace how exactly?"

"Sometimes we need to protect ourselves or those we're assigned to take care of. But most of our work usually requires little more than getting the precise amount of money into the right person's hands."

"Bribery?"

Kira nodded.

"I'm glad to know our tax dollars are going to good use," Nicole said sarcastically.

"Money's a powerful motivator, but it doesn't always work. Sometimes we have to resort to other tactics, especially when dealing with religious fanatics. It can take years to infiltrate such groups. Or we'll manipulate our target psychologically to acquire the information we need, and then we'll disappear from their life without any one being the wiser."

"You *torture* people?"

"Nothing that medieval in my line of work. We're very modern in our methodology, and I'll just leave it at that."

There was something calmly reassuring about her confident demeanor. And why else would Kira have been on the bus, if not to rescue her?

"You okay back there?" she heard Kira shout ten minutes later.

Nicole hadn't realized she'd fallen so far behind. "Coming!" she hollered hoarsely, jogging to catch up.

Despite her fatigue, she was still able to appreciate all the natural wonder that lay beyond the boundaries of the trail they were following. *Crazy how the mind is able to cope*, she thought, craning her neck up toward the sky. There were hundreds of colorful birds of unknown species singing in the giant camphor trees above them. The constant chirping of insects grew louder and louder still as the sun began to lower. Just beyond the impenetrable perimeter of vines and creepers curtaining the rest of the jungle from their view came the sharp, piercing cries and high-pitched squeals of creatures she suspected might be baboons or perhaps monkeys, but she dared not ask lest she was wrong and confirmed her ignorance of the country's native wildlife.

"Ready?"

Nicole wearily lifted her throbbing head. It felt like there was a little man in there with a hammer who wanted out. "For what?"

"I'll need your help."

They'd come upon a small clearing. The fertile earth beneath her hiking boots was so soft and moist her heels felt like they were sinking into warm butter.

"The soil and climate here are ideal for growing coffee," Kira remarked, observing Nicole's steps. She positioned her hands on one of three large boulders that looked to have been there since dinosaurs roamed the globe. "The rainy season ends in May, but the dirt retains the water for some time. Have you seen the movie *Out of Africa*? The setting was a coffee bean plantation here in Kenya."

"No, but I read the book."

Kira stared at her, an amused glitter sparkling within the depths of her clear blue eyes. "Ah yes, I forgot how much you love to read."

"How do you know that?" Nicole was beginning to feel a little dizzy. Perhaps she hadn't heard Kira correctly. The ground beneath her wasn't as sturdy as it had been a few minutes ago.

"C'mon, help me move this," Kira urged, ignoring the question.

This was a mammoth-sized stone that weighed more than both of them combined.

"You don't really expect us to lift that, do you? And why?"

"It's made from plastic and fiberglass but still heavy. The last time I tried to do it alone, I nearly strained my back. You'll see what I'm talking about in a second. Here, lift this side."

Nicole squared her shoulders and did as instructed. Her contribution to the effort wasn't much, but the rock slowly creaked open—like it was hinged. The large, vacant underside concealed a square steel door built into the ground. She watched in bewilderment as Kira once again punched a few buttons on the magical device around her wrist and pulled up on a rusty metal handle, revealing a deep cement well with an old iron ladder bolted onto its walls.

"No freaking way."

"You need to go down first. Pulling the rock back into place and locking the hatch can be tricky. It's dark, so descend slowly."

Nicole retreated two steps backward. The events of the day were way too much like the plot of a movie coming to life.

"You're pale." Kira was suddenly at Nicole's side, sliding an arm around her shoulders for support. "What's wrong?" she asked, her voice gentle and concerned.

"I have a colossal headache," she answered honestly. She lifted a hand to her temple, feeling self-conscious standing so close to Kira. She could smell the faint scent of her shampoo—something floral with jasmine.

"This is an underground bunker the United States uses as an intelligence nest. It's fully stocked with water, fresh fruit, and other provisions. You're dehydrated, Nicole." Kira patted the back of the Kevlar vest tenderly. "We need to get fluids in you immediately."

Nicole hesitated.

Part of her brain said, *Run! You don't know this woman from Adam, and she could be nuts*, but another part, that part that would give her right arm for a glass of cold ice water, said, *It's okay, trust her*.

"There's also a satellite phone you can use to call your mother and let her know you're okay." Kira had moved back to the rock and was waving her hand impatiently, petitioning Nicole to lower herself down the shaft.

The words spurred Nicole forward. She'd promised her mother an e-mail as soon as she made it to the hostel in Nanyuki—and she already was an anxiety-ridden, menopausal mess. Nicole wasn't going to be the straw breaking that camel's back. When she was halfway down, she looked up to see Kira still perched at the top, keeping the door angled at a certain position so that the waning light of the day could spill down into the hole to make rungs of the ladder visible for Nicole to navigate.

"Careful," Kira cautioned, her voice echoing about the hidden silo.

"I feel like I'm in a bomb shelter," Nicole said when her feet finally touched cement and she was standing in the shadows listening to Kira maneuver down the passageway.

"It's similar in design," Kira agreed, brushing past her and flipping a switch.

Beyond the narrow compartment they were confined within was a fluorescent-lit passageway with Russian lettering painted onto its two steel doors. It took a moment for Nicole's eyes to adjust to the lighting, but when they did, her heart dropped to her empty stomach.

"Relax," Kira advised as if reading her thoughts. "This bunker was built in the mid-seventies when the Soviets were still our enemies. If anyone discovered this facility, the engineers designed it so that the last country to be blamed for its existence would be the United States. Everything in it, including the ancient mainframes, was programmed in Russian." She walked down the stark corridor punching away at a tiny keypad on the gadget around her wrist, and a locking device hidden within some mechanism inside the doors clicked open loudly. "Reagan allocated most of his defense budget to his Star Wars program, leaving this place forgotten and untouched up until the late nineties when al-Qaeda began attacking U.S. embassies here in East Africa. From here, we can monitor all radio and cell frequencies as well as access Internet servers that service Somalia, Sudan, Uganda, and most other neighboring countries that harbor terrorists."

"You hack into computers?"

"Not the words I would use. According to all records, this place doesn't exist. If questioned, we're employees of a technology company with offices in California, Japan, and Pakistan."

Kira pushed through the unlocked doors. They were now in a large, round room that reminded Nicole of a hospital. Everything was steel, cement, and glass with more of the bright, fluorescent lighting overhead.

"Did you say *we*?"

No sooner had she asked the question than a woman emerged from another doorway. She was at least three inches taller and a decade older than Kira (whom she guessed was in her late twenties), with long black hair and dark, curious eyes.

"Well, looks like you succeeded in collecting your little stray." The tall, ebony-haired woman spoke with an Eastern Bloc accent, her voice low and silvery. "So, this is the little doe they're after?"

The woman's heavy-lidded eyes slowly examined Nicole.

"Easy, Shevchenko. She's way too young."

"Advice you might do well to heed yourself."

"She needs lots of water and a small meal," Kira instructed in a clipped, matter-of-fact monotone, disregarding Nicole as if she wasn't even in the same space. "Once she washes up and has a moment to reflect on all that's happened and where she is, she'll probably go into shock. If she does, come get me. I'm going to shower."

Nicole stood on rubbery legs as Kira walked out of the room without so much as a backwards glance.

"She's a cool one, eh?" Shevchenko prodded, her eyes watching Nicole's expression closely. "We call her the Ice Princess. Now come with me. I'll take you to your room. It has a hot shower and towels. You'll feel much better when you change your clothes. You two ladies don't smell as pretty as you look."

Nicole didn't know whether to laugh or cry. "I don't have any clothes to change into."

"What do you mean, you have no clothes? Come. I show you. And call me Stella."

Nicole followed the statuesque stranger down yet another

long, clinical corridor and into a small room simply furnished with a twin cot, a bureau, and a chair.

"All your things are right here, little one." Stella opened a closet to display everything Nicole had packed, hanging neatly from wire hangers.

"This can't be. My duffel bag? And my shoulder bag too?" The familiar beige canvas hung from a hook on the back of the closet door. Kenya was the identity theft capital of the world. Surely her belongings had been pilfered and a dozen loans had already been applied for using her good credit. She unzipped it and inside were her wallet, passport, driver's license, and notebooks, all untouched, just as they had been before she'd been forced to flee from the motorcyclists.

"But how? That's impossible! I left everything on the bus headed for Nanyuki!"

"No, nothing is impossible when you meet Bogie. He was behind you both the whole way. He grabbed your bags and covered your tracks so no one would be able to find us here."

"Bogie?" Nicole felt what little strength she had left draining from her. "How many of you people are there?"

"There's only three on this mission. You're looking ill. Here, sit down and hydrate while I run the shower. When you're done washing, I'll come back and check on you. You must drink lots more water and eat much fruit tonight. Kira remembered bullets but forgot to bring fluids. She's not as perfect as she thinks."

When she was finally alone, Nicole checked to see if the door had a lock and was grateful to find it did. She nursed the first bottle of water slowly, knowing if she drank too much too quickly she would be sick. Once in the shower, she found a bar of fragrant soap still wrapped in plain white generic paper and unlabeled containers of shampoo and conditioner. Fifteen minutes passed while she stood just absorbing the heated sting of the shower before she found the energy to lift a weary arm to scrub the muck from her bruised and scraped skin. Afterward, she brushed her teeth, combed through most of the knots in her tangled hair, and drank another bottle of water before collapsing into an unconscious heap on the edge of the bed with little more than the damp towel she'd used to dry off with as a makeshift blanket.

CHAPTER FOUR

Nicole was cold. Tiny crystals of snow fell from a drab, gray sky in blustery gusts all around her. She knew the street like the back of her hand, having walked the stretch of tree-lined blacktop ever since she was a little girl. Her house stood alone at the road's end. All the neighboring homes had disappeared. The storm was harsh, the winds howling, pushing her back. If she could make it home, she'd be safe.

The faint outline of a woman appeared in the distance ahead, beckoning to her without words, but the furious gales of the blizzard were strong. Stronger than her. Their invisible hands tugged at her from every direction, pushing and pulling.

"Mom?" she called out. "Mom, is that you?"

Suddenly, she was in her childhood bedroom. Warm. Too warm. Her mother's hand gently soothed her heated brow as soft, reassuring words were whispered into her ear. She didn't understand how it could be, but her mother was once again the strong, sturdy woman she'd been when Nicole had been a child, before her father had been killed.

A blast of frigid air tore through the room. She was lifted up and tossed outside into the storm, those cold winds snapping at her from every direction. Just as quickly, the sky cleared and calmed. She found herself alone in her backyard, standing just feet from the willow tree she and her father had planted for her seventh birthday. Despite the wintry weather, the magnificent tree was in full bloom. She took a hesitant step forward, not sure if what she was seeing was real or an illusion. The elongated leaves growing from the twisted boughs of the drooping sapling concealed the shape of a man.

"Dad!" she shouted.

She ran toward the tree, only her father had disappeared. In his place stood the regal figure of a faceless woman dressed all in white and wearing a brilliant crown made from diamonds and icicles. She claimed to be the Ice Princess and demanded Nicole tell her where her father was hiding the jewels he'd stolen from the king.

"The fever's almost broke, Shevchenko. I told you she'd be okay."

"I know that's what you keep saying, but I see the truth in your eyes. I'll go heat her soup."

Nicole blinked, trying to identify the voices speaking over her. Was she in a hospital? Had she been in a car crash?

"So you've decided to join us back on planet Earth? I was beginning to think you were staying delirious just to avoid me."

Reality flooded back into the foggy corners of Nicole's brain like a raging tsunami crashing onto an unsuspecting shoreline.

"I've been sick?" she asked through dry and chapped lips. Bits of hazy flashbacks flickered inside her head—painful reflections of her head throbbing violently and an insatiable thirst she couldn't quench.

"Quite. You've been in and out of it for almost two days."

"Two days?"

Kira was sitting on the very edge of the small bed. She was wearing a form-fitting baby blue sweater and faded Levi's. Her hair was parted on the side and hanging soft and loose around her face. Nicole caught her breath, and it had nothing to do with her poor health.

"I know you had to have all your shots and pills before embarking upon a trip to the Dark Continent—your school required proof before granting you permission to teach here—malaria, typhoid, yellow fever, hepatitis, polio, meningitis, even tetanus. I checked just to make certain they didn't miss anything."

Nicole grimaced, remembering.

"Ruling all else out, we think you might have picked up a simple virus on one of your overseas flights. Our jaunt through the forest probably helped the bug seize control of your immune system."

"A coup d'état?"

Kira looked down at her and something like amusement lit up her otherwise shadowed eyes. "Here, you need drink this. It was developed in Bangladesh to help treat infants with cholera." She lifted the straw to Nicole's lips. "It replaces electrolytes and helps treat dehydration."

"You don't have to feed her like a baby anymore," Stella reprimanded sternly, striding through the doorway carrying a tray laden with soup and bread. "And what she needs is food, not that nasty gruel you've been spooning down her throat for the past two days."

Nicole had to agree with her. The drink had the consistency of water mixed with baking soda and tasted horrible. But oddly enough, she found she'd be willing to drink a gallon if it meant Kira would stay sitting next to her and continue caring for her. She wasn't ready to analyze that just yet, but when the object of her gaze got up and coolly left the room just as she'd done when they'd first arrived, her insides swelled with disappointment.

Something was happening she wasn't at all looking forward to exploring.

"You work with Kira?"

Stella's full, brick-colored lips stretched across her swarthy cheeks in a wide smile. Something about the woman reminded Nicole of a cat she had while growing up. George had been an extremely clever feline, in many ways far more intelligent than the humans he allowed to feed and keep him.

"Little one, leave all questions for later. Right now, we need to get you healthy. Sit up and eat some of this soup I made. It's my mother's recipe from the country I grow up in, Ukraine." Stella lifted the tray and placed it on Nicole's lap.

"The last thing I remember was stumbling from the shower." She looked down, surprised to see she was dressed in one of the two sets of pajamas she'd packed—a pink cotton top and bottom with imprints of tiny kittens.

"Don't worry," Stella counseled, seeing the downward path of Nicole's eyes. "Kira cared for and bathed you while you were sick. She found you on the floor and stayed at your side the entire time you were in the fever."

Nicole wasn't sure how she felt about that particular revelation.

"You like?" Stella asked, her black eyes alive with eager expectation as she watched Nicole take a sip from the spoon.

"It's delicious," she answered honestly. The broth was tasty and warm.

"It has some rice, beef, egg, and carrot. It'll make you strong again like Popeye when he eats his spinach." Stella curled her arm to make a muscle.

Nicole laughed. She liked Stella Shevchenko. There was something quite charming about the older woman's manner.

"Kira mentioned a satellite phone. My mom hasn't heard from me since I called her collect during my layover in Brussels. She's probably ready to have a meltdown, if she hasn't had one already. I need to talk her, let her know I'm okay. Is there any way I can use that phone?"

"You needn't be troubled," a familiar voice replied. Kira was standing in the doorway, a mug of coffee in one hand. "Your mother believes you arrived in Nanyuki safe and sound. In fact, you've already sent her several e-mails detailing the delights of teaching a small tribe of Embu children the joys of the English alphabet. She seemed greatly pleased you were following in her footsteps. What does she teach?"

"Tenth-grade history," Nicole answered, numb with shock. Although she would never admit it, part of her was greatly relieved. The less her mother knew about what had really happened on a trip she'd repeatedly warned Nicole not to take, the better.

"And the teaching organization is cooperating with us fully, believing your absence from the program is a matter of international security."

"International security?" Nicole scoffed. "That's stretching it, don't you think? At some point, I'll need to provide an honest explanation why I missed orientation and my first few days of volunteering."

Kira shrugged, taking a sip from her mug. "It's the truth. And I'm sorry to tell you that you'll miss more than a day or two of teaching. You'll miss the entire internship." She turned to leave. "Shevchenko, when she's done eating, give her some of your special sleeping medicine so you and I can get back to work."

"What the hell? I'm not a lab specimen you can put back in a cage when you don't need me anymore." Nicole bit her lower lip. Kira whirled about, surprised. "And I don't want to sleep. I just woke up after being unconscious for two days."

A knowing look passed between Kira and Stella.

"What?" Nicole was losing her patience. "Why won't I be able to teach the kids? Would one of you please enlighten me?"

"In case you've forgotten, we're here to protect you," Kira said coldly. "You might try showing some appreciation."

"Really?" Nicole asked, lifting the tray with its bowl of sloshing soup from her lap and setting it down on the bed with care. "You've been trying very hard to convince me since you forced me from the bus, but something else is going on here."

Kira's blue eyes darkened. "Leave us, Shevchenko."

Stella reached over Nicole to grab the tray. Their eyes met, and a look of sympathy and warning illuminated Stella's smoky gaze. When Stella was gone, Kira closed the door softly behind her.

"And by the way, don't do anything as asinine as locking the door on us again. The locks are ancient and we have no idea where half the keys are. Luckily we had the one that opened your door. If you'd really been hurt, it would've taken a long time to get to you. The doors are made of solid steel."

Nicole clenched her fists under the sheets. She felt like a little kid being scolded for some silly transgression. A wave of heat ignited inside her and spread, slowly working its way up over each body part until all the circuits converged.

"You can't keep giving me the runaround. I think it's about time you tell me what's going on."

"I hardly think you're in much of a position to demand anything," Kira said as she sauntered slowly toward the bed.

A flicker of apprehension coursed through Nicole. She tried to sit up straighter against the bed's small headboard.

"The first thing I'm doing when I get out of here is filing a complaint with whatever organization you work for."

"Do I need to remind you I work for a technology company with offices in California, Japan, and Pakistan?"

"You forgot to mention the hidden underground lair in the foothills of Mount Kenya."

Kira was at the side of the bed now and Nicole felt a cowardly urge to jump from her blankets and run from the room. "You'd never be able to locate this place again in a million years." She smiled.

They were so close to one another, Nicole could see dark circles under her ice-blue eyes. She remembered what Stella had said, about her sitting at her side the entire time she'd been sick.

"What, no smart-ass comeback?" Kira reached down and lightly palmed Nicole's chin, tilting her face toward the glow cast from the metal lighting pendant dangling from the ceiling. Nicole was aware of Kira's thumb slowly traveling toward her mouth, its manicured tip softly grazing the dry, tender flesh of her bottom lip. Her body quivered, her heart now racing wildly inside her chest. A surge of desire rushed forth from some region in her lower abdomen to curl like a serpent around her insides, the sudden need easily injecting its elusive venom into her blood and leaving her paralyzed. Every muscle in her body went limp and her breathing grew shallow.

"We got a problem!" Stella came running back into the room, her eyes filled with terror.

"What is it?" Kira dropped her hands to her sides.

"They've been spotted less than eight kilometers from one of the villages!"

"Who?" Nicole asked.

"I'll go deal with it," Kira said. She turned to Nicole. "Now do you understand why you can't continue with your plans to be a part of the teaching program? We can't take the risk." She strode from the room.

"What's going on, Stella? Are those men that were following my bus now at one of the villages looking for me? What about the children—will they be hurt?"

Stella gulped, her serene manner shaken. "Try to sleep, kid. Your body's still very weak. I'll check on you later."

"Sleep? Damn it, Stella, you have to tell me what's going on! Please," she pleaded, "are there children in danger?"

As Stella closed the door, Nicole heard her softly reply, "Don't worry. Kira will fix this."

Nicole fell back against the bed and sighed. How could she possibly be expected to just sit here when who knew what was going on out there?

"What do those madmen on the motorcycles want with me and how'd they learn where I'd be?" she wondered out loud, lying back against the pillows. And just how did her father fit into this crazy puzzle?

She lifted a hand to her collarbone where the necklace he'd given her just before he'd left for that fateful trip to Yemen lay in a lazy coil atop her heated skin. It was a simple piece of jewelry, perfect for a little girl. The chain was sterling silver with an oval pendant dangling from its delicate length. On one side, the tiny ornament was engraved with a small willow, an acknowledgement of the tree they'd planted together, and on the other side an inscription that simply read, *In My Heart, Love Dad.*

"Dad," she said out loud, "what could they possibly believe you were involved in that would still matter twelve years after you died?"

CHAPTER FIVE

"Y ou awake, kid?" Stella opened the door and popped her head inside.

Nicole jumped at the sound of Stella's voice. "Are the children okay?" she asked, leaping from the bed. Roughly two hours had passed since Kira had stormed off.

"Fine. Kira said it was a false alarm. You should be sleeping."

"What time is it?"

"The trouble with an underground bunker," Stella said, smiling as she took a step into the room, "there aren't any windows. It's not quite twelve o'clock."

"Day or night?"

"Night. I saw the light under your door and figured you might want to join us. I just put frozen pizzas in the oven. You like pizza?"

Nicole's stomach growled in response, and she nodded.

Stella smiled foxily, wagging her finger at her. "You didn't eat enough of my soup."

Alone again, Nicole sat back down on the bed basking in the knowledge that no one had been hurt. Though she hadn't known Kira Anthony very long, the woman seemed to be quite proficient at her job, whatever that job allegedly was. Stella too seemed to hold Kira in high regard. Could Kira and Stella be lovers?

There was an obvious intimacy between those two women, perhaps one born from working closely together in tight quarters for long periods of time.

Or it could be one spurred by a deeper emotional connection.

The question nagged at Nicole. Now that she was contemplating the possibility, something ugly crawled up inside her. Could this be jealousy?

She placed a pillow under her head and pulled the thin wool blanket over her. In the past, when anything requiring deep introspection reared its big head, she packed it up in a tidy bundle and buried it in the back of her subconscious. For so many years, she'd done that with her sexuality, but she couldn't hide from the truth any longer.

Especially the way she'd reacted to Kira's careless caress of her cheek.

No, there was absolutely no use in denying, covering, or avoiding it anymore. It was time to pull that securely wrapped parcel out from its place in the dusty cobwebs of her mind, rip it open, and expose the fragile contents to the light of day.

She was attracted to women. And one woman in particular right now—one she wasn't even sure she liked all that much.

She'd always known she had a preference for women. She remembered the pivotal moment in her childhood when she realized she was different. She'd been nine years old, watching *Titanic* on the TV for the first time. But it wasn't Leonardo DiCaprio her eyes gravitated to whenever the movie's two stars appeared on screen together—but Kate Winslet and her cherry red lips and seductive, almond-shaped, blue-green eyes.

And so it had been for all other films and television shows Nicole watched. It was the heroine her eyes were drawn to, the pages with the female models she'd turn to in the clothing catalogs and innocently ogle when they came in the mail, or the young, pretty teachers in school she'd developed crushes on. Yet she'd never before found the courage to acknowledge her inclination, much less embrace it.

Not even after what had happened between her and Danielle.

Her thoughts ricocheted back to those five minutes in her life a few months back when everything between her and her roommate had changed.

Now was not the time for that skeleton to be dragged out of the closet, but now that she'd flung open the doors of the vault, the memories of her first and only semi-sexual experience refused to remain locked away.

She met Danielle one day last summer in the university bookstore. They'd immediately clicked, and by the second month of their friendship, Danielle had suggested they get their own apartment together. Nicole knew it would upset her widowed mother that she was moving out, but she was too excited to feel guilty for long.

By November, Danielle was occasionally accompanying Nicole to her mother's when she went home on the weekends, and other than going to their respective classes, they were rarely apart. But then came that somber Thanksgiving break and an ending to their brief friendship she never could have predicted.

"It's no big deal. You and I can bunk in your room together. I guarantee your sister will run back to her husband with open arms come morning when she realizes no one else is going to wait on her hand and foot like he does. C'mon, Nick, this will be fun."

Nicole could recall how uneasy her hollow laugh sounded when Danielle playfully tossed a pillow at her before disappearing into the bathroom to get ready for bed.

"You're awfully quiet. What're you thinking?" Danielle had asked as they lay inches apart on the worn twin mattress Nicole had slept on since leaving the crib.

"Nothing, just tired, I guess."

"Ya know, Nick, you never talk about guys. Why don't you have a boyfriend?"

She could remember tensing as Danielle turned toward her and placed one warm hand along the contours of her hip.

"I—I—I don't know. I just never—"

"God, do you even know how incredibly hot you are?"

Danielle's other hand reached out and pulled her closer. She'd been so nervous, scared, and simultaneously aroused that she thought her heart would literally explode within her chest. They kissed, and all the answers she'd been seeking seemed to fall from the heavens and into her being. At Danielle's urging, their kiss deepened, but then something changed; suddenly her friend's movements were no longer gentle but aggressive, almost painful.

"I've watched you for so long, wanting to fuck you so hard," Danielle admitted in a ragged murmur as she clawed at Nicole's pajama bottoms.

Nicole cringed. She'd never heard Danielle speak so crudely. It was like she was kissing a stranger. "Please stop," she had begged more than once, but Danielle would not be discouraged.

Finally, Nicole pushed her friend from the bed with a powerful shove, and she fell to the hard floor in an undignified heap.

"What the hell?" Danielle had complained groggily. "What's wrong?"

"Nothing," Nicole denied in a whisper, tightening the tie to her pajama bottoms and buttoning her top. "This just doesn't feel right."

Danielle shook her head. "Feel right? Nothing's ever felt better. Don't be scared. I know you're a virgin."

But she wasn't afraid. She was repulsed.

"I don't want this to ruin our friendship, Danielle." She'd grabbed a blanket and headed for the old lumpy couch downstairs in her mother's den. "Let's just pretend it never happened."

Only things were never the same between them after that

weekend. By Christmas break, Nicole had moved back into her mother's house, and she hadn't spoken to Danielle since.

Tossing the blanket aside, she wondered whether or not she had the fortitude to face Kira again so soon after their squabble. The thunderous rumbling in her belly told her she did—but not in kitty pajamas. As she bent to turn the water on to take a quick shower, her eyes caught sight of a green metallic bedpan leaning on the side of the toilet bowl. She'd not given a thought to how her bodily functions had been disposed of while she'd been sick, and the image of Kira overseeing such an obscenely intimate task set her reeling on her heels in horrified mortification.

"This nightmare can't possibly get any worse," she muttered under her breath as she ran a bar of soap over her body. As predicted, there was a large bruise along her arm where she'd collided with the metal frame of the bus. After drying off, she threw on a pair of jeans, astonished to see how loose they now were around her waist. Pulling a pair of socks over her feet was difficult, so she decided to remain shoeless. Her ankles were still red and chafed, but the blisters were starting to heal.

As she made her way from her bedroom down the stark concrete corridor, she wondered whether she was supposed to have waited for Stella to come get her. Visibility was hindered by the limited amount of wattage the tiny emergency lights mounted a foot from the floor generated. Hesitant, she wasn't certain in what direction she should go. It was as if she were in the catacombs of hell. One wrong turn and the devil would be waiting with pitchfork and fire.

And that's exactly what happened. She took a left when she probably should have gone right, coming face-to-abdomen with a real-life giant.

He was huge, close to six and a half feet tall, with skin the color of dark chocolate and biceps that challenged the seams of his shirt. His head was completely hairless and it seemed even his skull had muscles. The revolver he was aiming at her stole her attention.

"Relax, Bogie. It's only Nicole." Kira appeared from thin air.

"Ahh, yes." The black man smiled, transforming himself from merciless killing machine into gracious dignitary complete with a captivating South African accent. Nicole recalled hearing his name. Stella said he'd been the one to collect her luggage from the bus.

"Old habits," he offered, tucking the gun into the waistline of his camouflage-patterned pants, and extended a large, beefy hand. "A pleasure to finally make your acquaintance."

Nicole managed to reciprocate the engulfing handshake. *I must be getting used to having guns waved in my face*, she thought.

"Bogie's part of our team," Kira said casually, leading the way to another chamber. Her hair was pulled back into a ponytail, and the jeans she'd been wearing earlier had been replaced with a pair of dark athletic pants. The fabric molded itself to the length and form of her long legs. Nicole felt Kira's eyes assess her in return and was glad she'd taken the time for mascara and lip gloss.

"Good! Just in time!" Stella greeted them jubilantly, hunched over a large industrial oven.

Harsh, fluorescent tubes illuminated the room, momentarily blinding Nicole, who was still used to the dim lighting of the corridors. A round table and four austere chairs made from metal and plastic took up the center of the sparsely furnished space. Steel shelving units stocked with everything from Oreo cookies to self-heating emergency meals packaged in fancy colorful boxes lined the walls.

"Our provisions reflect our needs," Kira informed Nicole, responding to the direction of her curious gaze. "Bogie has a sweet tooth, Stella needs her salt, and I'm ashamed to say I'm a caffeine addict."

"No way. You have a weakness?"

Stella hid a smirk but Bogie rolled back his dark head and released a loud laugh.

Kira regarded her through half-lidded eyes. "I do like my coffee. It's not as detrimental to my well-being as some of my other cravings," she confessed, grabbing a can of Nicole's favorite diet cola from the refrigerator and handing it to her. "But I suppose we all have our monkeys."

Nicole drank her Diet Coke in silence, watching as the three pulled dishes and grabbed silverware. She studied Kira and Stella closely. So far, she hadn't seen any indication they were lovers; no smoldering glances or romantic love taps. There was an easy camaraderie between all three of them, as if they'd spent many a late night together just like this one.

So who exactly were these mysterious strangers awake at one o'clock in the morning and cooking frozen pizzas? It seemed unlikely any of them worked for the United States government. Two of them weren't even American.

Two weeks earlier, as Nicole and her mother had sat at the kitchen table discussing the details of her trip, her sister Liz had come bouncing in, eager to tell them about the television show she'd watched the night before. The show had been a news documentary about college girls disappearing while vacationing and studying abroad. According to Liz, some of the missing girls had turned up years later, claiming to be victims of an elaborate sex slave operation involving an intricate underground network of shady government officials, gangsters, and even drug dealers who would broker the girls to the highest bidders.

Nicole had never seen her mother's eyes bulge from their sockets quite like that before. Even now her toes recoiled, recalling the painful blow they'd dealt her sister's shin under the table.

She doubted these three were involved in something so deviant or sinister, but she also wasn't convinced they were part of any government-sanctioned operation. She'd spent the last five years commuting to school in Washington DC and had the opportunity to observe civil servants up close and personal. The image of the swashbuckling undercover spy secretly working to save the world was the stuff of fiction. Did Kira really believe she was that naïve?

For some reason, having her intelligence doubted by the haughty blonde was irritating.

She suspected Kira was the ringleader of whatever con they were scheming. Maybe they thought her family was wealthy?

Perhaps they'd already made demands for a ransom.

She snorted into her forearm. They were in for a sad surprise if that was the case. *Hope they take Visa*, she thought.

And they'd better get the charge preapproved first.

CHAPTER SIX

L et's eat," Stella said, slicing through the crust and melted cheese with a pizza wheel. "Usually we stay away from junk food, but sometimes it's good for the soul. But not my hips." She laughed.

They all sat down at the table and proceeded to devour the two pizzas while Kira explained how their groceries were delivered.

"We receive a text, in code of course, providing us with coordinates and a time when a helicopter will make a drop not too far from here. They're usually done in the early hours just before dawn."

"Sometimes those guys in the copters miss the drop point," Bogie complained in his deep voice. "You gotta look out for animals. They don't bother me none. They'll just tear open the food and have at it. But this area is teeming with illegal marijuana plantations. The type of migrant workers those farms employ are far more dangerous than any denizen of the wild. And if they found our net filled with boxes of perishables, they'd be very suspicious." He finished his fourth slice of pizza in one quick swallow. "You like Mallomars?" he asked Nicole, lifting his muscled mass from the chair and rummaging through the shelves crammed with boxes of cookies and cakes.

"Dessert can wait," Stella cautioned, placing the last slice of pizza onto Nicole's empty plate before placing the pan into the sink. "Little one here needs to eat more starch. She lost too much weight."

Nicole would have loved nothing more than a chocolate-coated marshmallow right then, but she wasn't about to undermine Stella. She genuinely liked the woman.

"So what happened tonight at the villages?" she asked, taking another bite of pizza while looking back and forth between the two other women.

"A false alarm based on bad intelligence," Kira was quick to answer. "It happens."

Bogie, who'd been studying the inventory of cookies with a scientist's intensity, confiscated an entire package of Walkers shortbread in one of his giant paws and vanished from the room without a word. Nicole looked around. Stella had disappeared as well.

"Where'd everyone go?"

"Stella and Bogie are involved in another project. By the way, I'm sorry about the way I reacted earlier. You had every right to be angry." Kira couldn't quite master the emotion she was trying for. Instead, her words came out hollow and forced, as if she were reading from a script. "You've been kept in the dark way too long. I'd planned on explaining everything to you as soon as we got here, but you fell ill, and now," she reached across the table, enfolding Nicole's wrist in a soft, warm hand before gently turning it so that she could read the time on her watch, "it's late. I'm on duty in a bit. We'll have to put that discussion off until morning."

Kira's fingers were still wrapped around her wrist and it was all Nicole could do to breathe. The sweet smell of baby powder and the fresh clean scent of soap clinging to Kira's skin filled the small space between them. The blood flowed from Nicole's chest to the crown of her head in a rush, and she was certain the action produced a surge of bright color along her cheeks.

"Are you feeling okay?" Kira's hand moved from Nicole's wrist to her forehead. "You look like you're still running a temperature."

The contact and their proximity to one another was simply too much for Nicole to bear. She felt her insides turn to mush and her senses start to short-circuit.

"I'm fine," she announced, standing up so quickly Kira was almost knocked from her chair. "Do you mind if I have another Coke?"

"You'd do better drinking water, but help yourself."

With her back toward Kira, Nicole stood at the refrigerator for a few seconds collecting her composure before pulling the door open and grabbing a soda. She placed the cold can up to her cheek, hoping it would cool her off. Had she seen a flicker of reciprocating desire in those ice-blue eyes boring into her own, or had it been a trick of the lighting overhead?

Or maybe just another part of Kira's act, she reminded herself.

"When you say you're on duty," Nicole's voice sounded hoarse and unsteady even to her own ears, "what exactly does that mean?"

Kira turned around in her chair, regarding her thoughtfully.

Grateful for the distance between them, Nicole leaned back against the refrigerator. The appliance was sturdy and she needed its support. She was feeling insecure in her shoeless feet, loose jeans, and damp hair. She wondered what it would be like to have a tenth of the confidence Kira possessed. Never had Nicole come across anyone so supremely self-assured, perhaps not even in any of the films she'd watched or the fiction she'd read. The woman was certain of her place in the universe, exhibiting a smooth polish in every aspect of her manner, be it as simple a gesture as the way she tucked her hair behind an ear, the subtle swagger in her step, or the precise enunciation of each word when she spoke.

"It sounds taxing, but it basically entails little more than sitting in a room filled with computers waiting for one of them to tell me they've detected something interesting."

"Like what?" Nicole popped the top on the soda.

"Let's say one of our country's enemies wanted to send information to a fellow terrorist across the Internet. Our highly sophisticated software programs monitor all the data traffic on computer networks in select countries here in Africa and the Mideast. The programs are called package sniffers. If one of these programs intercepts a message it considers suspicious based upon parameters we set, such as certain words or phrases, visits to specific websites or e-mail addresses, it spews the information out into yet another program. This other program filters everything collected and then yet another program analyzes the findings. Everything is in real time, so someone has to be on duty should a program alert us to a potential attack or some other imminent threat against our country or one of our allies. Ninety-nine percent of the time, false alarms."

Nicole nodded. Maybe she was wrong. Maybe Kira was really one of the good guys. *Only one way to find out.*

"So how'd you end up in Kenya working for the government?"

Kira was quiet for so long, Nicole thought she was going to avoid answering. Then finally, "Back in 1998, a group of terrorists bombed three U.S. embassies in East Africa. My parents were among the two hundred twenty-four victims they murdered."

Nicole gasped.

"My father was a consular officer with the Foreign Service in Nairobi. A desk job, helping U.S. citizens with lost passports and medical emergencies. My parents had moved to Kenya a year before to start a new life. My father had forgotten his lunch at home and my mother was dropping it off when the car bomb went off. The explosives were hidden in the beds of two trucks. As you probably already know, al-Qaeda claimed responsibility."

"Where were you when it happened?" Nicole whispered.

"I was thirteen at the time and in school. The city was chaos. Sirens and alarms. People running everywhere. Phone lines not working, electricity out. The school sent all the students home, fearful of additional bombings. When my parents didn't return that evening and no one came calling to whisk us to the hospital to visit them, my brother and I reasoned they were amongst those killed, yet to be or unable to be identified."

Nicole longed to reach out in comfort but she curbed the impulse, raising a fist to her mouth instead. This was no lie. She could almost see the vulnerable, grieving teenager still lurking in the shadows of the adult woman.

"My aunt and uncle raised us." Kira pushed a wave of hair from her eyes, revealing a deep sadness in their blue depths. "All other growing pains aside, they provided me and my brother with first-rate educations and a very loving home. However, whereas my brother was able to put our parents' deaths behind him and move on, I couldn't. The need for vengeance in me never waned. I knew almost immediately that I would devote my entire career and the rest of my life to seeing each individual responsible for those bombings either in jail or dead."

A chill ran down Nicole's spine. She wouldn't want to be on the receiving end of Kira Anthony's wrath.

"After graduating from college, I joined the FBI's counterterrorism division. I made al-Qaeda my sole focus, studying everything about them—their infrastructure, bomb-making techniques, and philosophies. From there, I was recruited to work for a division within the Defense Intelligence Agency."

Nicole's mind raced as it worked to assemble the chronology of Kira's career. "So did you help track down Osama bin Laden?"

"Shevchenko and I were on one of the dozens of task forces analyzing clues that ultimately led the CIA to his fortified compound in Abbottabad. That Ukrainian is a computer whiz," she added admiringly, and the haunted look instantly evaporated from her face. "Shevchenko created many of those package sniffer programs I was telling you about. Even though these fanatical idiots denigrate anything Western, they certainly have no issue using the technology we created to communicate with one another. Although bin Laden was wise and refused to use the phone or Internet, his people didn't. And it was ultimately his downfall. When his courier made a phone call in 2010, it led us right to bin Laden's doorstep." She sighed heavily. "But it was never bin Laden I was after. Ayman al-Zawahiri was the mastermind who plotted to bomb the embassies, as well as the World Trade Center. Now that bin Laden is dead, he's been appointed al-Qaeda's official leader."

She stopped talking, like she was afraid she'd said too much There was a reason the Ice Princess shared such a poignant event in her life—Nicole just didn't know why yet.

"So what about you? What are your plans after graduation?"

Nicole hesitated. She didn't want to talk about herself. Now that she'd been given a little peek behind the curtain, she was greedy for more. Where did Kira actually live when she wasn't hunting terrorists? What did she do in her free time? Or was every spare minute dedicated to seeking her revenge against al-Qaeda?

Doubtful.

There was another side to Kira Anthony. Nicole had seen it very briefly when she'd accidentally let her mask down. Did she share that smile with someone special? It wasn't Stella, of that Nicole was almost certain after watching them together tonight. More than likely, Kira was straight. This notion filled her with a sharp disappointment.

"Well?"

Nicole realized Kira was staring at her expectantly, waiting for an answer.

"Nothing nearly as exciting as what you do. I'm gonna teach," she tried to sound enthusiastic, "perhaps at my old high school. My mother is a history teacher there."

Kira nodded. "How'd you know you wanted to become a teacher?"

It was a very simple question, but one Nicole couldn't immediately answer. Once upon a time, not so long ago, she was a rambunctious kid with a head full of wild dreams, excited about the future. She'd always longed to do something adventurous, like joining the military or even volunteering for the Peace Corps, but feared what the emotional impact of such an undertaking would have on her widowed mother.

After her father's death, Nicole's mother had grown more and more apprehensive about the safety of her two daughters, so much so that Nicole found it difficult to take a trip across town, never mind one out of the country. Learning foreign languages on a laptop in her bedroom had been her way of appeasing both her mother's paranoia and her own wild wanderlust. By the tenth grade, she'd become bored with studying French and turned her attention to Arabic because she'd been told it was one of the hardest languages to learn. Despite its difficulty, she stayed with it all through college. Speaking it didn't come easy for her, but she'd had no trouble mastering reading and writing the complex script. Teaching had seemed a wise career choice for someone with her language skills. Lord knew, her mother thought so.

Yet it was time for Nicole to stop deluding herself into thinking life was just going to magically work itself out. Somewhere out on the horizon, she'd always believed she was going to get there, that place where she was free to live the life she chose. She didn't know how or when; it was just always there, beyond her reach, but waiting for her. But she had to face it. Soon she'd have to start looking for work, and the thought of devoting eight to ten hours a day, five days a week in an enclosed classroom adhering to the outline of some state-issued lesson plan filled her with a sudden claustrophobia, more than the reality of being trapped down here, ten feet under the ground in a cement tomb.

"I thought it wouldn't be too hard to find a job," she finally said, unaware of the melancholy that flitted across her features. "But now with all the budget cutbacks, it looks like I could be waiting tables a little bit longer than I'd planned."

Kira quirked a brow. "I thought you were going to tell me you found teaching rewarding or that you liked kids."

"I do," Nicole said defensively, feeling like a fraud. For some insane reason, she longed to earn the admiration of the woman looking at her with something vaguely akin to disappointment.

"Probably time for you to get some rest and for me to go to work." Kira pushed herself to a standing position. "It's easy to get lost, so I'll walk you to your room." Glancing down at Nicole's socks, she asked, "Do your feet still hurt?"

"How'd you know?"

"I was the one who treated your wounds while you were sick. Your feet were a mess."

Kira had seen her naked. How could she forget that? An embarrassing flush ripped through her entire body, surely turning her cheeks a bright red. She was prone to blushing and she hated it.

"God, Nicole, you seem so," Kira's blue eyes were intense as she moved closer, slowly growing puzzled as they scrutinized her, "innocent."

Innocent? Nicole said nothing, unsure how to respond to such an odd appraisal. Danielle had described her once as *wholesome*, and she wasn't sure if it had been a compliment or a judgment.

Kira stared at her for a bit longer, then abruptly turned on the heels of her running shoes. Nicole sensed the sudden tension between them. Kira had become irritated with her, but why, she hadn't a clue. Her moods seem to change with no warning. One moment she was concerned, and the next, she was back to being cold and distant.

Tomorrow. Tomorrow she would find out how she was involved in this lunacy and soon she would be free. But what was she really hoping to escape from? This underground crypt buried where no one could ever find her even if they tried, or the disconcerting feelings the mercurial, mood-swinging enigma walking so tensely next to her had awakened within her?

Their hands accidentally collided and they both shrank away in response, almost as if the intimacy of an inadvertent touch was too personal for either one of them.

"I want to show you something," Kira said a minute later as they made their way through the cement tunnels. She slowed as they passed an open room filled with a dozen or so prehistoric computers. All of them were dark and silent except for one. "That machine controls the generators," she explained. "The entire system runs on small solar-powered panels stationed throughout the forest. It's surprisingly quite efficient. There's always ample hot water and we've never been without juice for any of our electronic devices. Amazing to think they created this technology over thirty years ago and yet we refuse to move toward embracing the sun as a true source for energy."

Nicole glanced at Kira from the corner of her eyes as they continued on. Not only was she incredibly intelligent, but her beauty was like an addictive drug; once viewed, you were left with an incredible yearning for more. Yet there was something more…something raw, intangible, and primitively sexual that radiated from her inner being. Nicole knew she wasn't safe, and it had nothing to do with anyone on motorcycles chasing her. She was in danger of succumbing to a very severe case of something beyond mere infatuation.

"Since I can't stay and teach, I assume I'll be able to go home soon?"

They were standing at the steel doorway to her room, the one that Nicole had erroneously locked when she'd first arrived. It wasn't completely closed, and Kira pushed it open with the tip of her sneaker.

"If that's truly what you want," Kira replied, then disappeared into the black hole from which they'd just emerged.

CHAPTER SEVEN

The intoxicating aroma of brewing coffee woke Nicole. Unsure of the time, she reached for her watch. It was a little past nine in the morning, Kenya time. After taking a quick shower and dressing in jeans and a long-sleeved gray T-shirt, she managed to make her way to the kitchen without getting lost. Her hiking boots stayed behind, at the side of her cot.

"Good morning, kiddo." Stella was seated at the table alone nursing a mug.

Nicole did a double take.

She was wearing mauve-colored lipstick and false eyelashes and her swarthy complexion had been dusted with rouge and facial powder. Her coarse black hair had been straightened and there were small pearls in her earlobes.

"You look especially pretty today, Stella." Nicole was rewarded with a wide smile.

"You want coffee? The beans for this coffee were harvested right here in Kenya," the dolled-up Ukrainian proudly informed her as she filled a plate with eggs and toast and set it down before Nicole.

No one else was in sight, but Nicole could almost sense that Kira was lurking nearby. Although she hated to admit it to herself, the thought filled her with anticipation.

"I love the smell, but I'm not a fan of the taste. So what's the plan today?"

"I think you and Kira have that talk."

As if on cue, the subject of their conversation made her entrance, and a trickle of awareness coursed down Nicole's spine. She was dressed in a white button-down shirt with the sleeves rolled up to her elbows and its length tucked into crisp khaki slacks secured with a brown leather belt. Her heeled boots looked more stylish than utilitarian, and her silky blond hair fell in a soft cascade around her shoulders. She poured herself a cup of coffee, leaned back against the kitchen's Formica countertop, and drank it in stoic stillness, avoiding Nicole completely.

Not much of a morning person, is she? Then Nicole remembered she'd been on duty at the computers most of the night.

"Finish your breakfast, kid—you need the protein." Stella winked. One of her false eyelashes separated from the glue and dangled precariously from her left eyelid. "Bogie's turn to rest and my time to take watch. See you later, gator."

"Never fails." Kira refilled her coffee cup and walked over to the table where Nicole was seated. "Four days in this hole and Shevchenko starts to lose it. I always know I need to send her up for air when the eyelashes appear. On the other hand, you look much healthier today."

Nicole knew that was a lie. Her fatigue always showed, and last night had been a rough one. She'd tossed and turned for hours, fantasizing about Kira.

"Are you done with your breakfast?"

Nicole nodded, wiping crumbs of dry crust from her mouth with a paper napkin she retrieved from the center of the table.

"Good. Come with me," Kira said softly, placing her mug of coffee next to Nicole's plate of half-eaten eggs. "Time we got down to business."

Nicole followed Kira's slim figure down yet another corridor, trying hard to focus on anything besides the outline of the perfectly round derrière in tan slacks. They entered a dimly lit office space overwhelmed by a large gunmetal gray desk and two orange-colored upholstered chairs. Nicole looked for a framed picture of a loved one or some other personal artifact, but there weren't any in sight.

"It was chic in the late seventies," Kira said dryly before taking a seat behind the desk and indicating Nicole should sit in one of the orange chairs.

She did, but the chair had been designed before *ergonomic* was even a word. Sitting required her to keep her back ramrod straight, otherwise the hard plastic molding stabbed at her shoulder blades.

"Relax, Nicole. You act as if you've been summoned to the principal's office." Kira smiled, but it didn't quite reach her eyes. She was again distant and guarded. "So tell me," she reclined back in her more modern chair and asked in a controlled voice, "how is it that someone who's never even crossed a state line in her entire twenty-two years suddenly flies off to Kenya for six weeks?"

Bewildered, Nicole couldn't think of an answer.

Kira leaned forward. "Who'd you come here to meet?"

"Meet?" Nicole realized she sounded like a slow-brained idiot, but she had no idea what the hell was Kira talking about.

"Yes, Nicole Kennedy." Kira tapped a pen impatiently against the surface of the desk. Her face darkened. "Why are you really here in Africa? You don't really expect me to believe that bullshit story about coming here to teach orphans, do you?"

Nicole swallowed hard. She couldn't admit that the only way to win her mother's endorsement for traveling to another country was if it were under the guise of a teaching internship. It would sound juvenile.

"I came here to teach. I thought it would be fun," she lied. "And maybe I'd get some research done for my thesis."

"With no laptop?"

"I b-brought notebooks," Nicole stammered. "I wasn't sure if I'd have access to electricity. I was going to use the old-fashioned method of pen and paper." She felt a surge of adrenaline surge through her. "Is that now illegal?" She caught her breath and squared her shoulders. She wasn't guilty of anything, so why was she acting as if she were?

"Strange for an education major to study Arabic." Kira stood and came around the desk. "And Nairobi's a hotbed for all sorts of criminal activity."

Alarm bells were ringing in Nicole's head. She didn't recall telling Kira what languages she'd studied.

"What are you implying? That I came all the way to Africa to cook up some outrageous plot against my own country?" She released a mocking snort. "You and these guys on the motorcycles definitely have me confused with someone else. In case you haven't been paying attention to what's happened to the economy, the teaching field isn't exactly exploding with job opportunities these days, so I thought if I continued studying Arabic it would make me more marketable." Her voice had slowly risen in volume until it was almost a shout. "Do those sound like the plans of someone whose picture you'd find on a most wanted poster in the post office?"

"It seems like you have your future all sketched out. It sounds very"—Kira paused, her tone sarcastic—"exciting."

Nicole squeezed her fists, the tips of her nails biting into the tender flesh of her palms. "You just accused me of flying to Nairobi for some furtive meeting with God knows who, and now you're mocking me for being dull?"

"Let's just stop the pretense, shall we?" Kira crossed her arms and leaned back against the desk. "I know all about you and Danielle."

Nicole felt the color drain from her face. The seat under her thighs felt hot and there was a thundering in her ears. The scrambled eggs she'd eaten were doing a dance inside her stomach. How could Kira know? Was the small bedroom she slept in equipped with some sort of mind-reading mechanism?

"How do you know about that? Nobody knows about that," she mumbled loud enough for Kira to hear. She stared at the gray cement floor waiting for her world to stop spinning. Fragments of comments made over the past few days swirled about her head, but it was difficult to put them together into some semblance of sense.

Just how had Kira known about her and Danielle? She squeezed her head between her hands, as if the pressure would stir some neural activity. She lifted her head. "How long?"

"How long what?"

"How long have you people been stalking me?"

"Stalking? Don't be dramatic, Nicole."

"How long have you been eavesdropping on me?"

Kira's blue eyes sparkled. "I'm not admitting to anything—but electronic monitoring does allow access to conversations, e-mails, telephone conversations, and the like."

Nicole thought of that night in her bedroom with Danielle. Had Kira been listening? And why? A rush of angry embarrassment enflamed her face. "What right do you have to do that?"

"The Patriot Act gives us the right." She got to her feet. "Now tell me, who'd you come here to meet and why?"

"The Patriot Act? You can't be serious." She threw out a hand into the air, needled. "For kissing a girl?"

It was Kira's turn to look surprised, but she recovered quickly.

"I didn't think Danielle was your type." She leaned back against the desk. "Guess the old cliché is true." She pursed her lips. "There's no accounting for taste."

Nicole had a sudden violent urge to reach out and slap Kira across her cheek. Instead, she stood up. "You have the wrong person. Your computer sniffer thingamajig screwed up. Bad intelligence. I've never even had a speeding ticket. And if you want to know the truth, I sort of suck at speaking Arabic."

Kira remained motionless. "Did Danielle ever mention her father is a colonel in the army?"

The back of Nicole's neck began to tingle. She knew nothing

about Danielle's father. Danielle had always avoided talking about her family, changing the subject whenever she brought it up.

"So if I tell you that this colonel was one of the last people your father was seen with before that car bomb took his life, you'd agree that that's an awfully strange coincidence, wouldn't you, Nicole?"

The question sent Nicole reeling backward on the figurative heels inside her head, grasping for something mentally solid to keep her from falling and crashing, but her brain went blank. She was at a loss, empty inside and bereft for an answer.

"That's impossible," she claimed, stumbling back to the chair, unconsciously clinging tightly to her necklace.

"It is. And just what are the chances that twelve years after your father was killed, you end up sharing an apartment with the daughter of the very man we believe your father was about to turn evidence against? Danielle's father is Rhyse Taylor. Colonel Rhyse Taylor."

It was all too much. Reliving her father's death, the hijacking, the time changes, the fever, the realization she had no idea what she was going to do with her life, the attraction to a woman who was being downright hateful to her, and now these insinuating allegations involving Danielle. The next thing she knew she was buckled forward on her knees, face in her hands, trying to stem the sudden flow of tears that would not be denied.

CHAPTER EIGHT

I'm sorry if I was a little rough," Kira said, her voice gentle and sincere as she plopped down into the other plastic chair next to her.

"Do ya think?" Nicole asked. She rubbed her palms against her eyelids but stopped when a warm hand pressed against the small of her back. Upset and disturbed as she was, she was conscious of Kira's body so close to her own and the light scent of soap and jasmine. Part of her wanted to relish the physical connection, while another part wanted to flee in panic, while still another part was suspicious of this sudden concern. "So why the third degree?" She wiped away the last of the tears from her eyes.

"I had to be certain you weren't somehow involved with Danielle." Kira retrieved a box of tissues from a metal shelf and handed them to her. "You're not, are you?"

Nicole's sniffled into one of the tissues. "If what you're saying is true, I had no idea about Danielle."

She pictured Danielle, with her wheat-colored hair, large hazel eyes, and the sprinkling of freckles across the bridge of her tilted nose. "My God, are you absolutely sure?"

Kira nodded solemnly. "Danielle's father killed your father, Nicole. And there's no way you two coincidentally crossed paths one day and became best friends. Your meeting and friendship was planned."

Making friends with other girls had always been difficult for shy, introverted Nicole. But that hadn't been the case with Danielle. Danielle had pursued her, she now realized.

"During the short time you two lived together, Danielle never mentioned her father?"

Nicole shook her head. "She was reluctant to talk about her family. No one ever came to visit either."

"I was worried she might have told you a bunch of lies, tried to win you over. But I see I was wrong." Her eyes held Nicole's for a long moment. "And you're positive she never mentioned anything about her father?"

"You seemed to know what books I've read and what courses I've taken, so I'm sure you already know all the details of our conversations. And you must also know I haven't spoken to her since December."

"Sometimes we miss things. Not all discussions occur within range of our equipment."

"You mean the bugs you hid in my apartment," she snapped. *Thank you very much, George Bush, for your Gestapo politics.* "So if Danielle wasn't trying to recruit me to the dark side, what did she hope to gain by pretending to be my friend?"

"She was looking for something."

Nicole frowned, her tone dubious. "What would I have? And why now? It's been over a decade since my father died."

Nicole watched Kira pace back and forth in front of the desk before finally returning to sit next to her. "Look, Nicole, we both lost people we love at a very young age. Just as I'm seeking justice for my parents' murders, I'd like to help you do the same. Your father's death was no random act of terrorism by some religious zealot. It was a premeditated and deliberate homicide. And we know Colonel Rhyse Taylor was behind it—we just need to prove it."

Nicole tried to sit back, but the plastic wings of the chair jabbing at her reminded her she couldn't. A memory flashed in her head. On the mantel in her mother's living room was a picture of

Luke Kennedy holding a baby. A three-year-old Liz was standing at his side in a cardboard crown from some fast food promotion accompanied by a gaudy pink boa around her neck. She'd never forget her father's expression as he looked down into Nicole's baby face in that picture. She had always been the apple of his eye. They "got" each other. He'd understood her need to climb trees and build forts in the backyard. Or use her mother's makeup to paint a mural on the back of the house. And he'd been the one to introduce her to French as she sat on his lap in the den and they listened to the Pimsleur cassettes over and over. He'd even glued a giant map of the world on her bedroom wall, and together they would point at countries they were going to visit together when she was older. He always made it seem like the biggest cause for celebration was her birthday, making the twenty-third of April the most spectacular day on the calendar.

"It doesn't make any sense." She shook her head. "My father was a geologist for Davenport Petroleum. He gathered sand and soil specimens for possible oil exploration. Why would someone from the military have wanted him dead?"

"I'll start at the beginning and tell you all I know. And then maybe you can help me?"

"I'll try," she replied.

"About a year and half ago, I was part of a team reviewing car bomb attacks before 9/11. We were hoping to find some overlooked detail that would lead us to bin Laden. As you already know, an unknown anti-American religious group not linked to al-Qaeda claimed responsibility for the bomb that took your father's life, but we wanted to be thorough. In the past decade, technology has become a lot more sophisticated. And we've also become much more knowledgeable about terrorist groups. So when we reexamined all the evidence, we were quite surprised to find that this incident didn't fit the paradigm of a terrorist act—the area in Yemen where the explosion occurred was vacant. Most take place in highly populated areas. The more victims, the better.

The type of explosive used in the detonation wouldn't have been available on the black market at that time. And the parts used to construct the bomb were extremely high quality. Then we took a closer look at the group that claimed responsibility for the bomb and discovered no trace of such an organization before or after this attack. When I began digging into the victim's background, I grew even more intrigued. Your father's name surfaced as an informant in a case involving the sale of the army's own weaponry to terrorist groups in North Africa. In the report I read, Rhyse Taylor was investigated, but they didn't have enough evidence to indict. After the car bomb killed your father, the illegal trafficking of the weapons and ammunition immediately ceased. The trail was cold and the case suspended."

The air inside the small office space felt thick and oppressive. Nicole inhaled a deep breath, trying to take it all in.

"This is difficult, Nicole, but…" She paused and looked away. Her voice, usually so sure and confident, was small and hesitant: "We think your father may have been working with Rhyse Taylor." Kira held up a hand as if to say *hear me out.* "Your father spent a lot of time in the Mideast. Working for the oil company, he made many connections. He would have been the perfect candidate to act as the conduit between Taylor and those who wanted to buy illegal weapons."

"You didn't know my father," Nicole replied, setting her jaw stubbornly. "There's no way he'd commit treason."

"You're right," Kira soothed. "I didn't know him. I'm only reading old files and making calculated assumptions. Either way, it doesn't matter because your father eventually did do the right thing. We believe he was collecting evidence to incriminate Taylor. And somehow, he was found out."

Nicole felt queasy. "Dead men can't testify, right?"

"Yes, but now we believe your father hid that evidence before he was killed. You were a child, barely ten when your father was taken from you. But you two were extremely close.

Did he perhaps give you any papers or CDs or tell you to keep something for safe keeping before his death? I need your help, Nicole."

Nicole needed a chance to think. Kira was obviously not going to give her that courtesy.

"Crap, my head. It's killing me." Nicole bent forward, grasping her skull between her hands. "I feel sick."

She sensed Kira's skeptical eyes glaring at her. But after an awkward minute, Kira finally said in a resigned tone, "Let me get you some water."

"Aspirin too," Nicole mewed, her voice barely an octave above a whisper.

As soon as the door shut behind Kira, Nicole was up and pulling open desk drawers that had been left unlocked. She fumbled through dozens of army green office folders with a nervous haste, looking for anything that might provide her with a missing piece to this strange puzzle.

"Hurry!" she chastised herself. "There has to be something in here!"

But every folder she opened was either empty or filled with pages written in Russian. Nevertheless, she managed to discern a small blurb in English written in blue ink at the top of one of the memos stuffed within a thin folder hanging in the very front of the drawer.

United Airlines flight 423 arrives 10:00 a.m. Attack to take place at—followed by and the longitude and latitude numbers, which had to lead to a barren road just outside of Muranga. *Win her trust. Get to it before they do*, was scribbled alongside the flight info.

She could hear Kira's voice again, in her head.

"And still in other scenarios, we'll manipulate our target psychologically in order to acquire the information we need, and then we'll disappear from their life without anyone being the wiser."

"You torture people?"

"No, Nicole, nothing as medieval as torture in our line of work. We're very modern in our methodology, and I'll just leave it at that."

She pictured the passengers of the bus during the hijacking. Calm and quiet. No mad stampede down the aisle to get the hell off the bus and far away from the guys with the guns. The only hysterical screams ringing through the tinny interior of the bus had come from her because everyone else had been anticipating the crash, bracing for it. She recalled the bus driver—climbing on board the bus almost an hour late.

And, of course, Stella's frantic announcement about the children in one of the villages being in peril.

"Goddamn," she whispered to herself. "That's downright diabolical."

Everything that had happened, every last bit of it, had been a crock. Nothing more than a well-orchestrated theatrical production designed to convince her that she was in danger; that bogeymen were after her and closing in fast. But the question that remained was *why?*

Why the need to manipulate her?

"Evidence, my ass," she whispered out loud. Whatever they were after was much more valuable than her father's notes about some military wacko selling guns to nut-jobs in Libya.

Or wherever.

The sound of Kira's boots clacking on the concrete drew nearer.

She shoved the paper back into the drawer.

"Shouldn't you should be sitting?"

Nicole looked up, composing her features carefully.

"Actually, I'd just like to go back to my room and rest for a while," Nicole managed to mutter through dry lips, her heart pounding.

Kira scanned the desktop. "Sure," she replied coolly, peering toward the desk's drawers and then back to Nicole's face.

Do not crack! Breathe normally!

Despite her own admonitions, Nicole's last intake of breath seemed to solidify into a massive lump in her throat.

"No aspirin, but I found some ibuprofen."

Their fingers touched during the exchange of the small white packet. A tremor of awareness shot up Nicole's arm, straight down her spinal cord and into her soul.

"You've had a lot thrown at you. We'll talk more later. Can you make it back to your room by yourself?"

Nicole nodded.

"Nicole." Kira's voice was low, but it sounded like a roar in Nicole's ears. Reluctantly, she turned, certain guilt was written all over her face. "Don't you want something to wash down the pills with?"

Kira stood casually against the wall, holding a bottle of water in an outstretched hand. She grabbed the water, avoiding Kira's eyes.

CHAPTER NINE

Nicole bolted upright with a start, afraid she'd slept through the night and blown her chances of escape. She glanced at the time on her Timex. The tension left her at once. Not quite eleven at night.

She pulled the long string cord dangling from the ceiling light while reaching for the Ziploc bag Stella had dropped off for her earlier. The trusting Ukrainian seemed to have bought her tale about not feeling well—*"maybe a relapse, Stella"*—and left Nicole alone, urging her to rest. Under the guise of illness, Nicole had been able to spend the rest of the day in bed so she'd be fresh for tonight. Her sleep had been broken and restless, remembering her times with Danielle *and* her father as she tried to reconcile their memories with their new personas: spy and traitor.

She couldn't.

She also was afraid that at any moment Kira would come bursting through the unlocked steel door demanding to know where her father's hiding place was. But she stayed away, and Nicole did finally manage to get some sleep.

Famished, she pulled the soft sandwich from its protective plastic. As she ate a very American peanut butter with grape jelly on wheat bread, she pulled her duffel bag from the closet and shoved only the essentials she would need into it. The rest of her belongings she would have to leave behind. She tested the bag's weight. Good. Light enough to carry without becoming an immediate strain on her shoulders. She had a long walk ahead of her.

With some trepidation, she slipped her feet into her hiking boots. Her toes and heel were still a little sore, but she'd manage. At the bathroom sink, she drank greedily from the faucet. It might be a while before she found water, so she filled up the now empty bottle Kira had given her that afternoon. When she was done, she wondered if the water supply might not be safe to drink. Maybe they only used it for bathing. All of the water she'd been given to drink had been in sealed plastic bottles. She shrugged her shoulders. If she should become ill from any invisible organisms swimming about her gut, hopefully it wouldn't happen until she was far, far away from here.

If all went as planned, she'd be on her way back home by this time tomorrow.

Opening the bedroom door, she peered down the corridor to make sure the coast was clear. Somewhere in the darkness ahead was another windowless chamber where Kira lay sleeping. At least Nicole hoped she was sleeping. Kira had worked the late shift the previous night and should be dead tired.

Patting her thigh, she felt the securing comfort of the small lump hidden in the loose pocket of her jeans. That afternoon, as she lay awake wondering why now, all these years later, these people wanted whatever it was her father had hidden away somewhere, and what it was—because it certainly *had* to be something far more important than evidence incriminating a man who's been walking around free for the last twelve years—she'd remembered her pocketknife and started searching through her duffel bag for it. Last night, Bogie had warned her about the nearby marijuana farms. The dull, rusty four-inch blade wasn't much to defend herself with should she cross paths with a hungry lion or one of those plantation workers, but it was all she had and it was certainly better than nothing. Pulling her knife from its sheath, she gripped the weapon's handle tightly and cautiously made her break for freedom.

Creeping stealthily and hugging the wall, she propelled herself forward. She kept peering back, certain at any moment Bogie was going to rush from the inky shadows to tackle and drug her before locking her up for the rest of her life in this cement vault. A light emanated from the kitchen. She had to go past it. Hopefully no one was awake, indulging in a late-night craving for one of those boxed meals or tins of cookies.

As she drew closer, she dropped to her knees and crawled. When she reached the kitchen door, she paused to listen. All was quiet except for the steady swish of the air blowing through the ceiling ducts. With some hesitation, she poked her head into the room and did a quick scan. There was an open bag of chips on the table and an empty plate near the sink but not a soul in sight. Breathing a sigh of relief, she moved onward, her hiking boots occasionally squeaking as the rubber scraped against the hard stone. Every time they made the loud screeching noise, she'd cringe and stop, waiting for the discovery she felt was inevitable.

The fabric of her jeans provided a decent barrier between her skin and the cement, but there wasn't any padding to protect her kneecaps, which began to ache and grow sore from the impact with the hard concrete. Holding the knife in her right fist while she inched along on all fours was also irksome and uncomfortable. Minuscule granules of sand had become embedded in the sensitive surface of her fingers between the knuckle and the fingernail, and the pressure of her weight pressing down made it feel like she was crushing the small pebbles into her bones.

But those were just little things, inconveniences she could endure as she remained completely focused on getting to where the labyrinth of tunnels converged as fast as she could. From there, all she'd have to do was figure out which one of the tunnels would take her back to the narrow shaft with the ladder and then she'd be free.

Up ahead now, maybe only ten more feet to go. She crawled faster now, ignoring the pain in her knees and the cramping. Five more feet…

"Where do you think you're going?"

Nicole froze. *Kira.*

"Did you really think it would be as simple as walking out of here in the middle of the night, Nicole?"

She didn't have to turn around to know that Kira was amused. There was no telling how long Kira had been behind her, watching her with a smirk on her face before saying something. This infuriated her even more than being snuck up upon from behind and having her escape thwarted. She stood up, brushing the dust from her jeans and the fragments of cement from her hands.

"At least tell me how you were going to get through the steel doors?" Kira went on, a trace of laughter in her voice. "They're bolted shut and can only be opened with a code." She emerged from the shadows, her lips twisted in a mocking smirk. "A code, I might add, that's exceptionally intricate and hard to decipher."

Her hair was pinned up in a comb-like clip at the back of her head, long silky tendrils hanging loose around her face and neck in sexy dishevelment. Other women spent hours striving to perfect that fashionably careless look, but Nicole had no doubt Kira hadn't given her appearance more than a second's attention.

"I figured it all out, Kira. Not your imaginary code, but your game."

Kira said nothing. There was just enough light for Nicole to see one dark shapely brow rising in mute inquiry.

"The gadget around your wrist is just as much of a charade as every other thing that's happened to me since boarding my bus back in Nairobi. There are no bolts and codes. There are no sinister madmen with machine guns after me. The only thing keeping me here is my own delusional thinking—aided by you and your friends every step of the way. I gotta admit, it was a pretty good plan—waiting to strike while my stress level was at its highest and my body was weak from sickness and fever. Did you study theater at college? Because you're a great actress. Just like those people on my bus. They were all in on it, weren't they?"

"I suspected you'd been snooping when I left you alone in the office. You're very easy to read, Nicole. Although your daring impresses me, I'm more disappointed by your lack of planning. What would you have done if you'd managed to escape from here? It's pitch black outside and something tells me even if you did have a compass, you wouldn't know your north from your south."

Nicole didn't answer her—there wasn't any point. She hadn't really thought that far ahead—all she'd cared about was getting out of here. She bit her lip and dug her fingernails into her palms.

"Go back to your room and get some sleep." Kira waved her hand dismissively.

Nicole's hand tightened on her knife as anger surged through her, but before she could even think of making a move, Kira lunged forward. She caught Nicole's wrist, pressing her thumb against the muscles there in such a way that the knife fell from her grip and dropped to the floor.

"Let go of me!" Nicole demanded, trying in vain to shake Kira off, but the effort was useless. Her grasp was like a steel vise.

"There are cameras everywhere, but lucky for you, I'm on duty again tonight. I have to admit," she lowered her voice, "it was rather entertaining watching you skulk about like some character in a bad movie, but I was afraid you'd accidentally trigger an alarm and wake up Stella and Bogie. They both need their sleep, especially tonight."

The amusement in Kira's voice pushed Nicole beyond angry.

Provoked to her breaking point, she remembered the handwritten note on the Russian memo she'd found. "You failed!" she hissed. "You didn't win my trust, and you never will."

In response, her hand was gripped even tighter, producing a pins and needles tingling in the tips of her fingers.

"I hate you," she added childishly.

"You say that," Kira whispered as she took control of Nicole's hands and backed her roughly into the corridor's hard wall, "but your body tells me otherwise." Kira's looked down Nicole's shirt and jeans. In spite of everything—her anger and distrust, she felt her legs getting weak and her lower stomach fluttering with arousal.

Her body was indeed betraying her.

She could feel her nipples grow suddenly sensitive, grazing against the fabric of her bra as a curling vortex of heat traveled like a lit fuse across the inner lining of her loins. There were only six or so inches separating them, and Kira's subtle scent invaded the small space like a fragrant cloud. She wanted to shout a loud denial to Kira's all-too-accurate assertion, to break free and run, but her hands were suddenly released and a long, slender finger was placed against her lips to silence her.

"Shh, no more words between us," Kira purred in the dim light.

Nicole felt her resistance waning.

"I can't keep fighting it either." Kira's voice was like warm, liquid silk.

"Fight what?"

"This."

Kira's hands softly cradled Nicole's face in a tender clasp. Kira leaned forward and gently kissed her. Nicole melted in surrender, unable to stop herself from arching into Kira's warmth. She opened her mouth to accept the tentative tip of Kira's tongue, savoring the sweet taste and essence that was her.

All the tension of their encounters had been building to this moment between them, the tone of their kiss one second coaxingly sweet and the next punishing as they each struggled with the raw passion they roused in each other.

All rational thought seemed to have left Nicole completely, her physical being now nothing more than a wanton entity of tingling nerve endings and unfathomable aching, but then, suddenly, a rush of chilling cool air swooped in between them, jerking her down from the blissful realm she'd been floating within. She lifted her head, weak and bewildered, her lips still quivering from the unrestrained intensity of the kiss they'd just shared.

"Go back to your room, Nicole," Kira ordered, her voice strangled and guttural. She took an unsteady step backward.

The fluorescent lighting was flickering to life overhead. Dazed, Nicole blinked hard, adjusting to the blinding luminance with great difficulty. When she eventually did, she saw an icy contempt in the blue eyes that just a moment earlier had been feverishly bright with need and desire and passion.

"What's all the commotion here?" Stella asked reproachfully from somewhere beyond the haze of desire that was shaking Nicole's ability to think clearly. "It's very late, little one. You need to sleep," Stella suggested softly, closer now. "Soon you'll be able to go home."

When the fog cleared Nicole saw that Kira was already halfway down the passageway. Stella, her mouth a thin line of disapproval, was casting one very dark look at her colleague's retreating figure.

CHAPTER TEN

Once the door to her room was closed, Nicole tossed her duffel bag to one side and dropped down to her tender knees, gulping in several deep, ragged breaths of air. What had just happened? She put a hand to her lips. She could still feel the soft, warm imprint of Kira's mouth on her own. Trembling, she reached down to touch the cold cement beneath her in an effort to cool her burning desires. *This is what it must feel like to be struck by lightning and survive*, she thought. Her nerves felt jittery, her muscles weak and rubbery. What was wrong with her? How could this woman have such an effect on her?

The unsettling, frightening truth was that if Stella had not interrupted them, she wouldn't have been able to stop. She recalled her encounter with Danielle—and was amazed by how much that experience paled in comparison. *Now* she finally understood what was meant by sexual chemistry—that basic, primal attraction from inside that was impossible to resist.

An image flashed inside her head. With horrible clarity she recalled Kira's face when Stella had switched on the lights. She physically winced as she saw again the derision in the blue eyes staring back at her. Nicole felt her insides clench with humiliation.

What was I thinking? That the one they all call Ice Princess had become so overwhelmed by passion for me that she'd simply lost control?

It was almost laughable. It had all been just another of her twisted mind games—manipulating Nicole for her own purposes, using her sexuality as a means to an as yet unknown end.

Writhing in shame and mortification, Nicole curled into a tight ball and leaned back against the closed steel door only to feel something hard and obtrusive poking at her tailbone. It was her knife. She didn't remember bending and retrieving it during her mad exodus. She picked it up and stumbled over to her bed. She fell down atop the blankets despondently. There would be no escape. She was stuck here, a prisoner for as long as they wanted to keep her.

❖

At some point, she dozed off. One minute she'd been wondering just what information Kira had hoped to obtain from her tonight if their kiss hadn't been disrupted, and the next thing she knew, Stella was standing over her, one hand pressed lightly down upon her shoulder, giving it a gentle squeeze.

"Time to go, kid."

Nicole blinked.

"Get up. We've got only a few minutes."

"What's going on?" she moaned once she managed to remove her tongue from where it was plastered to the roof of her mouth. She pushed her tangled hair from her face, wiped a crumb of sleep from her eyes, and made to sit up, disoriented.

"You're going home."

"Home?" Nicole repeated with effort, trying to make sense of the word. Was she dreaming? She couldn't be serious, could she?

"C'mon, get up," Stella urged as she tugged the blanket from the bed. "Bogie's waiting."

"Bogie?" Nicole sat up sleepily. "But I just went to sleep."

"It's four thirty in morning. Bogie and I will hike with you to a spot where a helicopter can land. That's why we have to move fast! It will take you to Nairobi and," she flashed a bundle of official-looking papers in her face, "from there you'll get on a plane that will take you back to Washington DC."

Nicole was instantly awake. The events of last night came flooding back into her mind.

The kiss.

A blissful sensation rippled down her spine when she thought of Kira's lips upon her own; the taste of her, the wondrous feel of being pressed so closely against her.

"Don't you want to go home, little one?"

Nicole lifted her face to Stella, her eyes bright as she fought to control her emotions. "I've wanted out of here from the moment I arrived," she declared, tossing back the blanket and getting to her feet.

After washing her face, brushing her teeth, and tossing the rest of her clothes into her already half-packed duffel bag, she was strolling down the very passageway she had meant to use for her escape plans last night. She watched with wide, disbelieving eyes as Stella peeled back the sleeve of the black sweater she was wearing and began punching keys on the same type of electronic device Kira had worn around her wrist upon their arrival. In response, internal mechanisms churned and twisted loudly before the steel doors magically parted to allow them access to the rusty ladder leading up to the forest.

"Okay, so I was wrong. The bolts and locks are real," Nicole murmured aloud in a defeated voice only she could hear.

"Bogie's already above. Ready?"

Nicole cast a blank glance backward, confused by her own feelings.

She knew she should be ecstatic her incarceration was finally coming to an end, yet…it felt like some invisible force was telling her to stay. The rational part of her brain knew it was absurd nonsense, but as she watched the steel doors close firmly behind her, she felt like she was relinquishing hold of some intangible but extraordinarily significant dimension to her life.

She would never see Kira again.

Ever.

She shook her head.

The only explanation for this illogical sentimentality was a condition she'd studied in one of her psych classes—it was called Stockholm Syndrome. It was a psychosis in which hostages or kidnap victims slowly begin to feel affection for their captors.

"Yep, that's definitely gotta be it," she reasoned, climbing up the shaft with a manufactured enthusiasm.

Once outside, she pushed the tiny ache in her chest away from her thoughts and inhaled deeply. *Fresh air.* The perfumed breeze was filled with the uniquely pungent scent of Kenyan vegetation. Every pore in her body tingled. After several days inside the bunker and breathing recycled air, the cool splendor of the early-morning dampness was invigorating. She looked up. The sky was clear and the stars sparkled, but she didn't recognize a single constellation.

"The sun won't be up for a bit," Bogie informed her, shining an industrial-sized flashlight on the artificial rock so Stella could reset it back on its concealed hinges.

"We have a two-mile walk ahead, but without the benefit of daylight, the trek will be hard. Don't fall behind," he advised. "And stay alert. This isn't a park."

"Okay," Nicole replied, still too confused to make much sense of anything. For the first twenty minutes of the hike, as her body adjusted to the chill of the early morning as well as Bogie's rapid pace, her mind remained preoccupied with images of Kira and that earth-shattering memory of their kiss. She said nothing to her two hiking companions, not even questioning the details of her sudden release or the intricacies of her transport back to the Unites States. But finally her brain cells fluttered to life.

How do I know where they're leading me?

Her heart dropped into her empty stomach. All was serene and quiet, no sound other than their footwear falling softly on the dirt and the occasional crunch of foliage as they passed under or over a bush. The moon was a fading silvery crescent as the sky slowly began to lighten. Stella looked back at her and Nicole could see concern in those big dark eyes.

"Okay, kid?"

Stella. She liked Stella. The eccentric Ukrainian wouldn't do anything to hurt her, Nicole was sure of that.

She trusted Stella.

Wham!

It hit Nicole so quickly her knees went weak and she lost her balance.

Win her trust.

How stupid could she be?

Kira hadn't failed. She'd won.

Nicole had blindly followed Stella and six-foot-five Bogie into the African wilderness with no protection other than the knife bobbing up and down somewhere in the folds of her luggage.

"Here she comes!" Bogie suddenly announced.

They'd emerged from the forest into a flat, treeless valley glistening with the first brilliant rays of the dawn's warm red-gold light. Bogie was pointing a large ebony finger toward the eastern horizon. Nicole lifted her eyes to the sky, the warmth of the sun's yellow beams warming her cold cheeks as the sounds of a helicopter grew closer.

"It's beautiful," Nicole breathed in awe. Her fears and apprehension left her now that the helicopter was in sight. She really *was* heading home.

And she was trying to relish her first and only African sunrise, but Stella was now pacing in a circle, her eyes darting nervously back and forth.

"I must tell you something!" Stella shouted to Nicole over the increasing noise of the approaching copter.

Nicole recalled Stella's face last night when the lights flickered on. There was no doubt from her expression Stella had known something had occurred, but did she actually witness the kiss between her and Kira? What was it she wanted to say to her now? *Stay away from Kira, she is mine?* But there had been no glint of malice in those black eyes last night, no dull hurt shining from their depths; only disapproval mixed with censure, and those sentiments seemed to have been aimed at Kira.

"Shevchenko, it will work itself out in time!" Bogie shook his bald head. "Leave it alone!"

Stella volleyed back, "Time is something we don't have!" There was another comment, but her husky accented words could no longer be heard, dissolving into the blustering currents of air blasting across the grass. The helicopter was landing just a dozen feet away, making conversation near impossible. She continued to look imploringly at Nicole, her dark eyes intense. Frustrated, the dark-haired Ukrainian reached into a leather satchel she'd been carrying across her back, grabbed what appeared to be the airplane paperwork and a pen, and scribbled something on the outside of the ticket jacket before shoving it into Nicole's canvas bag. Bogie grabbed Nicole's hand and pulled her toward a tall, broad-shouldered man emerging from the helicopter's cockpit.

She looked back toward Stella and waved as if she were saying farewell to a friend rather than some fantastic character from the most bizarre episode of her life, which already seemed like a dream. Bogie winked at her before giving her a mock salute.

"Ready to go for a ride?"

Nicole nodded at the tanned, rugged pilot and within minutes they were airborne. The hilltop with its hidden underground burrow vanished from her sight. She reached inside her bag to retrieve the ticket jacket Stella had given her, searching for the words she'd written in such haste. There they were, scribbled along the frayed edge of an advertisement for an American Express card: *Remember the Tin Man.*

What the hell was that supposed to mean?

And what had Bogie meant about it working itself out in time? *What* would work itself out in time?

"You okay back there?" The dark blond pilot asked once

they'd been flying for a few minutes. She saw he'd removed his aviation headphones and was waiting for her to respond.

"Great!" she mouthed, giving him the thumbs up.

"We have a quick detour to make before we land at the airport!"

A frisson of alarm curled up inside Nicole's stomach as her mind ran wild with crazy possibilities. Yet her instincts told her the good-looking pilot with the gorgeous hair, American accent, and chiseled features was harmless. He practically reeked of sexy charm, from his perfect white-toothed grin down to the engaging twinkle in his dark blue eyes.

"Why don't you come sit up here next to me? It's a much better view, and this way we won't have to keep yelling at each other!"

Nicole maneuvered up to the cockpit.

"You can't leave Africa without having a glimpse of one of the most breathtaking sights you'll ever behold," he said into his microphone after handing Nicole an extra headset, watching as she placed it over her ears.

The domed windshield offered a completely different perspective than the rear passenger seat window. Miles and miles of unpolluted earth filled her view. There were no roads, no vehicles, not even one building to stain the majesty of the African landscape. The pilot reached under his seat and produced a pair of binoculars for her to use, a sly smile twisting his lips just before he grabbed the throttle and veered the copter south.

"Helicopters are noisy. So I don't disturb the animals, I'll have to stay up a good height, but you'll still get quite an eyeful."

Nicole nodded, pleased he was thoughtful enough to consider the well-being of the wildlife. She adjusted the scope of the binoculars to fit her face and settled back into her seat to enjoy the ride. When he pointed a tanned finger, she took a few seconds to focus the binoculars, and gasped. Less than twenty minutes later, she'd seen herds of gazelles galloping across the plains, a family of giraffe foraging through the sparse branches of an acacia tree, and a lone rhinoceros bathing in a pool of muck and glaring at them severely enough so Nicole was glad she was out of his reach.

"This is the Masai Reserve. It's protected against hunters and poachers. If we had time, I'd take you to the Mara River, but at least this morning you'll get to see the march of the wildebeests."

They were heading back north, and just to the left of the copter, Kira could make out a lengthy train of what looked like moose, and she said as much aloud.

"Those are actually the wildebeests," the pilot indicated with a jut of his square chin. "Each year, thousands of them begin their long trek from the Kenyan border to the Masai Reserve. They're constantly tracked by predators and circled by vultures, so their journey is dangerous and long. But they do it and most of 'em make it." His deep voice was filled with admiration. "Nature is a remarkable navigator."

"That was incredible," Nicole said when Nairobi's airfields came into sight. "I can't thank you enough. I'm sorry, but I don't even know your name."

"Mike. And it's not me you have to thank. Kira asked that I take you for a quick tour before dropping you at the airport."

A tender warmth rose up in Nicole's chest. Damn. Kira would have to go and do something nice like this to just mess with her mind one last time.

The helicopter descended onto a white circle painted atop the black tarmac.

"Your ears may ring for a bit," Mike informed Nicole jovially, helping her from the cockpit and taking her headset. "If you go inside the small blue building there and ask for Tom, he'll drive you over to the main terminal."

"Mike, if you see Kira, will you tell her…" And Nicole found she couldn't complete her thoughts, not sure what it was exactly she wanted to say. The horrible woman had faked a hijacking, caused Nicole to miss her teaching internship, accused her of treason, and labeled her father a criminal—never mind what had occurred between them last night. She shouldn't feel at all grateful for the brief excursion over the wilds of Africa, but she was, and the feelings fluttering about her heart left her tongue-tied.

"I'll tell her," Mike stated kindly, nodding his fair head in parting before disappearing into a maintenance hangar.

Nicole had the inexplicable feeling that she had not seen the last of the hunky pilot.

CHAPTER ELEVEN

The first thing Nicole's blurry gaze fell upon was a decade old N'sync poster featuring a very young Justin Timberlake in the center. It was mounted on the back of her bedroom door with strips of tape that had aged to a dusty urine-colored yellow. She stared hard at his boyish features and curly hair until her tired eyes were finally able to focus.

It wasn't quite seven in the morning yet, but it was already hot and humid. She'd come home to a good old-fashioned East Coast heat wave, and for some odd reason her mother hadn't yet switched on the air conditioner for the summer.

Placing a pillow under her head, she gazed up at the ceiling fan's motionless white blades and thought how wonderful its gentle breeze would feel, but she simply lacked the required amount of energy needed to get up and yank the cord.

Even though she'd arrived home before yesterday's sun had even dawned, and done little else but sleep and watch TV since, she was still suffering the disorienting effects of jet lag.

At least that's how she was trying to explain the strange emptiness that had opened up inside her, like a black hole in the center of her very being vacuuming out the remnants of the person she once was. Looking around her childhood bedroom, she expected to see the ghost of her former self hovering in one of the corners.

A lot had changed during the past week.

She had changed.

Lying there in her old bed amidst a sea of stuffed-animals she'd collected over the years, her faded pink and white gingham coverlet strewn across the bed in twisted disarray, she reflected upon the extraordinary events of the prior week.

It wasn't much different than if she'd been abducted by space aliens, taken to another galaxy, experimented upon, and deposited back onto Earth. No one would believe her if she told them her wild tale.

Straight to the looney bin she'd go.

"Did you enjoy the show last night?" she asked out loud.

She lay silent for a full minute, waiting for Kira to travel through some invisible portal and appear in the middle of the room. Were the microphones they'd planted still active? Had they even existed to begin with?

She rolled over on her side, recalling the excruciating and humbling conversation she'd had with her mother last night. After a calorie-laden delivery pizza with extra cheese, her mother had tentatively broached the subject of Nicole's sudden, unexpected return from Africa. Although Nicole longed to tell her mother everything that had happened, from the first moment Kira had entered her life to the last, she realized she couldn't. The real story of her few days away, even minus the kiss and sexual attraction, would frighten her widowed mother and would probably turn her already graying hair white.

Her husband had been killed in a strange foreign country, and twelve years later, her daughter had almost suffered the exact same fate. Yes, even though the hijacking had been a sham, her mother would never be able to listen to anything beyond gunfire and kidnapping.

No, this lie Kira had created about being deeply homesick was much better than the truth.

"You must've been laughing your ass off when you sent

those e-mails to my mom pretending to be me." She was speaking again to the ceiling. "I have no idea what you wrote to her, but I guess you can add creative writing to the list of your many talents."

"It's my fault that you've turned into such a homebody," her mother had said at the kitchen table last night, pursing her lips and averting her dark brown eyes. It pained Nicole to hear the guilt and self-reproach in her mother's tone. "All the hovering and worrying I did. You were always so much like your father, and I suppose I've tried to stifle that part of you."

Nicole had to bite her tongue. Her mother was having a breakthrough, and although it was a few years too late, it wouldn't help matters for Nicole to vent her long-suppressed anger and resentment right then. Whatever Kira had written in those e-mails had made her mother feel guilty enough. There was no point in adding to it.

"Even just last week, when Liz and I dropped you off at the airport, I was still begging you not to go." She shook her head, upset with herself. "I remember when you were only nine and already studying French with your father. Most kids were playing with Barbie dolls, but you were researching student exchange programs. You had *his* wanderlust, and it scared me."

The question lurking in Nicole's mind was at last answered. Her mother had known nothing of her father's dealings with Rhyse Taylor or with the government. If she'd had even the remotest sense of the danger her father had been in, there was no way she ever would have allowed her husband to leave the house, let alone the country.

But what if she had? What if she'd learned *some* of it after his death?

And maybe that was the real cause of her anxieties all these years.

Maybe her mother *did* know something. Not all of it, but maybe just enough to know someone out there still wanted something, whatever it was, and she was going to do everything she possibly could to ensure her two daughters didn't inadvertently stick their noses into it and put themselves into danger.

Yet that was precisely what Nicole had gone and done the very first opportunity she had.

"Lord, Nicky," her mother had lamented, "you were such a determined little girl. When you put your mind to something, anyone standing in your way had better just watch out. And to be honest, I didn't understand you. I thought maybe by just encouraging you to be more like your older sister, you'd have a happier life, and one day get married, have some kids." She'd sighed, a deep, melancholy sound that infused their small kitchen with a heavy sadness. "I messed up. I should have just allowed you to become the person you were meant to be."

It had taken every ounce of self-control Nicole possessed to keep the truth from spilling out from her lips when her mother slowly got up from the table and returned to her cold cup of coffee at the counter. Even now, remembering the sadness, the regret, in her mother's expression, seeing with a sudden clarity her mother's age in the lines and creases around her eyes and the slight sagging of her jowls, she felt a growing knot of tightness in her chest and a stinging in her eyes.

She rolled onto her back again after another minute and laced her fingers together under her head. "Well, aren't you listening anymore?" It took all of her self-control not to yell the words.

She knew she was acting like a fool, but in some strange way she found it oddly comforting to think there were some hidden wires running through the rafters overhead connecting her to Kira.

"And why I'm even talking to you, I really don't know. Or maybe I do," she said in a scathing aside to herself a minute later, tossing the sheets off in one violent motion. She rubbed her eyes and yawned. "Which means somewhere along the way I must have turned into a masochist."

Downstairs, she found her mother already made up and dressed at the kitchen table.

"Mom, why don't you have the air on?" she complained, reaching for a carton of orange juice and a glass. "It's hotter than Hades and it's only eight in the morning."

"That thing eats electricity like it's going out of style, Nicole. You kids seem to think money grows on trees."

That was when Nicole noticed what her mother was doing, crouched there with a ballpoint pen in her hand. She was circling want ads in the weekly flyer.

"Mom!" Her voice erupted from her as whining mix of outrage and shock. "You teach a bunch of rowdy brats all year. The summer's always been your time to recuperate. You can't really mean to get another job?"

"Just trying to keep myself busy," her mother replied awkwardly, as if she'd been caught doing something shameful. She got up from her chair to refill her empty cup from the sophisticated KitchenAid coffeemaker Nicole had given her for Christmas one year. The modern piece of kitchen equipment looked incongruous amongst the rest of the dated décor. "You know the old saying, idle hands are the devil's tools."

Nicole kissed her mother and went back to her bedroom, slipping into running shorts and sneakers and taking to the neighborhood streets with a zeal she hadn't possessed in quite some time. It had been over a week since she'd had any real exercise—other than the death march from the bus in Muranga and the short hike to the helicopter with Stella and Bogie. Even though it was hot and muggy, she found the run exhilarating. When she finished her three miles, she walked the last block back home, her legs throbbing with pain and awareness, and her shirt damp with sweat.

Somewhere nearby a lawn mower roared as it did its job and sprinklers made their strange thwacking noise as they sprayed water over grass. She could hear children shouting and giggling from another block, and there was a dog barking. It all was very comforting and familiar, the sounds of a quiet neighborhood in the summer.

But a part of her ached for one more run from an imaginary gunman.

After showering, she returned to her bedroom and opened a window to allow some cool air in to circulate. Her desk and her bed were part of a set that was a gift from her grandparents the year after her father died. Her father's parents had purchased many things for them that year, maybe thinking gifts could somehow fill the void they were all feeling. Atop the desk's chipped, ink-riddled surface sat her laptop and cell phone, neither of which she'd used since her return from Africa. She'd avoided both for the past day and a half, but she knew there were some things she couldn't keep dodging.

She pressed the power buttons to both devices, and as their screens came to life, she towel-dried her hair, gathered its thick wavy length into an elastic band. She put on a pair of khaki shorts and an old T-shirt. She decided to tackle the least challenging of all those on her list first—her finances.

Money had always been a frustrating issue for her. Now the lack of it literally made her stomach ache.

Not long after making her decision to teach in Kenya for the summer, she'd increased one of her student loans to enormous proportions to cover the program's travel and living costs, and quit her part-time job as a waitress at the Greek restaurant she'd worked at for years. She shook her head, thinking she'd have to borrow those want ads when her mother was done with them or beg for her old job back.

Logging on to her bank's website, she wasn't surprised to see she now had less than seven hundred dollars to cover her expenses until she started working again. Luckily, she could live here at her mother's house rent-free, at least until school started in the fall. *Only one more semester.* Thinking of school made her wince. At some point, she would have to address the subject of her abandoned internship with her school's advisory committee, but that wasn't as much of a priority for her as the other issues on her agenda.

She opened up Google on her laptop and searched for any piece of information about one Kira Anthony. She wasn't surprised when her searches turned up nothing. Next on her list was Stella's mysterious scribble about the tin man. After an hour, she still had no idea what it meant.

By noon, she couldn't postpone the inevitable any longer and directed her attention to the inbox of her student e-mail account. It was already overflowing with spam but she scrolled down until her cursor settled upon the three dated e-mails from Danielle. The first was sent in January, two weeks after Nicole had moved out. The next came in February, and the last was sent in April. They were all still highlighted in bold, black text. Nicole hadn't deleted them, but she'd never read them either. She took a deep breath and clicked on the first e-mail sent in January. It was brief:

Call me, Nick. We need to talk.

Then February:

Why won't you return my calls? This is important. Beyond what happened between us at your mother's house over Thanksgiving.

And the last one, sent in April and just as concise:

Nicole, I know you avoided me today outside of class. I am not stalking you, even though it might seem that way. There are things I need to talk to you about—matters of utmost importance. Please call me.

The coward in Nicole longed to delete the e-mails and pretend she'd never read them, but she knew she couldn't. With a less than steady hand, she picked up her cell phone and dialed the number that would connect her to Danielle. She was astonished to find she still knew the number by heart. Good thing—she'd deleted it from her contacts months ago.

Despite her resolve to be brave, she breathed a sigh of relief when the call clicked over to voicemail. She left a message, her voice shaky. If what Kira said was true and Danielle was involved in some insane intrigue relating to her father's murder, she had no doubt she wouldn't have to wait too long for a return call.

CHAPTER TWELVE

S o, Nick, did you meet some sexy native while you were in the jungle?"

Nicole wiped the sheen of sweat from her brow with the hem of her T-shirt and took a sip of bottled water before casting a glance toward her sister.

Weary of rummaging through her father's boxed belongings in search of a clue to the dead man's mysterious past, she'd decided it was too hot to spend a second longer in the tiny attic and had elected to engage in something as physical and mindless as mowing the lawn.

Yet even though her body had been out in the yard enduring attacks from mosquitoes and other annoying insects, her head was still up in the sweltering space of the attic, wondering if she'd overlooked something. As she was pushing the wobbly-wheeled lawn mower back toward the garage, she'd spied her sister on the patio lying atop one of her mother's aged vinyl lounge chairs in a skimpy bikini.

"I can tell something happened over there." Her sister's eyes looked her up and down before finally settling on her face. "There's something different about you."

Nicole stiffened in reflex, deliberating for a fraction of a second if she dared share the truth about what had really happened to her in Africa before realizing just how absurd that would actually be. She loved her sister, but Liz was more than a bit obtuse. Lucky for her, she was pretty, and it was her looks that had gotten her through life.

Nicole heaved a tired sigh and watched as her sister fished through an elephantine bag riddled with a designer's initials across its dimpled leather, her oily cleavage glistening in the sun. She wondered again for perhaps the millionth time in her life how she and her older sister could be so different. Not only did they disagree in their ideologies and political philosophies, but they were as different in appearance and demeanor as night was to day. Nicole sometimes found it hard to believe they came from the same gene pool, much less grew up under the same roof four years apart.

"C'mon, Nicole. Aren't you going to tell me if all the men in Africa were dressed like Tarzan and walked around in loincloths?" Liz joked, pulling her iPhone from her bag and updating her Facebook page. She placed the phone on the arm of the lounge chair and rubbed the last of the oil into her knees.

"What?" Nicole asked. She hadn't been paying attention.

Liz pulled her pair of expensive tortoiseshell sunglasses down from her blond highlights, turning a charming pout in Nicole's direction. "I asked you if you met someone while you were in Africa. You're acting weird. Weirder than usual, spacing out like a zombie. What's up?"

Nicole took a seat at the bottom of Liz's lounge chair, admiring the short, crisp rows the mower had scored into the lawn. There was finally a light breeze stirring in the late afternoon air, and the magnificent willow tree swayed gently back and forth with the wind. Nicole turned to her sister.

"Remember when you carved that heart into my tree?" she asked absently. "I wanted to kill you."

Liz made a face. "Why are you changing the subject? Why will you never talk to me about guys? I swear, Nick, sometimes I wonder about you." She removed her sunglasses and arched a perfectly shaped pale brow upward, her attention focused on an invisible chip in the bright red polish of her recently manicured nails. "Truth is, sis, it *is* a bit peculiar that you've never shown much interest in the opposite sex. And by the way, I denied it then and I'll deny it till the day I die. I never touched your stupid tree. And what was the big deal anyway? So some kid cut a heart into it? It's not like they chopped it down. And look at it—it's none the worse. It's grown almost as big as the house. Really, Nick, could you ever picture me with a knife in my hand messing up my nails and risking a splinter?"

Liz's question haunted Nicole the rest of the night. The willow in the backyard had always been a symbol of her father's love. She'd treasured the memory of helping him dig the earth to plant it, shoveling dirt over its roots and watering it every day throughout that spring. Days after he died, she'd discovered someone had chiseled a heart with some boy's name into its very center. Naturally, she'd blamed her stupid sister, and they'd fought about it for months. But now, as she readied herself for bed, she finally realized that what Liz had said was the truth. Although her sister's affection for boys had always been a bit obsessive, never in a million years would she have gone to all the effort and sweat it took to hew a heart into the tree's hard, brittle bark.

But then who did?

The answer came like a bolt out of the blue. In preparation for a quick shower, she'd removed both her watch and earrings and was just reaching for her necklace's clasp when she caught sight of the oval pendant hanging from its long, silver chain. With trembling hands, she held the side with the engraved willow to her before slowly turning it over to read the inscription.

In My Heart, Love Dad.

"Oh my God," she whispered as she grasped the significance of the five words. Liz really *hadn't* carved the heart into the tree!

Donning her robe, she ran to the bedroom window to look out at the willow silhouetted in the moonlight.

Her father had left a clue to whatever it was both Kira and Danielle were after in the trunk of the tree.

For her to find.

Nicole nearly flew from her bedroom down to the kitchen. Under the sink, hidden behind cans of open Ajax and bottles of Pine-Sol and other aging cleaners, she found the flashlight. When she pushed the rusted power switch forward and a bright beam of light erupted from its corroded head, she almost jumped with joy.

In just her robe, she ran out into the warm June night, her heart hammering almost painfully against her chest as dewy clumps of damp grass clippings collected between her bare toes. The neighbor's dachshund appeared at the fence, determined to wake the entire neighborhood with his annoyingly shrill yapping.

"Quiet, Henry!" she scolded, and the little dog scampered back toward his house. When she reached the willow, she pointed the flashlight up and down its trunk but couldn't find the heart. A wave of apprehension swept over her.

Twelve years had passed and she wasn't sure how long tree carvings lasted. But then she aimed the dull beam of light higher. There it was! Its shape was a tad contorted and the letters faded from weather and time, but the five letters were still legible.

Gavin.

The unusual name had meant nothing to her back then, but now it was everything.

She ran back into the house as fast as her legs could carry her, lurching clumsily through the backdoor and into the kitchen, almost crashing into her mother.

"Nicole Anne Kennedy, it's almost eleven o'clock at night!"

Nicole clutched the ends of her robe tightly together, suddenly conscious of her state of undress.

"What on earth is all the ruckus?" Her mother stood at the kitchen sink in her nightgown looking down at the open cabinet doors and the toppled bottles of cleaners, then back to the flashlight in Nicole's hand. A shrill, electronic beep pierced the tense quiet.

She was clutching Nicole's cell phone in a tight fist. Someone had sent a text message, and unless a button on the phone was pressed, the harsh irritating buzzing would repeat all night.

"Sorry, Mom." Nicole was still panting from her exertions. "I thought my necklace fell off while mowing the lawn today and went out to look for it. Then I remembered I'd taken it off to shower."

"Here, take this darned thing and shut it up, please."

Nicole grabbed the offending device from her mother's outstretched hand and silenced it, but not before casting an inquisitive eye to the screen. *Danielle.* She fought the urge to read it, shoving the phone into one of her robe's deep front pockets.

"You girls and your phones," her mother grumbled softly, organizing the cleansers in the cabinet. Nicole bent to help.

"Are you hungry, Nicky? You hardly ate any dinner tonight. I can't let you get any thinner. Those few days in Africa already took too much from you. You're skin and bones."

"I'm fine, Mom." Nicole grabbed a paper towel and wiped blades of grass up off the floor. "I was thinking of heading over to the high school in the morning. Summer school's in session now, right?"

"Classes may have started, but why?" her mother queried, uneasiness in her voice.

"Since I won't be teaching in Kenya, I'm hoping I can get the same credit if I help out at the high school." Nicole was pleased with her ability to create such a plausible lie on the spur of the moment.

"Do you think that's wise?" Her mother straightened, nervously plucking at her nightgown collar. "Don't you think the rec program at the elementary school would be better? Those kids at the high school for the summer, well, they're not like the other students. It's more like being a warden in a prison than being a teacher."

"I'm gonna stop by and talk to Principal Thomas in the morning, run the idea past him."

"Mr. Thomas is a busy man. I'll call him first, see if I can set something up for you."

Nicole knew there had been something of a chaste flirtation between her mother and the high school principal for the past few years, but it wasn't something anyone ever spoke about. She certainly didn't want her mother meddling in this, finding out her lies.

"Nope, I'm good, Mom," Nicole said, hurrying toward the stairway. If she'd turned around right then, she would have seen that her mother's face had gone an ashen gray, but she was too preoccupied with reading the text message Danielle had sent.

Meet me at Zorba's @ 6 Wednesday. Need 2 talk 2 u!!!

Zorba's was the restaurant where Nicole had worked up until May. It was as good a place as any to learn just what Danielle's involvement might be in all this weirdness.

While I'm there, she humorously mused, *I might as well apply for my old job.*

❖

The next morning, Nicole dressed in a white blouse with crisp pleats, charcoal slacks, and leather sling back shoes. The temperature was supposed to climb back into the upper eighties, so she decided to leave the matching jacket in the closet. She needed to look the part if she hoped to accomplish anything at all.

An ornate, gilded-framed mirror hung at the bottom of the staircase. It had been there for as long as she could remember, and since childhood she always quickly glanced at it when she passed, but this time, she paused. The image in the reflection was not the one she was used to seeing, the one she expected to see. She wasn't the meek child hiding behind her mother's legs or the tomboy in torn jeans climbing trees anymore. Her stance radiated confidence and her lightly tanned skin seemed to glow with an inner light.

Even her large amber eyes looked *seductive.*

She remembered what her sister said. *"You look different."*

"Nice outfit, Nicole," her mother acknowledged fondly from the threshold of the kitchen. "Go on and see Louise at the grade school. I told her you'd stop by. No need to bother Mr. Thomas. Louise has all sorts of programs she needs help with since the state cut her budgets."

Embarrassed at being caught admiring herself, Nicole rushed from the house to her decade-old Civic in the garage, where she'd stowed it for the summer. As she drove the five miles to her former high school, she pictured Kira, which she found she was doing whenever she allowed her mind to wander. The blond temptress teased and taunted her dreams. Even when Nicole was fully awake, Kira floated near the perimeter of her consciousness, tugging at her ability to concentrate on anything other than the memory of the achingly sweet kiss they'd shared.

She wondered what Kira was doing right at that moment.

CHAPTER THIRTEEN

Turning into the school's parking lot, she surveyed the one-story brick building with less than nostalgic eyes. She hadn't made a trip back since graduating. High school wasn't a pleasant memory for Nicole. There had been no dances, cheerleading competitions, or love letters exchanged during the four years she'd slouched through the gloomy hallways, a painfully shy, blemished-faced geek with no interest in the silly shenanigans her fellow female classmates engaged in to attract boys.

"You have to sign in. I'll need to see some identification," said a squat-shaped, forty-something female security guard with a large potbelly busting the buttons of her uniform after Nicole asked to talk to the principal. "Is he expecting you?"

Nicole hesitated.

"Nicole Kennedy? Is that you?" A gravelly male voice echoed in the hallway. She turned and faced the man she'd known more than half her life.

Mr. Thomas was tall and attractive. He was a bit thicker around the waist than the last time she'd seen him but still in good shape for a man in his early sixties. Her first memory of the silver-haired administrator was when her mother had introduced Nicole to him at her father's funeral.

"Look at you, all grown up. Every time I see one of my

former students, Mavis," he said to the guard, "I realize just how old I'm getting. Come with me back to my office, Nicole," he said with a dapper smile as he straightened his tie. "First period is about to end and it'll be mayhem here in a minute. School ends tomorrow and I'm sorry to say some of these kids will be back for summer classes."

Nicole was bewildered. "I thought summer school started already?"

"We had to extend the school year." He shrugged his shoulders. "Too many snow days this past winter. Department of Education regulations. Everyone is miserable—the teachers as well as the students." He wiggled his gray brows. "They all want to be at the beach."

"But my mother's been off for the past few weeks. I don't understand."

A distressed look marred the principal's weathered features. "I thought you knew." His voice was solemn. "Let's talk."

Disturbed and confused, Nicole followed his distinguished form into the main office and through a half door cut into the laminate countertop. The school smelled exactly as she remembered—a faint, musty scent mixed with lingering odors from cafeteria food and floor wax.

"No phone calls please, Rita," Mr. Thomas told a harried-looking secretary before closing his office door and taking a seat behind a huge metal-gray desk littered with stacks of papers. It was a small, messy room with pictures of various graduating classes adorning the plain white walls and a large window overlooking the baseball fields.

"What's going on, Mr. Thomas?" Nicole took a seat in one of the chairs on the other side of his desk. "If school is still in session, then why isn't my mother here teaching?"

"Please, Nicole, let's dispense with the formalities. We're both adults now. Call me Gavin." He cast a quick glance toward the door. "I shouldn't be talking about any of this with you. Legally,

I could get in hot water for sharing any information concerning the termination of a school-district employee, regardless of your relationship. But I think you know I have a special fondness for your mother and I'm deeply worried."

"Termination? *My mother was fired?*" Nicole was aghast. What the hell was going on?

"In a manner of speaking, yes."

He remained quiet for almost a full thirty seconds. "The school district called my secretary one day about three months ago to inform us that your mother's teaching certification had been revoked. I thought the situation nothing more than an administrative glitch, but when I addressed the situation with Dorothy, she became flustered and agitated. A few days later, I broached the subject again, but she refused to talk to me about it. She began calling in sick, and then one day, she simply stopped reporting for class altogether. You know how much the kids love her. They were devastated. I dropped by the house but she wouldn't answer the door. When I called, she'd hang up on me. As I am legally bound to do, I sent her several registered letters, but she never responded. I tried to find out what had happened with her teaching certificate, but the school board wouldn't provide any clarity either. After two months, they simply closed her employment. Your mother is sorely missed, by her students and fellow faculty, but by me as well."

"How strange," Nicole remarked.

"That's why you've come to see me, isn't it?"

"Actually, no." She saw a muscle in his square jaw clench. "I was hoping you could help me with something else, although my mother's teaching license may somehow play a role in all this."

"I fear it might," he agreed in a steely voice.

"You know why I'm here?"

The room was deadly quiet. Nicole could hear two women laughing in the main office and the faint chiming sound of Microsoft's Windows theme as a computer sprang to life.

"Yes, Nicole, I believe I do." He leaned back in his chair, a pensive frown marring his aged but timelessly handsome face. "At one time, your father and I were close. I don't know what he got himself mixed up in or how this involves your mother, if it does at all, and I'm not sure I want to know. Your father came to me a few weeks before his death asking for my help." Nicole watched as he pulled his wallet from the rear pocket of his gray trousers. He reached for something from the inner confines of the worn leather billfold and held it out to her. "This is what you've come for."

"A key?" she asked upon seeing the small piece of silver metal. It felt as if a hand were slowly tightening around her throat. "To what?"

"A safe deposit box. Your father said he needed a place to store some extremely sensitive paperwork, but he couldn't have anything in his name. He was nervous and scared, mumbling something about corruption. I thought perhaps he was delusional or on drugs, but just the same, I agreed to do as he asked. The box has remained untouched since he passed away."

Nicole shook her head. "I don't understand. Why didn't you just give me the key years ago or give it to my mother?"

"Luke was very specific. It could only be you, and I would know when you were ready. Look, Nicole, all these years, the only time I'd remember I even had the key was when I changed wallets. I never thought anything would come of it. Take it," he ordered as he handed her the key, "something tells me your father wasn't as paranoid as I once believed him to be."

❖

"You say you're listed as a deputy?"

Nicole tried to quash her momentary panic. "Deputy?"

"Meaning you're authorized to have access to the box," the middle-aged redhead clarified in a bored monotone as she pecked at the keys on her computer. Her creased eyelids were coated with a layer of blue shadow and her chubby cheeks bore a heavy stroke of pink blush.

When Nicole arrived home yesterday after her visit with Mr. Thomas, she'd found the house hot and empty. She'd used the time alone to search through her mother's desk, hoping to learn exactly what was going on in her life—only to be horrified by what she found.

Tucked into the bureau's tiny drawers were several menacing letters from the IRS inquiring about deductions her mother had taken on past tax returns, a notice from the Social Security Administration informing her that she'd been overpaid eight thousand dollars in survivor benefits, at least three overdraft notices from the bank, the registered letters Mr. Thomas said had been sent from the school board, and a notice from the school's insurance company stating benefits would be terminated now that her mother was no longer an employee of the school district.

At least she knew the reason her mother had been circling want ads in the local flyer.

Nicole noticed something peculiar about the dates on all the correspondence. All the mail had been postmarked in the month of March. How could her mother's entire world simply fall apart in the span of one month?

Kira Anthony and her henchmen.

Dinner had been a practice in patience. It took every ounce of restraint she possessed not to tell her mother that she'd met with Mr. Thomas and now knew she was no longer teaching. And she'd wanted to question her mother about the letters hidden in her desk.

"Do you remember if your signature is on file? If we don't have your signature, you can't get to the box without the renter being present."

They were seated in a small glass cubicle just off the bank's main lobby in the heart of Washington DC. With all the mergers and acquisitions in the banking industry over the past decade,

Nicole had been surprised to find the financial institution still existed.

"Signature?"

"Oh, never mind," the redhead said, bringing a plump finger to her rouged lips, "here it is." She smiled. "I'll just need you to sign the electronic pad here." She pulled a device across the desk that looked similar to the machines retailers used for processing credit cards. "And I'll need some identification."

After showing her driver's license, Nicole nervously scribbled her name and waited with bated breath. *This is it*, she thought, *they'll know I'm a fraud and have me arrested. Right now, she is probably pressing some secret button under her desk to alert the authorities.*

"The number of the box is 423. I'll get the guard key. And you have your key? We need both to open the box."

"I have it," she gulped with relief. She wondered how her father had managed her signature twelve years ago. And who had been paying for the box all this time?

423. The box number was the same as her birthday, April twenty-third. The room with the safe deposit boxes was a secured area tucked deep inside one of the bank's vaults; the steel- and copper-colored receptacles lined up from floor to ceiling much like post office boxes.

"How much time will you need?"

"Five minutes," Nicole answered, almost breathless with anticipation after the small metal bin had been pulled from its tracks and carried over to a private desk. Once alone, she peered inside the container and saw her name written on an envelope in her father's recognizable scrawl. Under the envelope were two bundles of cash bound by rubber bands. She quickly thumbed through the bills. They were all hundreds. There had to be at least twenty thousand dollars there. Under the money was a stack of official certificates, but she placed them aside and returned to the folded manila envelope. Clinging to it was a tiny piece of paper like those inside a Chinese fortune cookie. On one side it was blank, and on the other it read, *Your best friend is often in the mirror.*

She stuffed it into a zippered pouch in her handbag and opened the envelope. It contained nothing more than a single sheet of old computer paper, the kind with holes along both sides and perforated edges. Random letters were printed on it in a dot-matrix font. It looked similar to the incomprehensible jargon her printer spewed out when she changed the ink cartridge. None of it made sense. She flipped the sheet over, and on the other side, in her father's almost illegible handwriting was a list of names. All had a line through them except for two: *Taylor* and *Kohl.*

Her attention returned to the certificates. They were all in Chinese. She recognized the symbols. *A Chinese fortune and these strange-looking documents that looked like Chinese stocks.* Why had her father been hiding these items? *Internal Share Certificate* was stamped across the top of the stocks in English and *Sempco Industrial* directly under it.

"Everything okay, miss?" the bank associate asked when she reappeared.

Nicole felt like she was going to shatter into a million tiny pieces and knew she probably looked it. She swiftly placed everything back into the safe deposit box, hesitating slightly when her hand touched one of the cash bricks. She recalled the mail she'd found in her mother's desk. This money could come in handy right about now, but her gut told her to leave it. She didn't know where it came from, and for all she knew, it might be blood money—or worse. It might be marked and the minute it the currency reappeared in circulation, the Department of Treasury might come knocking at their door.

"Do you need a few more minutes?"

Nicole shook her head. She couldn't speak. Her father was someone she thought she'd known, but it was turning out that he'd been a man of much mystery and many secrets. And Kira had been right. Judging from the contents inside the safe deposit box, her father might very well have been a criminal.

Shoving the key into her wallet, she watched as the box was returned to its slot. On her way out, she glanced at the bank's clock and remembered it was Wednesday. She was supposed to meet Danielle at Zorba's tonight.

Hopefully by then her legs wouldn't feel like overcooked spaghetti.

Outside the bank, she noticed the change in the sky. It had grown dark. The wind had picked up and the smell of rain was heavy in the summer air. The disc jockey on the car radio that morning had mentioned a coming storm would bring some relief from the record-breaking heat wave, and it looked like he'd been right. She'd had trouble finding a place to park, and had to park her Civic several blocks away. With any luck, she'd make it back to her car before it started to pour. She'd just started across the crosswalk when a large black Chevy Suburban nearly ran her over. She cast an angry glower at the driver but froze when she saw a familiar face at the wheel.

Stella Shevchenko?

It couldn't be!

Her momentary shock was all the time Bogie needed. He jumped out from the passenger door and shoved Nicole into the backseat. She started to scream, but before she could, the Suburban was already barreling down Massachusetts Avenue, Bogie right beside her. The seats were leather and slippery. She struggled to get her balance.

"What the hell's going on?"

Bogie's large, meaty hands were clenched securely around both her wrists, and her angry attempts to kick free from him did little good. He held her down and pulled the hems of her white linen pants up and removed the pocketknife she'd strapped around her right calf before leaving her mother's house that morning.

After the hijacking in Kenya, Nicole swore she'd never be caught defenseless ever again.

Bogie grinned.

"I'm impressed," he said in his South African accent, holding her knife up in the air like a trophy. "Easier to reach than having to fumble through your pocketbook."

"I thought I was done with you people!"

But deep inside, Nicole had suspected they'd be back—especially after she discovered the heart in the tree.

"Calm down, kid," Stella implored from the driver's seat. "You're not in danger. We just want to know what you found in the bank."

Nicole's blood boiled. "You don't really expect me to tell you, do you?"

Stella's eyes meet Bogie's in the rearview mirror.

"It would make life easier for all of us," Stella replied wearily in her crisp Russian dialect.

A mobile phone rang and Nicole watched Stella bring a shiny black handheld to her ear. "We have her." She snapped the phone shut.

"Was that Kira?" Nicole demanded.

"Tell us what you find, little one," Stella repeated as she turned onto the highway.

"How were you able to follow me?"

She'd purposefully pulled the battery from her cell phone that morning, just in case anyone might be tracking her whereabouts. Obviously, it hadn't mattered.

Bogie answered Nicole's question by pulling her knife from where he'd slipped it under his belt. He removed a small piece of tape from the blade. She could see that a bunch of tiny black wires ran the length of the clear strip, unnoticeable against the gray of the blade until now.

"Embedded into this tiny piece of tape is a transmitter sending me a signal. I placed it there when I grabbed your bag from the bus back in Africa.

"Don't even think of it," Bogie warned, seeing Nicole's eyes stray to the door handle. He pulled a set of handcuffs from a bag on the floor and placed one metal cuff around his huge wrist and the other around her smaller one. "I think it best you and I make this journey together."

CHAPTER FOURTEEN

How much longer till we get to wherever it is you're taking me?" Nicole finally gathered the spirit as they left the congestion of DC and crossed over the state line into Virginia. She wasn't scared. Even though she knew these people weren't with the government, instinct told her they wouldn't harm her—especially since they seemed to want what she'd found in the safe deposit box.

"Providing we don't hit any more traffic and we're able to outrun the storm that's heading up the coast, at least another hour or so," Bogie answered, eyeing the metal cuffs that bound them to one another.

"Once you're done eating, you should rest," Stella suggested as she pulled off an exit and into a fast-food drive-thru. "It will be a long night."

After eating a grilled chicken sandwich and a large Diet Coke with her one free hand, Nicole found herself doing just that. Her sudden fatigue outweighed her stress over being abducted yet again. She suspected Stella might have slipped some of her magic sleeping medicine into her Diet Coke before she passed the Styrofoam cup to Bogie.

When next her eyelids opened, they'd left the busy highway and were traveling down a winding, isolated stretch of dirt road. Flashes of lightning scored the early evening sky while booming claps of thunder rumbled all around them. The private path dipped low through a lush green valley before curving and snaking around endless lengths of bright white fencing until they turned onto a long gravel driveway. A magnificent three-story-house stood nestled in the center of a large lawn and surrounded by acres of rolling hills. Its floor-to-ceiling windows were ablaze with a warm yellow light.

"This is where you're taking me?" She was wide awake—if they'd drugged her, it had been a small dose that had already worn off.

Neither Stella nor Bogie answered her. The vehicle rolled to a stop in front of the house. Bogie uncuffed himself and attached his empty manacle to Nicole's free wrist so that both of her hands were now secured together on her lap. He and Stella climbed out without a concerned glance back in her direction. A minute later, Stella returned to the car by herself and led Nicole inside.

The house was like something featured in a home and garden magazine. The first floor was open, with no walls to mar the rustic simplicity of the architecture. A huge stone fireplace with a raised hearth dominated the center of the expansive room, and a stairway made from rough-hewn logs led to an upper level. All the woodwork looked to be a red cedar accented with iron and slate. Several three-foot-tall floor hurricane lamps, their candles flickering welcomingly, were positioned between two very cozy-looking brown leather sofas placed invitingly in front of the fireplace. "You've taken me to a bed-and-breakfast?" she asked sarcastically. "How thoughtful. And here I was thinking you two were bringing me to some vacant warehouse on the outskirts of town where no one would be able to hear my screams. Okay, you can remove the handcuffs. Very funny. I'd like a wake-up call around eight, if you don't mind."

"Good, you still have a sense of humor." Stella looked exhausted. Her dark eyes were red and swollen. "The winds are causing the power to go on and off. Not sure we have enough candles," she added absently. "Now come on, kid, tell us what you found in the bank. You know we'll eventually get it out of you."

She smiled into Stella's fatigued features. "I was just beginning to like you, Stella. Why would you do this? You're a good person. I can see it in your eyes."

"What was at the bank, Nicole?" This time the question came from Bogie, his tone impatient.

"Can I use the bathroom before the interrogation? My bladder's about to explode. And would it be possible to have my bag? It's still in the car."

Stella looked at her suspiciously.

"I have nothing to hide. Feel free to go through my stuff. As much as I wish I'd thought to pack a stick of dynamite on my way out this morning, being taken hostage wasn't on my agenda for the day."

"I'm sure you'll understand if I don't take you at your word." Bogie went to retrieve Nicole's handbag, and when he returned, she watched him rummage through its contents. She stiffened slightly when he unzipped the compartment in which she'd shoved the Chinese fortune, but he didn't spare a second even to read it. He did examine a travel-sized container of toothpaste Nicole kept in her purse before warily depositing the bag into her bound hands.

"No escape attempts," Stella warned, unlocking the handcuffs. "We know you're capable of it."

Alone in the bathroom, Nicole let out a stream of profanity that would have made the underpaid line cooks at Zorba's proud. She'd been considering breaking a window and making a run for it, but she realized how idiotic such an endeavor would be.

They were watching and listening to her every move.

After using the toilet, she washed her hands with a squirt of scented soap from a decorative dispenser next to the hand-carved marble sink, then dabbed some of the toothpaste Bogie had just inspected onto her index finger. The nap in the car—or whatever it was they'd spiked her Diet Coke with—had left a funky taste in her mouth. She rubbed the toothpaste around her gums and teeth while studying her reflection.

"Your best friend is often in the mirror."

"What were you trying to tell me, Dad?" she asked her reflection. "Why did you leave that for me, instead of Liz or Mom?"

She rinsed out her mouth and stared again at the face looking back at her, hoping to find an answer. But all she saw was her ten-year-old self, a little kid grieving for the one person in her life she'd felt had completely understood her.

"C'mon, kid. Hurry up," Stella called through the bathroom door.

Knowing she had no other choice, Nicole opened the door.

"Back at the fast-food place, did you spike my soda?" she asked. Stella ignored the question, grabbing her by the arm and dragging her back into the main room of the house.

"Please don't lock me up," she pleaded with Bogie. He didn't say anything in response as he gathered her hands together and pulled her to one of three wood columns that ran from the vaulted ceilings to the hardwood floors. "I promise I won't run. Look at where we are, for God's sake! How far do you think I'd get?"

But neither Bogie nor Stella appeared to hear a word she spoke. They pushed her back against the wooden post and cuffed her wrists together behind it. There was no possible way she'd be able to get away.

"This sort of hurts."

"So tell us what you found in the bank." Bogie tightened the cuffs another painful notch. "And you'll be free."

"You know I won't, so just go ahead and do whatever it is you're going to do to me. I guess my instincts are more off than I realized. I didn't take either one of you to be a terrorizing sadist."

"Oh, we're not, are we, Stella?" Bogie asked as he laid the

key to the handcuffs down on an intricately carved wooden end table just out of Nicole's reach. "But you'll be soon reacquainted with someone who is."

"You had your chance, little one," Stella said in a low foreboding voice, her dark eyes filled with a sad mixture of regret and guilt as she and Bogie walked out the front door into the darkening evening.

"Hey, wait!" she called out "You can't just leave me here imprisoned! What if I have to pee again? Or what if the house catches on fire? I'll be trapped!"

Or what if my nose itches, Nicole thought lamely as their footsteps fell heavily on the wood porch, followed by the crunching of gravel before the Suburban's engine revved loudly, then slowly faded into the distance. She tugged at the handcuffs, but she only succeeded in removing more skin from her wrists.

A crack of lightning and another round of thunder pummeled the evening. The lights flickered. Nicole cast a curious gaze around the room, taking in the opulence of the expensive throw rugs and the exotic African wall hangings. She was not at all surprised to see Kira's winsome face in many of the pictures positioned at perfect angles atop the fireplace mantel. She'd already surmised that the luxurious castle belonged to the Ice Princess, but she *was* shocked when her eyes fell to one of the silver-plated frames and saw the woman with her arm casually draped over a familiar set of squared shoulders. Nicole felt her heart drop into her stomach. It was the helicopter pilot from Africa!

Mike.

As painful as it was to do, she couldn't seem to stop herself as she sought out the next picture and the next. He seemed to be in almost every one of the snapshots. She cast another gaze around the house, but this time with different eyes.

Was this *their* home?

A deep, unaccustomed pain erupted within her breast. For all her daydreams about Kira, Nicole never would have imagined that the woman was married to a *man*!

In her mind's eye, she saw a happy couple curled up romantically in front of the stone fireplace. She tried to smother the ugly, bile-inducing images of Kira and Mike laughing, touching, kissing, but they continued blinking inside her head as vividly as the lightning flashing outside the house.

She shook her head, berating herself for wasting energy on such thoughts. A nervous breakdown must be heading her way. Rather than worrying about being tied up in some strange house with no one knowing of her whereabouts, she was consumed by a ferocious jealousy. If one of her hands was free, she'd use it to slap herself out of it.

There were windows everywhere, and Nicole could see that the rain had finally begun to fall, large, heavy drops that splattered violently against the huge panes of glass. Over the sound of the rain, she heard what sounded like a garage door opening and a car door slamming shut. Nervously, she bit her bottom lip as a wave of fear swept through her.

It wasn't Kira she was afraid of, but rather her response to seeing her. She'd fought her emotions the entire week, torn between despising the deceitful woman and falling in love with her.

CHAPTER FIFTEEN

W e meet again."
      Nicole lifted her head and felt her breath catch in her throat. If possible, Kira was even more beautiful than she remembered. She looked ethereal, almost unreal in the dim light. She was dressed in a simple white cotton sundress that revealed the suntanned length of her legs, her silky blond hair stylishly windblown from the stormy weather.

"Far too soon for me," Nicole spat defiantly, despite the fact that every atom in her body seemed to explode with a quiet elation.

"You're angry." The beginning of a smile tipped the corner of Kira's pink lips as she tucked a wave of hair behind one ear. "And here I was hoping you might be happy to see me."

"Happy? I was never as happy as the day I left Kenya and thought I'd seen the last of you," Nicole heard herself reply viciously. She had to be careful. *Thou doth protest too much*, an inner voice warned.

"Surely you didn't think I'd let you go so easily." Kira looked at her intently. "Not when I knew you would lead me to exactly what I've been searching for." She sauntered nonchalantly into the room, stopping mere inches in front of Nicole. "I see Bogie and Stella felt it necessary to tie you up?"

"Yeah, right. As if you didn't order them to do it."

Kira's eyes slid to the key on the table. "I'd free you, but I'm beginning to see the wisdom of their decision." Her expression turned stern. "You can save us both a lot of time and unnecessary anguish by simply telling me what it is you found in the safe deposit box. C'mon, Nicole," Kira reached out, gently cupping Nicole's chin in her hand and searching her upturned face, "what was in it?"

Nicole tried to breathe.

Kira's proximity and touch was overwhelming. For the first time since leaving the hidden bunker in the hills of Mount Kenya, Nicole felt alive again. It was as if her soul had been closeted in some cold, dark abyss and was now free to drink in the abundant warmth of the sun.

"If it's a contest of wills you want, so be it," Kira said, dropping her hand and retreating a few steps backward. "But you'll lose. I'm quite a skilled interrogator, and I warn you now, I won't play fair."

"That I can believe."

Kira seemed amused. She turned her back and Nicole watched as she slid her sandals from her feet before falling gracefully into one of the leather sofa's thick cushions. "You've a very low opinion of me."

"Need you ask why?" Nicole tugged at her handcuffs to remind the woman that she was being held against her will. "Never mind the fact you've kidnapped me twice now, what you did to my mother was horrible!"

Kira looked bewildered.

"The letters from the IRS, the Social Security Administration, the numerous bank notices. Preying upon a widow? That's pretty low, even for you!"

Kira chose to ignore the allegation altogether. "Just tell me what you found, Nicole. We don't have much time."

Nicole recalled Stella yelling those exact words at Bogie before she got into the helicopter. "What's the rush? Are the feds after you?" She watched for a reaction but there was nothing.

"Forget it, Kira. No matter what you and your people do to me, I'm never going to tell you anything."

"My people?" Kira questioned with a raised brow, lifting her feet off the floor and propping them atop the iron and wood coffee table juxtaposed between the fireplace and sofa. "You make it sound as if I'm part of the mafia."

"I know you're not working undercover for the government like you've claimed to be."

"Really? And please tell me just how it is you've arrived at that conclusion?"

"No federal employee would ever be able to afford a place like this." Her brown eyes darted around the room. "And no government agency would authorize this type of commando operation."

"Ah yes, I forget you're still living in the blissfully naïve two-dimensional world of textbook and theory." Kira's mouth twisted wryly. "Do you want me to call Amnesty International and report my misdeeds?"

"I'd prefer you call the police. You and your husband belong in jail." Nicole tossed a lock of dark curls away from her face. "By the way, Mike mentioned it was you I had to thank for the scenic tour I received before I left. Glad I got to see something of Africa after blowing almost four thousand nonrefundable dollars"—she paused at each syllable and raised her voice to give the number more weight—"for an internship I didn't get to even start, let alone complete. So, thank you."

"Husband?" That perfect mouth broke into a wide, white smile and Nicole hated herself for being captivated by it. "Studly Do-Right? The human Ken doll? Whatever." Her gaze went to the pictures atop the mantel. "You'd think you would've remembered to remove anything of a personal nature before bringing me here. Although I'm surprised someone as cold as you even has someone who cares about her."

Kira rose from the sofa in one fluid motion. She stretched her arms wide, stifling a yawn. Nicole watched her smooth feminine biceps go taut and again wondered how long ago it was they'd flown in from Kenya—all three of them had that worn, jet-lagged look.

"Oh, Nicole, I do admire your wild imagination." Kira's movements were languid and relaxed like an advancing cat's as she slowly moved toward her. Lightning shattered the night sky and the lights powered off and on. They both stared at each other until Nicole had to break the spell by looking away.

"Do you think I would have kissed you the other night," Kira's blue eyes were now a shade darker and fixed unwaveringly upon Nicole's lips, "if I was married or otherwise romantically involved?"

Nicole felt her mouth throb and tingle, but she cleared her throat, pretending not to be affected. "I think you'd do just about anything to get what you're after."

Kira's gaze moved from Nicole's lips to roll lazily down the creamy expanse of collarbone the yellow blouse she was wearing revealed. "My actions have always been in line with my code of ethics."

"You act as if you have morals."

"I have more than some people."

"And just who might they be? Hitler? Saddam Hussein?" Nicole boldly challenged her, her tone heavy with sarcasm.

"Your girlfriend, for one."

"Girlfriend?"

"I see you could hardly wait to make contact with Danielle Taylor," Kira cast a withering glare at Nicole. "You're in over your head with that one."

"You're still listening in?"

"Never stopped."

"And I suppose you'll tell me again that the Patriot Act entitles you to commit acts that are blatantly unconstitutional?"

"I could, *if* my goal was to eventually file criminal charges against you. But I'm not."

"Because you're not with any government agency, are you?

If you were, you'd simply obtain a search warrant and access the safe deposit box yourself. Or use the Patriot Act."

Kira shrugged. "You don't understand what's at stake. To go through legal channels at this time simply isn't possible. We'd be showing our hand, and we can't afford to do that right now. We're this close." She held out her hand and made her index finger and thumb form a C. "But you're about to blow all of our hard work. Rhyse Taylor is on the move. No doubt he now knows all about your discovery as well. He's heading this way. He's coming for you, Nicole. He wants what you found."

Nicole's eyes widened in fear. She pictured the computer paper with the jumble of letters and numbers, the bundle of cash, and the Chinese stocks. She wished she'd had a chance to Google the name of the company on them. Why were they so important to everyone?

"All I need to know is what was inside the box," Kira went on implacably. "If the evidence your father collected isn't in there, we need to move on. Quickly."

A lightbulb flickered on inside Nicole's head. This was her modus operandi. Incite terror and fear to extract information from victim.

"Yeah, sure." She rolled her eyes. "I bet he is. How would anyone else know about the safe deposit box?"

"They're watching you. They've been watching you, just like we have," Kira replied smoothly. "But we're the ones wearing white hats."

"Then show me some proof you are who you claim to be! But you can't do that. Because you're not. If you really were legit, we'd both be sitting in an office down in DC right now and a bunch of guys in suits would be tossing all sorts of legal threats my way."

"I've already explained why I can't go that route," Kira replied, her voice growing strained. She stood up and pulled a disposable lighter from an end table's drawer and began lighting a dozen smaller candles set in an iron candelabrum within the woodless fireplace. "As I said earlier, you really do have a wild imagination. No matter what I showed you or told you, you'd always be skeptical, always thinking I was up to no good. I won't waste any more precious time trying to prove to you otherwise. I need a drink. Do you want something?"

"A hacksaw would be nice."

Kira smiled at the comment and walked out of the room.

Nicole replayed the last few minutes of their conversation. Could Rhyse Taylor really be coming for her? A tiny chill ran down her spine.

"Why not spare us both the pain that'll no doubt result from your refusal to cooperate?" Kira returned carrying a tray laden with two wineglasses overflowing with a golden yellow liquid. "C'mon, Nicole. I'm not asking you to do anything that would betray your father's memory. All I need to know is what you found locked up inside the box. You'd be free to go within minutes." As she lowered the tray onto one of the end tables, she spilled some of the wine but quickly dabbed at the liquid with a napkin.

"Do you give the maid a day off when you know you'll be bringing a captive back to the house?"

The storm was still raging violently, and every so often a burst of thunder would shake the frame of the expansive structure. Nicole could actually feel the vibrations of the booming explosions filter down the wooden beam and reverberate against her backbone.

"Anyone I bring back here comes willingly. Very willingly," Kira answered in a silky, mocking tone. "You being the exception, of course."

"It's my turn to ask *you* a question." Nicole tried to appear calm and poised but was in fact recovering from the unsettling vision of Kira strolling through the front door and kissing another woman. "Why would my father have hidden evidence in a safe deposit box in a bank? Why not mail it to the police or CIA or leave it in a conspicuous location so it would be found?"

"Finally, we're getting somewhere." Kira took a sip of wine.

"Maybe he didn't really think he'd be killed. And maybe he didn't know whom he could trust with whatever he'd collected. What did Luke leave for you?"

"Will you undo these handcuffs?"

"I get the feeling you're toying with me, Nicole." She took a step closer and another sip of wine, her blue eyes narrowing speculatively. "What was in the box?"

Nicole leaned back against the wood beam. Those stocks must be worth a fortune. It could be the only reason everyone was doing cartwheels to get to them. Again, her eyes took in the craftsmanship of the house and the opulent artifacts hanging from the walls. "I'm sorry to disappoint you. There wasn't any evidence inside it. No folders filled with incriminating pictures, no lengthy list of gun deals to Arab sheiks."

Kira frowned into her glass. "I knew you would make this difficult." She sighed, shaking her head as if in regret. "Here, have some wine. It's been a long day for both of us. Maybe you won't remain so stubborn with some alcohol inside of you."

Nicole drew herself erect.

Normally, she found the taste of wine bitter, but her mouth was dry. With her hands bound behind her back, she had to depend upon Kira to hold the glass to her lips. She felt an electric jolt as a warm, feminine hand was placed along her jawline and some of the sweet liquid was slowly poured into her mouth. The act was intensely intimate and Nicole swallowed with difficulty. She watched as Kira then took a sip from the same spot on the glass her lips had just touched. A powerful flutter as strong as the thunder pounding the house shook her innards.

"I'll give you one more chance to tell me."

"Get a warrant," she sneered defiantly. Liz had been right. She had changed. She was done with ducking and hiding. From the truth, from everyone, even Rhyse Taylor. If he was coming for her, she would face him head-on.

"So be it, you leave me no choice." Kira set the wineglass down atop the table.

"What're you going to do?" Nicole asked. "Beat me up?"

"At some point tonight, you'll probably wish I had." A burning determination glittered brightly within her blue eyes. "With the way it is between you and me, I suspect a soft, lingering touch will coerce you into telling me what I want to know far more proficiently than any amount of brute force."

CHAPTER SIXTEEN

Nicole's eyes rounded in panic, Kira's words and intent ringing loud and clear inside her head. Her heart slammed wildly against her rib cage.

"You can't mean to—to—" she stuttered, shook then bowed her head, her brain unwilling to even sort through her vocabulary to give utterance to the notion.

"Seduce you?"

"Not possible!" Nicole hissed, more frightened by her body's reaction to the picture Kira's threat evoked than if the woman had told her she was to be tarred, feathered and dumped in the Potomac.

"Is that a challenge? Anyway, I think we're at a point where we can admit that if it came to the actual act," Kira stated in her low throaty voice, the dark fringe of her long, black lashes concealing the emotion in her eyes, "both of us would be willing participants."

Nicole felt her face color. "You're delusional!"

"You want me, Nicole," Kira finished confidently, "far more than you'll ever admit. Even to yourself."

Nicole raised her eyes only to find Kira studying her. "I don't!" she practically yelled.

"Liar."

The softly spoken accusation had more of an effect

on Nicole's frazzled nerves than if a hot branding iron had emblazoned the word into her skin. Was her need so obvious?

"We're both strong-willed," Kira said, her gaze soft as a caress, "but you maybe more so than me, if such a phenomenon is even possible." She reached forward, lightly fingering a loose tendril of chestnut hair curling along Nicole's cheek. "You've spent your whole life hiding, Nicole, and I've spent mine running. I sense we're equally fearful of this power we have over each other. I know I've never experienced anything like it, and I confess, it scares me."

For one long, blissful, gullible moment, Nicole found herself falling for it hook, line, and sinker, but she remembered who she was dealing with.

"You really are incredibly arrogant," Nicole said scornfully. "Did you really think I'd be that easily duped? You'll have to do better if you expect me to swoon at your feet."

"Tell me, Nicole, what is it I'd have to do to make you *swoon?*"

Nicole became flustered. She hadn't expected her remark to be thrown back at her like that. "Okay, I get it. You worked up a psychological profile on me, discovered what would make me tick, and played me like a sheet of music: Quiet, introverted graduate student, death of my father at a young age—"

"Attracted to women," Kira added huskily, folding her arms across her chest and drawing Nicole's admiring eyes to the inch of alluring cleavage the cut of her dress displayed.

"That needn't be a factor, especially to you," she responded testily. She suddenly realized she was in way over her head and way, way out of her league. If she weren't tied up, she would've taken off running, even if the storm outside was a category four hurricane.

"So you're finally going to admit your sexual preference?"

"In case you're trying to use that particular angle to get me to capitulate to your demands, let me save you some time and energy. You're not my type."

Kira's blue eyes turned hard. She turned her back and took another long sip of wine. "I'll just go forward then with the business at hand, which is to get what I want."

Another round of lightning illuminated the house. The lights flickered several times before finally fading to complete blackness. They both stood quietly in anticipation of the electricity returning, but it quickly became clear the storm had at last won the battle with the power lines. The candles that had been lit earlier bathed the darkened room in a warm yellow glow. At once, the air became thick and the mood portentous.

"Will you tell me what I want to know?"

Nicole physically recoiled. "You'd actually go through with this?"

"And here I thought you finally understood my true nature." Kira spoke tersely, her face in the shadows. She took a step forward into the candlelight, a certain menace in her gait. Nicole was alternately thrilled and frightened. Try as she might, she couldn't keep fighting the magnetic pull between their bodies. It was if every molecule in her had an intelligence of its own and each wanted nothing more than to surrender to the overwhelming longing that had plagued her since the day they met.

"Whatever you do to me," Nicole rasped in an unsteady voice, "I'll never tell you—" but she was silenced as Kira moved in, reached out, and grabbed hold of her necklace all in one fell swoop. "What are you doing?"

Kira held the delicate piece of jewelry in her palm, carefully examining both sides of the small silver pendant before allowing it to gently fall back down upon Nicole's chest without comment. The smooth knuckles of her hand, however, remained still against the bare skin of her sternum.

Nicole dared not breathe, fearful that the air in her lungs was the only thing keeping her heart from exploding inside her chest. Surely, if Kira couldn't hear it pounding violently against her ribs, then she could certainly feel it.

"I really hate you," she heard herself growl with unbridled hostility, hating the woman for making her so weak.

A sly smirk twisted Kira's mouth, as if Nicole's sneering declaration greatly pleased her. "I seem to recall you telling me that once before. Right before you let me kiss you." She then proceeded to trail one slender fingertip from Nicole's necklace up to the delicate hollow at the base of her neck, pausing as if mesmerized by the small indentation there. With a soft, almost feather-like touch, she traced the delicate outline of her clavicle, following the fragile bone even as it disappeared under her blouse.

A wave of heat rippled inside Nicole. She couldn't contain the broken gasp that escaped her lips. Kira ignored her reaction and continued the sensual caress, her finger mapping a heated path to where the bra strap hugged her shoulder. Their eyes met and locked. Kira placed that one agonizingly arousing finger under the elastic fabric, gave it a gentle tug, then lazily followed the silky band of flimsy material downward until both her finger, and the heat of her hand, rested just above the swell of Nicole's breast.

"Do you even know what your eyes are saying to me, Nicole?"

Nicole childishly squeezed them shut. She tossed her head back and inclined her chin challengingly. "My hands are chained behind my back and I'm being openly fondled against my will!"

Without pause, Kira took a step backward, grabbed the key Bogie had left on the table, then leaned all her slight weight into Nicole as she leisurely reached around the wooden beam and fumbled with the handcuffs. A loud click indicated the locking mechanism had been undone.

"You're free," Kira whispered into her temple, but Nicole remained motionless, unsure what part of her ached more—her wrists from the ordeal with the tight metal still encircling one hand or her loins from the brief but unforgettable collision of their bodies.

"Let me see your wrists," Kira implored quietly, grasping both of Nicole's arms in a strong but tender grip and bringing them carefully around the wooden support. After gingerly removing the other cuff and laying the shackles, along with the key, back down on the end table, she bent to examine the soft tissue the hard, cold steel had irritated. Her brows drew together in an angry frown.

"The skin isn't broken but your circulation has suffered some. Bogie will have some explaining to do." The pads of Kira's thumbs stroked the vulnerable undersides of Nicole's wrists. It felt as if she'd been given a dose of opium, or at least what she imagined the effect of the euphoric drug would feel like.

"Are you okay?"

Nicole shook her head. Her voice was lodged somewhere in her stomach and if she attempted to speak now, nothing more than a high-pitched squeak would have sounded.

"What is it?" Kira questioned, genuine concern in her voice as her fingers continued their intoxicating magic, slowly traveling up and down the sensitive flesh of Nicole's forearms.

"What are you doing to me?" Nicole demanded, her mouth dry and body throbbing in places she never knew existed.

"Besides proving you're a liar?"

Nicole lost her battle with gravity. She had no choice but to use the beam that had imprisoned her for balance. "This isn't fair, Kira."

"I warned you already that I don't play fair. Are you finally ready to concede defeat?"

"You'd do this to me just to get me to," her voice was pained, filled with hurt, "to tell you what I found at the bank?"

"You misunderstand, Nicole," Kira divulged in a sexy drawl. "I don't care about anything else outside of hearing you admit you want me, hearing you beg in a voice ragged with need for me to take you and then pleading with me to do it all to you again and again until your body shakes from exhaustion. Morning will come soon enough and then you and I will take a trip to the bank. But tonight is all about this," she paused, as if searching for the right word, "chemistry, electricity, whatever label you want to use to describe what this energy is between me and you. If I don't kiss you soon, I may go crazy with this want, but if you think I'm going to force you, no matter how much you unconsciously try to make me, I won't."

Nicole felt that old familiar heat seeping into her cheeks. Kira had seen right through her charade. But she was even more shocked by Kira's staggering revelation that her own desire was so intense, she'd be willing to lay her proverbial scepter down and call a truce until morning's light.

Still she struggled.

She wasn't the type of person who could casually engage in a one-night physical encounter, particularly with someone whose ethics were so ambiguous. And then there was the little matter of her heart...

"Must you deliberate every decision you make, Nicole?"

Was it Nicole's imagination or had Kira taken a step even closer?

"Surrender to it," Kira purred somewhere close to her ear. "Let me hear you say you want me."

Nicole's senses seemed to go into nuclear meltdown. She felt herself begin to sway, falling into forbidden arms, yielding to some unidentified law of physics that had yet to be discovered and studied. "I do," she heard herself whisper.

"You do what?" Kira persisted, reaching out and tracing the soft line of Nicole's cheek with the back of her hand.

Nicole closed her eyes, reveling in the warmth of the light, magical touch. Nothing mattered anymore. The bogus hijacking, the threatening letters to her mother from the IRS, the tapping of her phone lines. Every lucid thought vanished from her head. There was no yesterday, no tomorrow, only the now.

"I do. I want you..."

Kira gently pulled Nicole into her arms and simply held her in a loose embrace for a long moment. Nicole remained absolutely still, absorbing her heat, breathing in that wonderful perfumed scent of her hair and skin, delighting in and memorizing the supple, delicious curves molding into her own feminine contours.

"Come with me," Kira commanded, her voice thick and unsteady as she took Nicole's hand and pulled her the short distance to the sofa. The votive candles in the fireplace candelabrum flickered luminously, casting shadowed swaths of gold and orange across the room. Nicole's entire body was aching with want, making the muscles in her limbs weak. She fell back against the plush leather of the cushions like a rag doll, the lack of light making her mahogany-colored eyes large, dark pools of desire as she watched Kira carefully drop down next to her.

"I could get lost in your eyes, forget everything," Kira admitted, her gaze intense as she turned slightly to close the space that separated their bodies.

Nicole moved closer, just as eager, but nervous and shy, unsure of her next move. Her breathing was shallow and uneven, her heart thudding wildly. One of Kira's hands found the small of her back, propelling her upward, while the other languidly cradled the tender column of Nicole's neck, tilting her face.

"If you don't want this, tell me now."

Nicole fluttered her lashes shut, saying nothing. She felt the warmth of Kira's breath a second before the slight weight of her moist, pink lips pressed down upon her own. The kiss was light, like a sigh. Kira moved leisurely, grazing feather-like kisses along the bottom swell of Nicole's mouth while her fingers moved from their position around her neck to brush up and down the curvature of her spine. The contact was tantalizingly persuasive and she fought to restrain her desire, savoring the sweet fragility of the intimacy for as long as she could, but her hands seemed to have a will of their own, a need that couldn't be curtailed. She reached out, but Kira sensed her intent and covered her hands with her own, then held them tightly to her.

"If you touch me now, I'll lose what little control I have."

Nicole shivered. The husky declaration was almost as arousing as her touch. Kira reclaimed her lips, her kiss more urgent now. Nicole released a low, drawn-out moan when Kira pushed her down into the sofa, her heated length coming to nestle horizontally atop Nicole, their pelvic bones converging. Kira's tongue entered her mouth, its velvety tip tentative at first, exploratory, but then it began a coaxing rhythm, flooding Nicole with a hot, liquid fire. They moved against one another, matching the measured cadence of their tongues.

A few minutes later, Kira broke the kiss, raising herself slightly and looking down into Nicole's flushed features. There was a glint of something indefinable within the blue eyes boring into Nicole's, a curiously deep longing that had absolutely nothing to do with the physical demands of their passions. Nicole opened her mouth to speak—what words she'd been about to confess she had no idea but Kira silenced her with a smothering kiss that removed any ability she had to access that part of her brain where language and words were cached.

Nicole's hands were released and she delighted in the freedom, running shaky fingers along the sexy lines of Kira's back, her waist, her hips before slipping them into the loose, lustrous strands of blond hair framing the oval of her face and taking great pleasure in their silky texture.

"I want you so badly," she heard Kira murmur into her ear as she slipped a hand underneath Nicole's blouse. It fluttered lightly across her abdomen, then situated itself underneath one cup of her bra. With an exacting aptitude no doubt born from experience (just how and upon whom such skills were perfected, Nicole pushed from her mind), Kira began fervently massaging the fullness of her breasts, lightly teasing the taut nipples with her thumbs. Nicole instinctively arched her body. She wanted to reciprocate the heavenly torture, reaching out and unbuttoning the front of Kira's dress with a clumsy haste.

In that instant, they were both lost to the wild hunger that could no longer be curbed, both of them hot with desire. Nicole didn't know how it had happened, but she was suddenly in nothing else but her panties, as was Kira, who was now looking down at her with eyes bright with admiration and hunger. She placed her palm flat along the inside of Nicole's thigh, tracing a small circle against the sensitive flesh with her fingers. Ever so gradually, her fingers slowly moved upward, closer and closer to the wet core of Nicole's femininity.

Nicole couldn't contain the sob of yearning. She watched with something akin to terror and bliss as Kira's head dipped low, replacing the coolness of her hand with the heat of her mouth. She trailed her lips along the sinewy juncture where Nicole's hip and thigh merged. Nicole was now writhing in ecstatic agony, dismayed by her body's abandon. She didn't think her lust could grow any stronger but then she felt the tip of Kira's tongue dart provocatively against the elastic of her silk underwear, pressing against the damp fabric so that the warmth of her tongue was at once tantalizingly painful and exquisitely enticing.

Uncomfortable with her desperate need, Nicole tried to close her legs. But Kira's will was stronger and she would not relent, pulling the last of Nicole's clothing from her so that no barrier remained between them as she continued her amorous assault, her expert fingers joining her mouth's licentious ministrations.

Nicole felt herself soaring higher and higher until at last, she burst, shattering as her release drained her of everything. When she fluttered back down to earth, she realized Kira was holding her tight, a slight smile tugging at the corners of her lips.

"You're amazing," Kira said in a voice that seemed to come from a long way off.

They lay quietly entwined in each other's arms until Nicole could no longer check her need to rouse a similar response from Kira. With a cautious boldness, she repositioned their bodies so that she was now on top and Kira lay with an acquiescent curiosity beneath her.

"What're you doing?" Kira asked, a gleam of both amusement and arousal glowing within her eyes.

"Wait and see."

Having Kira Anthony so weak and vulnerable underneath her filled Nicole with a primitive power and confidence. She leaned forward, the tips of their naked breasts colliding as she reached for Kira's hands. She imprisoned both, lifted them up over Kira's head, and held them there. She then traced the outline of Kira's lips with her tongue, tasting her own musky scent before deepening their kiss. With her free hand, she explored every inch of silky soft bare skin available to her inquisitive fingers. When at last she raised her head, she was satisfied to see no trace of amusement lingering in Kira's searing gaze.

She continued to kiss a sensuous path from Kira's pink lips, down the graceful column of her neck to her nipples. She took each one in her mouth, then positioned the hardness of her thigh between Kira's legs. She continued her brazen descent across the flat perfection of Kira's midriff. Perhaps realizing Nicole's intention, Kira refused to stay passive a moment longer. She jerked her hands from their confinement and pulled Nicole toward her.

"I'm already about to explode." Her breathing was loud and uneven. "Are you trying to torture me?"

"I want to taste you," Nicole whispered shyly, disappointed.

"Later, Nicole. *Please.* Right now I need you, more than anything!"

Nicole wasted no more time teasing. She slipped her fingers into the wet folds of Kira's womanhood, massaged and pressed, awkward in her movements at first and then growing more certain. In seconds, Kira was panting breathlessly and calling her name in a voice raw with need. And when Nicole felt the woman thrashing beneath her quiver, clench then tighten and shudder, she too felt a surge of satisfaction for being able to bring the one they called the Ice Princess to orgasm.

After a few minutes, Nicole went to retrieve a decorative throw she'd seen draped across one of the armchairs and covered their cooling bodies with the thin, burgundy-colored fabric. When she pulled Kira close against her, she was surprised to find the woman was already sound asleep.

CHAPTER SEVENTEEN

Nicole woke with a start. All around her was dark and quiet. For one long, very bewildering minute she couldn't remember where she was but then she felt the warm, delicious weight of a female's perfectly proportioned form pressed snugly into the curve of her spine.

Was the dream true? Had she and Kira actually made love?

The events of the evening projected forth onto the screen in her mind like a movie being fast-forwarded. In an instant, she was wide-awake and the peaceful lethargy that seemed to have hold of her spirit vanished into thin air. When her eyes finally adjusted, she cast an uncertain gaze down at the woman's arm possessively encircling her rib cage.

Yes, now she remembered: The storm, the loss of electricity, Kira's artful seduction.

No, it hadn't been a dream. In fact, she was naked and Kira's silky smooth legs were still tangled with her own. Their passions had quickly escalated to such a frenzy that neither of them could stand on their own two feet and had simply sought the nearest piece of furniture that would allow their raging desires complete liberty. The mere recall of their intimate encounter caused a flood of warmth to surge anew between her legs, but this was certainly not the moment to reflect on the magnificent awakening of her body under Kira's practiced tutelage.

She had to get out of there—*fast!*

Come morning's light, Kira would simply push aside the incredible physical intimacy they'd just shared as if it had never happened and go about business in her usual dogmatic manner, steadfastly determined to learn what Nicole had found inside the safe deposit box. Now that Nicole had experienced the magic of Kira's gentle touch, there was no way she was going to be able to deny the woman anything.

Her wristwatch was a simple Timex Ironman, and it had served her well. If she moved her arm too abruptly to check the time, she might wake Kira, and the hastily concocted scheme she'd just hatched would be derailed before it had even started.

Instead, she ever so cautiously shifted her weight until she was able to reach the outer dial of the plastic timepiece. Having forgotten about her encounter with the handcuffs, she flinched when she accidentally poked the raw, tender skin near the watchband. Kira grumbled an immediate objection to the disturbance in her sleep.

"Slowly," she silently admonished, pressing a tiny button until the face of the watch glowed brightly with an iridescent blue light. *12:55 a.m.*

With painstaking care, Nicole gingerly wriggled her body from Kira's ardent grip. Once liberated, she looked down, suddenly maudlin as her eyes traced the lovely bones of Kira's profile. A weak moonlight filtered into the house through the last of the sapped storm clouds, providing just enough light for Nicole to commit the graceful lines of the woman's face to her memory. She stood there, chilled and naked, taking in Kira's uncharacteristic vulnerability as she slept so peacefully, like a botanist might do having discovered a rare flower during a trek in the woods. She stared lovingly at the heart-shaped pout of Kira's lips, swollen now from their kisses, the perfect curve of her brow, the sweep of her closed lashes fanning their thick length against her lightly tanned skin.

It took every ounce of willpower Nicole possessed to quell

the sudden urge to gather Kira into her arms and hold her for as long as the waning night would allow. She straightened. There was no time for such ridiculously reckless thoughts. Imposing an iron control on herself, she turned away and went about searching for her scattered clothing. After locating the pants, blouse, and undergarments she'd discarded in passionate oblivion just a few hours before, she dressed hastily in the dark, then retrieved the handcuffs and their key from where Kira had placed them earlier.

Next, she crouched down next to the coffee table.

With a hearty intake of breath, she pushed the mammoth piece of furniture across the floor. Thankfully, the thick luxurious rug under the table absorbed any sounds the movement might have made, but just the same, she cast a wary eye toward the sofa. Kira was still sound asleep, no doubt exhausted from the long flight from Nairobi; one toned, unclothed arm conveniently dangling over the side of the cushions, her long, delicate fingers curling up against the polished hardwood flooring.

Nicole's lips twitched with self-satisfaction. If her plan worked, she'd be miles away before Kira woke.

Taking another deep breath, this time to calm her nerves and gather her weakening courage, she attached one handcuff to the ornamental iron framing the underside of the table, then turned to connect the other half of the steel bracelet to Kira's exposed wrist.

All at once, a series of high-pitched beeps and wails permeated the silence as electricity to the house was unexpectedly restored, its current surging through the wires and reengaging all the appliances and electronic contraptions.

Nicole tensed. *Hell's bells. Please don't wake up!*

Kira stirred ever so slightly but, after heaving a sleepy sigh, continued to doze.

Releasing a shaky, pent-up breath she hadn't even realized she'd been holding, Nicole quickly chained Kira's hand to the table without another second's falter.

Now where to hide the key?

She had to position it somewhere that would allow her enough time to implement the rest of the plan. Her eyes darted around the large space in frustration until falling to the massive staircase in the center of the open room. She placed the key on the lip of the seventh step, far enough away but not impossible to retrieve. Even though Kira was in prime physical condition, the table was solid wood and quite heavy. If all went as designed, it would take her a fairly decent amount of time to drag the table through the house, then manipulate it up three or four stairs until she was able to reach the key and free herself.

But how would she know that the key was there?

As unpleasant as the prospect was, Nicole would have to leave a note. She found a pad of paper and a pen inside one of the end table drawers and wrote a quick, impersonal missive explaining that the key was on the seventh step and apologizing in advance for taking her car.

Yes, this might just work! Not only would Kira be chained for who knew how long to the coffee table, but then she'd be stuck here without a vehicle, no doubt dependent on Bogie and Stella to come back from where ever they were to collect her.

Morning's light was certainly not going to find Kira Anthony in a very good mood.

Nicole couldn't help but cast one last look back. Her heart lurched with pained regret. If only Kira *really* was one of the good guys wearing the white hat. She swallowed hard and bit back tears.

Go, Nicole, she urgently whispered to herself. *Now! You're in love and your heart is playing tricks with your sanity. Need you be reminded Kira is involved with the helicopter pilot in the pictures on the mantel and that she attempted to destroy your mother's life? The woman is void of a conscience, and no amount of whimsical fantasy is going to change that fact. You're acting like a lovesick fool.*

She almost tripped over her own feet as she grabbed her

bag and ran toward the back of the house to find a long, slate-tiled hallway leading to a door that opened into the garage. The vast, industrial-like space looked big enough to house two tractor-trailers, but there was only one compact car parked on the white polymer-coated flooring—a sleek white Lexus sedan. She lifted the chrome handle, ecstatic to find it unlocked. With a grateful nod to the universe, she slid into the supple leather of the driver's seat, found what appeared to be the garage door's remote clipped to the visor and a set of keys dangling from the ignition. Her Honda Civic was nearly a decade old, but this luxuriously modern machine looked like it had just come off the assembly line. She remembered driving in her sister's leased BMW and recalled her fascination with the round button labeled *Start Engine*. She located the same mechanism to the right of the speedometer and pressed it. Sure enough, the vehicle powered on and the steering wheel robotically advanced forward like some innovation from the far-distant future.

CHAPTER EIGHTEEN

Her stomach in a tight knot, Nicole backed out of the garage while adjusting the position of the seat. Kira was about two inches taller, and the difference made it hard for her to put pressure on the pedals properly. The rain had stopped, but deep puddles of black water had pooled along the road's edges, and as she drove through them their murky debris splattered against the windshield.

Once she was a safe distance from the house, she gunned the accelerator. About a mile later, the wet dirt merged with solid asphalt. Nicole grabbed the rearview mirror and angled it so she could get a good view of the backseat. A part of her half expected to see Bogie or Stella lurching at her from the interior shadows.

Although the mirror showed the backseat to be empty, it did little to ease her frazzled nerves. Once she reached a main highway, she decided to head east. After a few minutes, the tension in her head lessened from a loud, painful hammering to a tolerable dull thud. The digital clock indicated it was half past two in the morning. She was making good time but needed to keep her foot to the pedal. Such a costly automobile surely came equipped with some sort of high-tech tracking system. Pinpointing her exact location would be just a matter of Kira making a call to the company that provided roadside and navigational assistance. She needed to dump the car as soon as possible.

As she drove, her adrenaline level gradually began to taper off and her eyelids grew heavy. Images began darting out from the darkness—flashbacks of Kira touching her, kissing her, unbuttoning her blouse, and slowly, seductively removing her bra. She pushed the gas pedal even harder, trying to keep from recalling the tender strokes of Kira's fingers along her legs and the feel of the woman's hot lips pressed erotically against her inner thigh. She felt her pulse quicken from the memory.

The night air was now warmer than the ground after the rain, causing a mist-like fog to slowly creep over the road. Her detailed reflections were interrupted when a concrete overpass appeared from out of the mist. Stifling a yawn, she took the exit, ascending the on-ramp at well over the suggested twenty-five miles per hour listed on the sign she shot past. She needed to slow down. The last thing she needed while driving a stolen car was to draw the attention of the police—who surely wouldn't believe her story. There was a truck stop with a bright neon light blinking in its steamy windows advertising it was open twenty-four hours. The parking lot of the truck stop was littered with huge semis and other equally intimidating rigs. She maneuvered the Lexus far away from the bright industrial lighting fixtures towering above the gas pumps before turning off the ignition. Grabbing her bag from the passenger seat, she fished through all her junk until she unearthed both her cell phone and its battery. Should she take the risk and connect them? No, she decided, dropping them back into her bag and surreptitiously surveying her surroundings. Who knew? Bogie might be monitoring her calls or tracking the phone's location. It wasn't worth the risk. She'd seen his skills with a piece of tape and a knife.

The sight of other people, even if they were an odd assortment of weathered, chain-smoking, boot-clad truckers was oddly comforting after driving through such isolated farmland. Grabbing her bag, she left the plush sumptuousness of the Lexus and nearly ran to the lone pay phone located next to some newspaper bins and the ice machine. She reached for the phone's handle. It was wet from the rain. She cautiously lifted it to her ear, but there was no dial tone. It probably hadn't worked in years.

She strode quickly into the truck stop. It was empty save for an older woman in a red, smock-like uniform eyeing her warily from behind the counter. After grabbing a toothbrush and deodorant, she found a shelf filled with an assortment of disposable cell phones. She only needed to make two calls. She picked one that offered usage for one hundred and fifty minutes. As she passed an end cap filled with packaged doughnuts and crème-filled cakes, her stomach reminded her it needed refueling. She grabbed something chocolate and a bottle of water from the refrigerated cooler.

"You okay, girlie?" the haggard-looking clerk asked when Nicole placed her items on the counter. "Look like you running from the devil."

Nicole gaped open-mouthed, not knowing how to respond. "Um—"

"Your shirt's inside out," the woman pointed out with a harsh laugh. Nicole looked down at her blouse. The seam of stitching was indeed facing outward.

"This time of night, only customers I git are eighteen-wheelers, lawbreakers, or spooked girls fleeing their men. Which one are you? Lawbreaker or spooked girl? You sure ain't no trucker."

Both, Nicole almost admitted out loud. She'd stolen a car and she was running, just not from a man. "I figured as much," the clerk grumbled when Nicole didn't answer, scanning the chocolate-frosted cake's bar code with a laser gun. "Been there myself once. If you need a place to hole down for the night, there's a motel on the lake 'bout two miles from here my sister runs. With that storm tonight, I suspect even the Lord might be wantin' a dry spot to sleep. You fancy, I'll rouse her out of bed for ya and by the time you get there, she'll have a room ready for ya."

"I don't have a car," Nicole replied. It wasn't a lie—she couldn't risk driving the Lexus any farther. It was just a matter of time before Kira freed herself from the handcuffs and came after her. "I'm sort of stranded until morning." She directed her gaze to the phone entombed in a hard plastic shell. "I was just going to call a friend to tell her where she can find me."

The woman's faded blue eyes seemed to see right through her, but Nicole didn't flinch. She was exhausted, and the prospect of laying her head down on something soft and somewhere out of harm's way for a few hours was worthy of a white lie or two.

"Hmmph," the store clerk snorted, giving Nicole another once-over. "Forty-two dollars and fifty-nine cents."

Nicole still had cash left over from her doomed trip to Africa in her wallet. Credit card transactions could be traced, she realized as she handed the money over.

"I am really tired—and there's no telling how long it will take my friend to get here," she said, stifling a yawn. "Do you think your sister has a free room? I really appreciate your help."

"Well, all right," the clerk said. "I'll lock up here and drop ya there myself, seeing as how you ain't got no ride." She gave Nicole a conspiratorial wink. "We ain't that busy this time of night anyway as most'a my guys are pulling a few z's in their cabs." She was missing a few teeth. Her hair was white with faded streaks of pale orange. "Yer mister ain't out there in the parking lot, is he?" she asked, pulling a shotgun from under the counter and limping forward.

"I don't think he was able to follow me, but I can't be sure." Nicole gulped nervously.

"Bastards." The clerk grimaced, checking the firearm's chamber. "Think they can do whatever they want to women, but this little baby puts us all on an even playing field. My ex tried to run me over almost thirty years ago and I got this mangled limb to remind me of it for the rest of my life. Since then, I don't go nowhere without protection."

Nicole remembered thinking exactly that when she'd tied

her knife around her calf that morning. "He's in jail, I hope," she said.

"Jail was too good for that varmint. By the way, my name's Gladys, honey. You ain't gotta tell me yours." She put her gun down and hobbled over to the coffee station. She began merging one pot of coffee with another before turning switches off and wiping the counter down with a damp blue cloth. "Anyways, a little backwoods justice was how we took care of him."

Nicole decided she didn't need to know any more about Gladys' life. "I know this sounds strange, but can you tell me where we are? I mean, what city?"

"You get beamed up by spacemen and dropped off in a cornfield?" She chuckled, a harsh throaty sound that eerily harmonized with the sad voice of country coming from a radio playing somewhere in the back of the store. "You in Delaplane, 'bout a stone's throw from DC, sweetie, just a tad off the beaten track is all."

Delaplane was a fairly exclusive area in Virginia filled with antique shops, wineries and horse farms. It was about an hour's drive west of the capital. When she'd woken up in the back of the Suburban, it had felt as if she'd been out longer than an hour.

"Now, be straight up, you ain't packing any heat, are you? The last thing I need is you robbing my kid sister in the dead of the night. I'll never hear the end of it. Though you're sweet as apple pie in the face, I've been fooled a time or two. I don't let the bad ones stop me from offering help when I want, otherwise they win, if you get my drift. Someone done show me kindness when I was in your shoes, and I try to return the favor when I'm able."

Nicole shook her head. "No gun, no weapons at all," she answered honestly. Bogie had confiscated her knife.

"Now, Sally can be a bit suspicious of folks, so don't try any funny stuff with her. And you'd best be heeding that advice. My shotgun ain't nothing compared to her two Rottweilers," Gladys counseled a few minutes later as they raced down a dark, unlit road in an old Chevy Blazer with all the windows open. The clerk was already on her second cigarette and it appeared the floor of the vehicle doubled as her ashtray.

"Light's on there in the office. She was just headin' to bed after a night out at the tracks with her old man when I called but she said she'd wait up a bit longer when I told her you'd pay in cash," Gladys wheezed through nicotine-stained lips when they pulled up in front of an L-shaped cinder-block building that looked like every other motel built during the 1950s. "I know it don't look like much," she took a long drag from her cigarette before flinging the butt out the window, "but there's a fully stocked lake behind it and this land was worth a ton of dough a few years back. Too bad the market took such a turn, otherwise we'd be living pretty dang good right about now. Sally mostly rents to hunters and truckers. Used to be vacationers, but the big highways took away that business. Go on now, get. My sister needs her beauty sleep. The longer you keep her from it, the more those of us who have to look at her'll suffer."

Nicole placed one hand on the door handle and grabbed her belongings with the other. "I don't know how to thank you for helping me, Gladys. You'll never know how much—"

"Never you mind all that. Just tell me what you want me to do with that shiny new car you left back in my parking lot."

Nicole's eyes widened in surprise.

"Saw you drive back and forth a few times before you pulled in, sweetie. Is someone going to come lookin' for it? Like the po-po?"

"Probably," Nicole admitted with a troubled frown. "Hadn't given it much thought, but now that you brought it up, yes, someone will come and ask questions…questions I'm hoping you won't be entirely up front about answering. I didn't do anything illegal, just needed to escape from a bad situation, and that car was my only means of doing so."

"No worries. I know me a bootlegger whose son runs a chop shop." Her foot pumped the brake pedal. "Good luck to you, honey! And don't go back to him—no matter how much he begs!"

Watching the Blazer's only working taillight disappear from view, Nicole hoped that the damned Lexus would be dismantled and its parts on their way to Trinidad or Turkey or some other foreign land before sunrise.

A wave of profound weariness invaded her bones. Her stomach heaved. Perhaps it was a combination of everything she'd been through all rolled into one massive body slam aimed directly at her intestines. Mercifully, the queasiness passed.

❖

Sally was indeed waiting for her as Gladys had promised and none too pleased to be doing so; one very frayed, slipper-shod foot tapped impatiently beneath the stained pink robe she was wearing, two salivating Rottweilers panting at her side. "I ain't like Gladys, taking in strays and whatnot. You bring me an ounce of trouble and my dogs here will have you for breakfast."

"No trouble, I promise. Just need a place to sleep tonight," Nicole assured her as she paid for her room with three crisp twenties and took the key from pudgy fingers.

"Last room to the left. Room 423."

Nicole stared down at the room key with wide, incredulous eyes. Had she heard right? Yes, she had. The diamond-shaped red plastic was inscribed with the number 423 in faded gold ink, the same number as the safe deposit box at the bank.

"Room 423?" she asked aloud, almost to herself. The motel didn't have more than twelve rooms total. It was too surreal to be a coincidence. She shook her head and walked out of the lobby to her room. She unlocked the door and flipped the light switch just inside the door. There was a mirror on the other side of the room, and her reflection was frightening.

It was three thirty in the morning. She was a nameless stranger the woman's toothless sister had dragged over from a truck stop. Her shirt was on inside out. After riding in the Blazer with windows rolled down, her hair had been blown into a wild, messy snarl of tangled curls. And her mascara had bled, leaving two crescent-shaped, coal-colored smudges beneath her bleary eyes. For the first time in what felt like days, Nicole laughed. She felt a deep empathy for celebrities who'd had their mug shots taken at the worst possible moments in their lives and posted on the Internet for the entire world to view. This wasn't an image she would want anyone else to see, much less remember.

The motel room was clean but felt damp, probably from the storm and the lingering humidity. A tacky lithograph of a random seaside adorned the wall next to the bed. The paneling was a dark shade of brown and the synthetic orange carpet looked relatively unsoiled. When she slipped off her sandals, she envisioned all the strange bare feet that had come in contact with the stiff, brittle rug and wondered if she was going to catch something—athlete's foot, ringworm, there was no telling what the rug was infected with. On the tips of her toes, she peeled the paisley blue bedspread away from the pillows, plopped down on the clammy sheets, shoved a piece of stale chocolate cake in her mouth, then took one of her Honda's car keys to puncture the disposable cell phone's near-impenetrable packaging and tore it open. The tiny device came already precharged. After pressing a code to activate it, she sat back against the warped, particle-wood headboard, took a long swig from her bottle of water, and dialed the first of two calls she had to make, even though it was the middle of the night and the sun would be coming up soon.

She was certain her mother would answer before the black cordless on the table at the side of her bed even had a chance to ring. She would be lying there in her bed, wide-awake and worrying about her youngest daughter's whereabouts. Nicole had never stayed out all night before. Even when she was living with Danielle, she usually called home every evening before bedtime so her mother could relax, knowing she was okay.

But for the first time in twelve years, Nicole was developing an insight into her mother's neuroses and overprotective worry about her daughters. The vague suspicions bouncing about since her return from Africa were slowly coming together into a pattern that began to make sense.

Dorothy Kennedy *knew* about the existence of the stocks and cash. She might not know *where* they'd been hidden for the past decade, but Nicole now realized her mother wasn't just paranoid or delusional. Her mother had feared someday someone would come looking for the things in the safe deposit box. It was why she'd always been so overprotective, constantly worried about her and Liz's safety.

But where was she now?

The phone rang until finally the robotic female voice programmed into the answering machine picked up. Nicole hung up without leaving a message and called back twice just to be sure. There was still no answer. It wasn't like her mother. Nicole hoped that she had taken a sleeping pill and fallen asleep on the couch in the den. But how likely was that if her daughter hadn't come home yet?

Kira had claimed Rhyse Taylor was on his way. Had he already been to the house? Was *that* why her mother wasn't picking up the phone?

She chewed at her bottom lip, tasting sugary remnants of the frosting as she pushed the keys of the phone, still amazed that after all this time she could remember the number. "I need your help," she said when a familiar feminine voice she hadn't heard in over six months answered the phone groggily.

Silence. And then, "You stood me up."

"I didn't intend to, Danielle. I just hadn't planned on being kidnapped yesterday afternoon."

"Kidnapped?" Danielle sounded instantly alert. Nicole pictured her sitting up erect in bed, her long, wheat-colored hair tousled and uncombed. Was her mother somewhere nearby, hog-tied to a chair and waiting for rescue?

"I escaped—I had to steal a car, but I don't have it anymore.

It's a really long story and your phone might be tapped. Can you come get me?"

Danielle didn't seem the slightest bit put out by the fact she was calling her at three thirty in the morning, nor did she seem to be taken aback at the possibility that her phone line might be tapped, Nicole's claim of being kidnapped, or the fact that she had stolen a car in order to escape.

Danielle didn't seem to have any doubts at all about this strange call at almost four in the morning.

Instead, after another long pause, Danielle asked, "Where are you?"

CHAPTER NINETEEN

Nicole managed to rouse herself from bed after only four hours of a very restless sleep interrupted by bouts of paranoia and anxiety about her mother. Several times throughout her brief slumber, she found herself wide-awake, laying in wait, listening for stealthily placed footsteps on the cement outside her door or pondering the revving of a car motor in the distance. Now tired and anxious, she stared up at the ceiling's water stains, wondering if she was really there—in a muggy motel room in the middle of the boonies, yanked from her quiet existence and thrown into the center of an international conspiracy involving the murder of her own father.

With her eyes closed, she could pretend she was deep in the throes of some wild dream.

But then she'd open her eyes.

While eating the remaining chocolate cake she'd been too sleepy to finish last night, she called both her mother's landline and cell. There was no answer at either number. She called her sister, but that too went right into voicemail. It was Thursday morning. It was highly unusual for her sister to have her phone off. Liz didn't have a job. She usually woke late and spent the hours when she wasn't shopping either talking or texting.

Ted.

She should call Liz's husband. Except the only way to get

his cell number would be to power up her own, and that might mean the possibility of Bogie being able to trace her location. She could call Ted at the insurance firm where he worked, but she couldn't remember the name of the company.

From the prepaid disposable, she dialed into her own cell phone's voicemail to check if she had any messages, perhaps from a hospital. There weren't any, and she wasn't sure if that was a good or bad thing.

She pushed aside her apprehension the best she could. Taking a hot shower helped her mood some. After putting the same wrinkled clothing she'd worn the day before back on, she stood looking out of the room's dingy window from behind a panel of musty gold curtain, scanning the vacant parking lot and wooded perimeter. Part of her was caught up worrying about her mother, and now her sister, and another part of her was still back at the house with Kira, watching her darkly fringed lashes flutter open as the morning sun streamed its warm light onto her far-too-pretty face, sensing her confusion when she felt the cold metal encircling her wrist, imagining her sudden anger staining her high cheekbones a dull red as she read the note on the table.

A car door slammed, jolting Nicole from her reveries.

It was Danielle's blue Ford Escape.

She let the curtains fall back into place, ran nervously to the door, and pulled it open. The minty scent of toothpaste on her breath mingled with the fragrant perfume of the June morning, replacing the mildewed smells of the motel room. The storm had chased away the heat wave.

"I wasn't sure you'd come."

"You asked me for my help." Danielle stopped mid-pace, her car keys in one hand as she tossed Nicole the T-shirt she'd been carrying with the other. "And a clean shirt."

"Thanks." Nicole caught the garment. "Let me change real quick." She receded into the motel room, leaving the door open as an invitation to come inside. Alone in the tiny bathroom, she released a tight, drawn breath.

Now what? Am I really going to jump into a car with the daughter of the man who may have killed my father? What was I thinking to call her?

All her false bravado from the previous night seemed to have disappeared with the appearance of Danielle's Escape. While removing her blouse and pulling on the borrowed Old Navy flag-emblazoned navy tee, she caught sight of her reflection in the cracked mirror over the rust-stained sink. It made her pause.

"Your best friend is often in the mirror."

What the hell did it mean? Maybe it wasn't the words that were important. Maybe it was the significance of the Chinese stocks *with* a Chinese fortune. *No*, she shook her head, looking at her face, *that conclusion doesn't feel right.*

Boy, I'm looking haggard, she thought with an internal wince. The lack of food and sleep were definitely taking their toll. The only makeup she had with her was an old stick of black eyeliner—and all it had done was emphasize the thin streaks of red marring the whites of her eyeballs.

She closed her eyes, gripped the sink, and took a deep, calming breath. The girl waiting for her in the other room was someone she'd lived with for four months. They'd shared shampoo, bars of soap, meals, and what Nicole had thought at the time was a pretty solid friendship. Danielle hadn't been the one responsible for the relationship coming to an end. Yes, there *had* been that awkward kiss in the middle of the night, but it was Nicole who ran away, who refused to answer Danielle's calls and e-mails.

And all because she'd still been ducking and hiding, not yet ready to admit to herself what Danielle had already known for a while—Nicole had been attracted to her roommate.

"Let's just cut to the chase," Nicole said, surprised at how even and calm her voice sounded as she walked out of the bathroom to face Danielle. Her fear for her mother had inspired her to be braver. "I know everything."

Danielle was still standing in the doorway, her willowy

form silhouetted by the day's bright sunshine behind her, car keys tinkling together as they dangled from her fidgeting fingers. She'd had at least four inches of her long, thick pecan-colored hair trimmed off since Nicole had last seen her in December. Danielle looked ready for a picnic or some other carefree activity dressed in a white tank, blue cotton shorts, and white canvas sneakers. She looked like she hadn't a care in the world, and for a second Nicole doubted herself.

Maybe it was all just part of Kira's mind games, she thought as she looked at her former roommate.

"Good." Danielle remained motionless, but her being seemed somehow lighter and relaxed. Her features were no longer pinched. "Believe it or not, I'm relieved. We can talk about this here or in my car on the drive to the airport. My father's flight lands in two hours. I think we both need to hear what he has to say." So that much of what Kira had claimed was actually true. Rhyse Taylor was coming. She felt relief flood through her rather than fear of what his coming meant.

If Rhyse Taylor was sailing through the air thirty-six thousand feet above them, that meant he didn't have her mother captive somewhere.

"Well?" Danielle urged. "Come on, we have to hurry."

Nicole watched her suspiciously. *The clock is ticking.*

Time running out seemed the common thread linking all the parties involved in this strange convergence that she found herself directly in the center of.

Kira would probably be finding the Lexus soon—it wouldn't be hard to track, after all. Gladys would be questioned, and soon Sally's sausage-like fingers would be pointing the way to room 423.

"Let's go," she said, following Danielle out of the room and shutting the door behind her.

Without a word, Danielle reprogrammed the coordinates of the GPS unit suctioned to her windshield from the motel's address to those of Dulles International Airport. Before long, they were driving past Gladys's truck stop to get to the interstate. Nicole had anticipated the parking lot would be littered with cop cars and crime-scene tape around the Lexus, but everything looked remarkably normal—no different than when she had left it only a few hours earlier. Big-rig drivers and blue-collar workers were busy injecting gas into their tanks and caffeine into their bellies. But Kira's sleek sedan wasn't where she'd left it—in fact, it was nowhere to be seen. As the Escape went down the on-ramp, Nicole nervously looked into the mirror mounted on her side of the car, almost expecting to see the front end of the Lexus accelerating toward them, but there was nothing there.

"I heard you were in Africa for the summer," Danielle finally said a few minutes later as she pulled onto the highway.

"And I heard you've been looking for something." Nicole turned slightly to study the effect of her words, but Danielle's face remained carefully blank. "Is it true, Danielle? Was our friendship—was all of it, just a lie?"

"It started out that way," Danielle confessed, not taking her hazel eyes from the road. "There's no way to say this without it sounding really bad, but I can explain—if you'll let me."

"I'm listening."

The interior of the Escape was unnaturally quiet. No radio played in the background to break the tension. Just the whirring of cars as they sped past, the drone of the air-conditioning, and the rhythmic thumping of the Ford's big Michelin tires pounding the asphalt as the vehicle traveled east.

"I didn't have much choice," Danielle finally asserted weakly. "I had to do as I was told. She wanted the stocks, and I truly believe she was willing to do anything to get her hands on them."

Nicole felt the blood drain from her face. *She.*

"Yeah, the stocks your father hid before his death. I know all about them, Nicole. They're issued in bearer form, which means that physical possession of the certificates is the sole evidence of ownership. You found them, didn't you?"

Nicole turned her head away to look out the passenger window in case her face betrayed her reaction to Danielle's words. After all, no one knew for certain what she'd actually discovered inside that bank vault yesterday. She tried focusing on the landscape passing by the car windows—the hotels, the industrial parks, the occasional rooftops marking the entrance of a subdivision built close to the noise of the highway, but she didn't see any of it.

All she could see were the official-looking documents under the manila envelope.

"It was my job to find them," Danielle's fingers tightened around the steering wheel, the knuckles turning white, "or at least a clue as to where they were hidden, before you inevitably stumbled upon them."

"Who the hell are you?" Nicole spat the words out angrily. She felt violated. She'd trusted Danielle, thought they were friends. It had all been a lie. "Who the hell are you working for?"

"I told you this was going to sound bad, but let me finish before you freak out, okay?"

"Yeah, whatever." Nicole felt ill, sick to her stomach. She hadn't wanted to believe Kira's stories about Danielle—but she'd been right.

Nicole had never felt so betrayed and deceived in her life.

CHAPTER TWENTY

Whenever you'd invite me to spend a weekend with you at your mother's house, I would wait until you and your mom fell asleep, and then I'd spend the entire night digging through desk drawers, old letters, mail. I searched everything you owned looking for something, anything, that would tell me where your father might have hidden the stocks: books, photographs, old diaries. Please don't look at me like that," Danielle pleaded, unwilling to glance over and meet Nicole's eyes. "I'm a pawn in all of this, just like you. If I didn't cooperate, she said they were going to hurt him."

She again. Nicole wanted to ask the name of this *she* but couldn't bear the thought of hearing Danielle say Kira's name out loud.

"Him?" she questioned instead.

The Escape swerved slightly toward the rumble strips along the shoulder of the highway, sending vibrations reverberating through the car's metal frame. "My father. The three of us—we've all become involved in something very dangerous."

Nicole searched Danielle's features, looking for some telltale sign that she was lying, but there was sincerity in her voice and her manner looked too authentic to be contrived. She felt her heart softening.

"I was living in Miami. I wasn't really a student at your

school. I enrolled in one evening class just so I could get the lay of the land, know my way around the campus."

"But why?" Nicole asked, her mouth dry. "Why all these lies?"

"Haven't you been *listening*, Nicole? For credibility, to gain your trust—so I could find the damned stocks and save my father." She flipped on her turn signal and headed for the exit for Dulles Airport. "Last summer, I received a call on my cell. It was some woman claiming my father would be hurt if I didn't do exactly as she said. I hung up, thinking it was a prank. She called back. I just kept hanging up on her. And then one night later that week when I returned home to my apartment, a man was waiting there for me. He wasn't big, but he was scary in a street-thug sort of way. He was just sitting there on my couch watching my television." Her face had gone pale. "He didn't say a word, just handed me a piece of paper with a phone number on it and walked out my door. I've never been so scared in my life. If he could get into my locked apartment, I wasn't safe anywhere. Of course, I immediately called the number, and the woman's voice was the same as the one I'd hung up on. She never told me her name—she just said that my father had engaged in some very questionable behavior while working for the military, done things that could be considered treasonous, and if I didn't want him imprisoned for the rest of his life, I should do as I was told. At first, I was skeptical, but she knew too many things about my family—things an outsider would never know. I only wanted to protect my father—you would have done the same," she added defensively.

"Weren't you curious about what *things* your father may have done?" Nicole asked.

"I know my father is no saint." Danielle's gaze ricocheted back and forth from the traffic to Nicole. "But he's my father and I love him. And this woman told me you and your family probably didn't even know the stocks existed, so no harm, no foul, right? A clue to their possible whereabouts would most likely be right in plain sight and all I had to do was find it, whatever the heck it was. She promised me no one would be hurt if everything went as planned. After many sleepless nights spent snooping through your stuff, I didn't find a damned thing. And then, you and I weren't even talking." Remembering the cause of their conflict, that kiss over Thanksgiving break, they both briefly turned their heads from one another. "I kept thinking she would send another one of her goons after me, punish me for my failure. Remembering that greasy guy waiting for me on my couch, I didn't go back to Miami. I rented a place in Reston and I hid. It was really more like waiting than hiding. Days turned into weeks, and weeks into months. I called my father almost every day to ensure he was okay, that no one had hurt him. But it was as if I had dreamt the whole crazy experience. Nothing happened. Nicole," her voice was shaky, "I wanted to tell you the truth, to warn you, but you wouldn't return my calls or e-mails. I was just putting my life back together when I got your voicemail the other day. I realized something must have happened for you to just call me out of the blue like that, especially when I thought you were teaching in Africa. I didn't know what to do. I called my father when you didn't show up to meet with me last night. I finally broke down and told him everything. That's why he's flying up from his base in Florida."

They were pulling into the airport's hourly parking lot. Danielle lowered her window and grabbed a stamped ticket from the automated machine. "So tell me about your kidnapping. What happened? Did they hurt you?"

Nicole gave her a brief overview of her recent adventures as they walked to the main terminal. She didn't give too many details, just the relevant pieces of her story from the moment she'd landed in Nairobi to her abduction the previous afternoon, all the while trying to sort through Kira's involvement in her mind and contemplating the gruesome reality of coming face-to-face with Rhyse Taylor—who might have killed her father.

Then again, everything Kira had told her could have been lies.

Kira Anthony claimed to work for the government yet possessed outrageously expensive tastes that couldn't be satisfied on a civil servant's salary. The expensive state-of-the-art Lexus and the palatial three-story house built on prime real estate just outside of DC were well beyond the means of any government employee, even at the highest federal pay grade. Add in the hijacking in Kenya, attempts to blackmail both Danielle and her mother, and yesterday's kidnapping—and it made absolutely no sense that any federal agent, let alone agency, would go to such lengths to achieve their end. Even if they played the "suspected terrorist" card, they wouldn't have taken her to a palatial estate in the country for an interrogation. So, it stood to reason that *she* was the criminal architect behind all of this intrigue. Yet Nicole's heart told her otherwise. Did she dare trust her instincts despite the evidence to the contrary? She ran a finger over her bottom lip, remembering the feel of Kira's mouth upon her own. Love could make one lose every ounce of common sense, couldn't it?

Maybe.

But if Kira was the one telling the truth, then Danielle was lying—and she didn't seem like she was being untruthful. The terror in her voice had been too real.

"We have to go to the police," she said as they passed a Starbucks. She was hungry.

"Police?" Danielle's voice was high-pitched, and she looked at Nicole as if she'd completely lost her mind. "What are you talking about? We can't involve the police!" They maneuvered past a slow-moving group of Japanese tourists. "This woman has access to the system. There's probably an all-points bulletin out on you right now for something far more serious than stealing a car. Go to the police and our fates are sealed."

"What do you suggest? We can't run forever. And if this woman," a cloudy image of Kira's beautiful face drifted into her mind, "tried to get to you through your father, something tells me she may try to do the same with my mother. If she hasn't already."

"He said he wasn't checking any bags," Danielle murmured absently without acknowledging Nicole's concern. "Let's wait by the shuttle." Her hazel eyes darted from a wall of electronic screens listing arrivals and departures to a security checkpoint manned by three TSA agents. "His plane landed early, so he should be here." She jumped and began waving her hand excitedly. "Dad, over here!" she shouted to a tall, clean-shaven man in his late fifties exiting one of the trains.

Rhyse Taylor had broad shoulders and a closely cropped head of gray hair. His starched khakis were perfectly creased and a large green canvas duffel was tucked under one beefy arm. Everything about the man screamed military. Nicole looked from father to daughter. The two looked nothing alike.

"You're Luke's daughter, aren't you?"

Nicole nodded, shocked by the contempt and anger in the man's manner. She'd been contemplating how she was going to rebuff his handshake. The thought of touching the hand that might have played a role in her father's murder had filled her with revulsion. Apparently there'd been no need to be concerned.

"Well, you're lucky," the colonel growled through a mouthful of bright, unnaturally white teeth, "because if anything had happened to Danielle, I would have held you personally responsible."

"Dad, please!" Danielle was visibly upset and confused by her father's outburst. "Nicole is just as much a victim in this insanity as I am."

"I'm sorry." He was instantly contrite, embarrassed. He attempted to comb the short hairs on his head with a rough, calloused hand. "It's—well, terrifying to get a phone call from your only child, hear the fear in her voice and know that you're over a thousand miles away and there's little you can do to help her."

"Dad, I'm okay." Danielle affectionately squeezed her father's forearm. The crowd around them grew thicker as passengers claimed their luggage and surrounded them on their way to the shuttles, parking lots, and busses.

"Let's find a restaurant," she added, raising her voice to be heard over the tumult. "We can grab something to eat and talk there."

The colonel agreed with a curt dip of his square head. Nicole followed behind, not knowing what to make of Rhyse Taylor. Was he her father's killer, or had that all been part of Kira's schemes and lies? She didn't know what to think anymore.

"Dad, tell Nicole what you started to tell me last night," Danielle urged once they were seated in a booth inside the airport restaurant and the waitress had taken their drink order. "The whole story."

Nicole watched the colonel take a sip from his glass of ice water. She braced herself, suspecting she was in for yet another wild ride. The colonel leaned forward, the lines in his forehead above his shaggy gray brows deep and ruddy from the Florida sun. His nose wasn't big, but its ball-shaped tip was ravaged by broken capillaries.

"Luke, your father, and I met at a bar in Madrid back in the late eighties," he began. "Two Americans in a foreign country who got to talking and discovered their lives were quite similar, with two little girls almost the same age. We'd meet up every six months or so, either in DC or abroad. Over the years, we developed quite a good friendship. Luke first introduced himself as an engineer for a petroleum company. As time passed and his trust in me grew, he confided that he was also doing some undercover work for the government."

Nicole was silent, but she was certain her eyes revealed her astonishment.

"He didn't tell me much other than it wasn't dangerous." The waitress returned with their drinks. Nicole ordered a cheeseburger well done and reached for her Diet Coke the way an alcoholic does vodka. She was hoping the caffeine and carbonation would curb the headache that was waiting to pounce.

"We got to talking that night." The colonel continued telling his story, but not without casting a scrutinizing eye at the occupants of neighboring tables every few minutes. "He said he was paid rather well for his services, but he had to hide the extra income from his wife. He didn't want her worrying about him."

Nicole flinched. That sounded like her father.

"He told me about an intricate arrangement he'd worked out with the agency that employed him. Rather than receiving a paycheck for his efforts, he'd asked that they purchase stocks in a certain company on his behalf. I don't know all the details, maybe he told me, I can't remember, but two years into it, he said he was ready to quit both his job with the petroleum company as well as the agency. He was tired of the travel and wanted to be home with his wife and children. A year or so passed before I heard from him again, and when I did, I was scared for the guy. He was gaunt and thin, nervous. I thought he might be on drugs."

Nicole remembered Mr. Thomas had said the same thing.

"When I confronted him, he laughed and said he wished his problem were one as simple as chemical dependency. He reluctantly explained that he'd uncovered something big involving the sale of the military's weapons to anti-American radicals. The fraud was massive in scope." He lowered his voice. "He feared it might be an internal operation. He didn't get too much into it, which was probably for my own protection, but he did mention that he'd discussed it with his go-to at the agency. They were going to meet in Yemen the following afternoon." He took another drink of water.

"A week later, I'd read that Luke had been killed by a car bomb. I thought, hoped, it might be just a coincidence. Car bombs are an everyday occurrence over there. Maybe a month after the car bomb, I was ambushed by two brutes at a hotel in Syria. They beat me up pretty good, took out all my teeth…one at a time. These are dentures." He pointed a finger with a well-bitten nail toward the pink flesh of his gum line. "They asked me all about Luke—where'd he hide the stocks—what did I know about an investigation he was working on, and so on. I didn't know anything so there was nothing for me to say. I was in bad shape." He massaged a knuckle into his temple, as if reliving the experience, the pain and fear. "They left me there, in a stairway, bruised and bloody. I never told anyone and never would have if Danielle hadn't called me and told me what they'd forced her into."

The food arrived and for a few minutes they were busy with the task of unwrapping their silverware from sealed paper napkins and salting their fries. The mood was solemn. No one seemed to have much of an appetite. Nicole lost hers as soon as her eyes fell upon Rhyse Taylor and it hadn't come back. She took a few bites of her burger, then glanced at her watch. It was close to one o'clock in the afternoon. She needed to check on her mother.

"Excuse me," she said, getting up from the table. "I have to use the restroom."

"Danielle, go with her," the colonel grumbled, a mouthful of food balled against the side of one cheek. "We can't take any risks. They may be watching, waiting for their chance to grab her again."

"No, I'll be okay. Really," she added firmly when she saw Danielle start to rise.

It took a moment for Nicole's eyes to adjust from the restaurant's dim mood lighting to the brightness of the main concourse. Once they did, she spied a shadowed nook harboring a row of seats with Internet portals. She glanced back to ensure no one had followed her, then pulled the disposable cell from her bag and dialed her mother's number before she'd even disappeared behind a concealing pillar.

"She's not there."

Nicole didn't need to lift her eyes from the phone to know

who was standing behind her. Every nerve ending in her body was tingling with electricity. The muscles that ran down the backs of her legs felt weak and her heart was racing. There was only one person on earth who could make her body react this way.

Kira.

CHAPTER TWENTY-ONE

Nicole turned. High heels and sleek straight-leg sharkskin striped pants with a matching jacket, blond hair pinned into an elegant chignon at the back of her head, and a rolling carry-on suitcase sitting at the heels of her pointed pumps—Kira looked every inch the professional career woman strolling through the airport on business travel. If she'd expected to blend in with the masses, she'd made a grave miscalculation. The simple line of her slacks accentuated the perfect shape of the faultless body within them, and the prim hairstyle pulled back from her face only accentuated the perfect bone structure and the beautiful eyes.

Their eyes met. With a shiver of vivid recollection, every detail of their last encounter filled Nicole's head, making rational thought impossible. She remembered the weight and feel of Kira's naked breasts brushing up against her own; the taste of her mouth; the gentle, seductive caress of Kira's fingers gliding along her inner thighs before skillfully dipping between her legs.

White-hot liquid heat seemed to flow from some region in Nicole's lower stomach to spread like wildfire across her loins. She fought for control but both her mind and body were refusing to cooperate. Part of her yearned to reach out and pull Kira into her arms. She fought the desire, the need, and pushed it to the back of her mind by reminding herself that this woman had placed her mother in danger.

"Where's my mother? Where have you taken her?"

"Calm down, your mother is safe, but if you don't do as I say, things may not end up well."

"If you lay one finger on her, I'll—"

"Not here. Put the phone away and go to the ladies' room. It's just beyond the American Airlines ticket counter, on the left."

"Where's my mother?" She crossed her arms, still holding the phone.

"Still as stubborn as ever." Kira rolled her blue eyes. "Go to the ladies' room, Nicole," she went on in a harsh whisper, glancing at the lone traveler seated at the end of the tables trying to connect to the Internet. "Danielle is bound to come looking for you. If she finds us here together, this entire operation will be blown!"

"You're sticking with that same bullshit story you've been feeding me for the past week?"

Kira raised an eyebrow. "You do want to see your mother again, don't you, Nicole? Then go to the ladies' room!" Kira was clearly growing more agitated with each passing second. "Now!"

With no other choice, Nicole walked to the ladies' room but discovered it was blocked off by two orange safety cones and a sign that read *Closed for Cleaning*. An airport janitor stood outside the door, a bucket of dirty water on wheels at his side and a wet mop in his hands. Nicole felt herself starting to panic. Maybe Kira had meant another ladies' room?

"The ladies' room is open…for you." The janitor's baritone voice was deep and familiar. It took a moment for her to realize it was Bogie dressed in gray coveralls. He inclined his bald head in greeting, then pushed the door slightly ajar so she could go inside.

The restroom appeared vacant, but she checked each stall just to be certain Stella wasn't hiding in preparation for another kidnapping attempt. At the last stall, her heart finally slowed to an almost normal beat and the fog encircling her brain gradually cleared. She tapped her foot angrily. Had she fallen for another one of Kira's tricks? She'd just voluntarily isolated herself in a restroom with no chance of escape, not with Bogie guarding the door.

"When are you doing to learn to trust me, Nicole?"

She whirled around.

Kira was washing her hands at one of the sinks and watching her by way of the reflection in the commercial-sized mirror.

"Where's my mother?" Nicole covered the short distance between them in three long strides. "What have you done to her?"

"Saved her," Kira stated in her maddeningly nonchalant manner as she pulled a paper towel from the stainless steel dispenser bolted to the wall and casually dried her hands. "I warned you Danielle was up to no good, but you just wouldn't listen."

"You haven't answered me. Where's my mother?"

"Right about now," Kira checked the diamond-encrusted silver watch encircling her slender wrist, then tossed the used paper towel into the garbage, "she's probably having lunch with the distinguished senator from Virginia and his wife. I said she was safe, Nicole." There was a curious longing in Kira's blue eyes as she turned to face her. "Why do you continue to doubt everything I tell you?"

"You're kidding, right? Should I start from the moment we met? Everything about you has been a lie."

"That's not entirely true. Okay, yes, we fabricated the attack on the bus in Muranga and, yes, lied about the threat to the village you were assigned to teach. Simple psychological tactics I initially employed to gain your trust and cooperation. You were alone in a strange country and I needed to take advantage of the situation. When people are frightened or in shock, it's easier to obtain the truth. At that point, I didn't know how you were involved in all of this. But," her tone grew softer, "I've been honest with you ever since."

"Honest? As in telling me my mother is safe? If she is, why not let me talk to her?"

Kira pulled a tiny cell phone from her pocket and pressed a button.

"Nicole wants to speak with her mother," she said. "You don't believe me? Here. Talk to her yourself."

Nicole grabbed the phone. "*Mom? Mom*, are you *there*? Are you okay?"

"Hello, dear, of course I'm okay. In fact, I'm marvelous," Nicole heard her mother declare in the high-pitched, melodious voice she only used when she was trying to impress someone or had imbibed one too many cocktails. The last time Nicole could remember her mother adopting the tone was when they'd run into the wife of one of the executives from her father's petroleum company at the mall. The affectation in her dialect was usually accompanied by a sudden change in posture and bearing, as if her body had suddenly become possessed by the spirit of a pampered Southerner.

"I just cannot tell you what a delightful time I've had today, and it's all thanks to you. First, the personal tour of the White House and now this elaborate luncheon. You should see the table setting! I wish you were here, Nicole, there's a handsome young gentleman, the senator's nephew, and he is so polite and courteous. Excellent husband material," she revealed in a hushed overtone. "By the way, did you know your car was towed? Someone left a message yesterday from an impound lot. Oh—I have to go, they're serving the first course and I don't want them to think me rude. Good-bye!"

Nicole was thunderstruck. She leaned her weight against one of the sinks and lowered her head into her hands. "What's going on? How is it my mother is having lunch with a senator?"

"There's not enough time to explain." Kira plucked the phone from Nicole's limp fingers. "Suffice it say that your mother was going to be used in a scheme to extort your father's stocks from you. Yes, I've known about the stocks for some time now," she said when she saw the look of surprise on Nicole's face. "But we were hoping you'd found something much more valuable to us inside that safe deposit box. Anyway, we had to get your mother before they did. Although I don't believe they would have physically hurt her, you and I both know the mental stress of being taken from her home by armed men in the middle of the night might have sent your mother over the edge for once and for all."

"Who would dare do such a horrible thing? And why?"

"The stocks are worth a bundle. The two men tasked with abducting your mother are already in custody, but they're little more than hired hands. As far as who would dare do such a thing? It's only the two sitting at the restaurant awaiting your return that need be of any concern to us at this moment."

"Danielle?" Nicole was incredulous. "Are you sure?"

Danielle had appeared so convincing. But then again, so did Kira. In fact, Nicole had yet to see something absolute that would confirm that she was on the law's side as she continually proclaimed to be. No badge, no government-issued windbreaker with the letters of her agency emblazoned upon its back with bright gold letters, and certainly no supportive sidekicks from the local police milling about in the background.

But somehow she'd arranged the luncheon for her mother.

Kira glanced down at her watch. "We've no more time for discussion. Pull up your shirt."

Nicole's jaw dropped.

Kira laughed at the look on her face. "As much as I'd like to see you naked again, this isn't the time or the place. I need to fasten a piece of surveillance equipment to you."

Kira lifted her suitcase, placed it on the countertop, and unzipped it. She withdrew a tiny device no bigger than a jeans button and as flat as a credit card from inside. Five inches of black wire dangled from it.

"This is an audio and video recorder. We'll be able to monitor and record everything they say to you. Bogie will always be within transmitting distance, but I warn you now, Nicole, this might become dangerous. I'll do my best to make sure nothing happens to you, but you need to know what you're getting yourself into if you agree to wear this."

"Of course," Nicole replied, her head still spinning. "What about my father? Rhyse Taylor said he'd been working undercover. If that's true, it means he wasn't a criminal, right?"

"I'll fill you in on all of that later, when we have more time. Right now, we have to hurry," she said, turning back to the gear inside her suitcase. "You've already been gone five minutes. If we delay much longer, they'll grow suspicious. And we don't want that, Nicole, believe me."

Nicole watched as Kira methodically took a pair of scissors to a roll of flesh-colored tape. She then grabbed a hand-sized tool that looked like a hole-puncher to cut a tiny segment of fabric from her shirt just under the crew-neck collar.

"Can you move your necklace?"

Nicole pulled the silver chain so that its length hung across her left shoulder.

"It cuts clean, no tearing or fraying of the fabric, so that the hole is invisible to the eye," Kira explained, her hands softly brushing against the skin of Nicole's sternum while adjusting the camera lens to align with the hole, then taping it to the shirt.

"The camera is flimsy but it does the trick. The microphone is more important anyway, but sometimes noises get confusing, so it's better if we can watch what is going on as well."

They were standing close to one another, almost as close as they'd been as lovers, but now Kira was all business.

It disappointed Nicole just a little bit that Kira seemed so unaffected by their proximity.

"It's Danielle's T-shirt anyway, so cut away."

This comment garnered a raised brow from Kira.

"I asked her to bring me a clean shirt," Nicole explained. Standing so close to Kira was pushing Nicole's willpower to the breaking point. Kira seemed impervious, though, and not the least bit jealous about how she came to be wearing Danielle's shirt.

"So how'd you manage to escape from the handcuffs?" she asked, somehow managing to keep her voice steady. How could someone have such an incredible effect on her? In the middle of an airport restroom, no less?

Kira lifted her eyes from her task, a faint glint of humor on her face. "Lucky for you, I had an extra key. Otherwise, who knows what might have happened to you today? I'm sure you will be pleased to know it still caused me a lot of discomfort. Shevchenko is the one who had that key."

Nicole pictured the scene: the Ice Princess nude and vulnerable, most likely seething; Stella, amused but respectfully deferential as she released Kira.

"Here." Kira pulled a slim, oblong piece of black plastic that looked like a ballpoint pen from the suitcase when she was finished. "It's a stun gun. Press the button at the top and the bottom will emit 100,000 volts of electricity. It has to make contact with skin to work."

"Why would I need that?" Nicole looked at it distastefully.

"Chances are you won't. We'll be watching and listening the entire time via the camera and mic, but sometimes things don't go as planned."

Nicole sighed, placing the pen in the pocket of her linen pants. She felt suddenly like the weight of the world was on her shoulders. "I don't know if I can do this."

"Relax." Kira patted her on the back platonically—too platonically for Nicole. She wanted something more than that. "You're doing a great job. Far better than any of us would have ever believed for someone just off the street and untrained. You're a natural, Nicole. Now listen carefully. Danielle will take you to the bank to get the stocks. When you return—"

"How do you know this? And why would I go with her? And why do I need a stun gun?"

"They want the stocks more than anything. They'll come up with some reason and Danielle *will* take you to the bank. Their plan is that when you return with the stocks in hand, the two guys that we have in custody now would run her car off the road. They would jump out of the car flashing weapons and demand the stocks in exchange for your mother, whom they would have tied up in their backseat." Her blue eyes kept darting to the tiny hole above the shirt's Old Navy graphics, studying the placement of the lens to ensure it wasn't noticeable. "All the while, Danielle acts the innocent. But when the plan goes awry, she might react violently, so I'd feel better if you had something on you to defend yourself with."

"How do you know all this?" Nicole shook her head, trying to get it all straight in her head.

"Did I mention I work for the United States government?" Kira smiled.

"I believe I heard you mention that once or twice." Nicole managed a wan smile, adding in her head, *but you've never offered any proof.* "Danielle told me a woman claiming to belong to the government forced her hand, blackmailed her," she added, somewhat reluctantly. There was still a tiny nugget of uncertainty about Kira's role in all of this lingering in the back of her brain. *Please convince me.*

Kira leaned closer, gently cradling Nicole's chin in her hand. "Answers will have to wait, Nicole. Our time now is at an end. Can you trust me," she asked in an unbearably tender voice, "just this once?"

Nicole felt desire mixed with love race through every vein in her body. She felt weak, unable to even nod in acquiescence.

"I'll try," she whispered.

CHAPTER TWENTY-TWO

Nicole walked through the airport on shaky legs, her palms sweaty. She tried to concentrate, but her nerves were playing havoc with her train of thought. She imagined she could hear the *Mission Impossible* theme music playing as she made her way through the concourse.

"Focus!" she berated herself as she almost tumbled over a wheeled golf bag carrier an Asian teenager was towing behind him as he hurried toward one of the electronic check-in kiosks scattered throughout the terminal. The cold feel of the plastic taped to her chest felt alien. It chafed against her skin as she moved. She glanced down, looking for the hole. Was it visible? How sensitive was it? Could Bogie hear her heart pounding?

"Where've you been? We were getting worried!"

Nicole lifted her head only to find that she'd somehow made her way back to the restaurant on autopilot. Both Danielle and her father were both staring at her. The father's expression was unreadable but she recognized the look on Danielle's face. Nicole had seen it before—when she told Danielle she was moving out; concern and worry were etched in the lines wrinkling her brow, but the hurt in the depths of those green eyes back then was missing now.

Nicole quickly relayed a tale about the restroom being closed and her inability to find another without a lengthy line.

She watched their reactions, searching both of their faces for a flicker of—what? Disbelief? Doubt?

Perhaps criminal justice or psychology course or two might have helped prepare her for this crazy situation that still seemed unreal.

"Dad and I have been coming up with a plan," Danielle announced excitedly as Nicole slid back into their booth. "No doubt, they know where the bonds are hidden. It's just a matter of time before they try to get them before you do, so we have to move first. Beat them to the punch, so to speak."

"They?" Nicole turned and fixed her eyes on Danielle's father. "Do you have any idea who these people are?"

"They're high up, that's for sure," Rhyse murmured vaguely.

"So why remove the stocks from the bank at all?" she persisted, more than a little unnerved at how prophetic Kira's words had been. *That has to count for something*, she thought. "Isn't that the safest place in the world to keep them right now?"

Father and daughter quickly exchanged a glance, and Nicole could have bitten off her tongue. She'd just confirmed the stocks were indeed at the bank.

"Remember who we're dealing with. These people are professionals of a caliber equivalent to the CIA," Rhyse said. "They've probably already obtained a warrant or some other sham document to get inside the bank. Everyday working stiffs are easily conned. If someone looks the part and acts with confidence and authority, no one questions them. Combine that façade with bogus credentials, or maybe even real ones, and they're in."

No doubt spoken from experience, Nicole thought. The waitress came and placed the bill in the center of the table. A shiver ran down her spine as she watched the colonel's long, thick fingers grab the check. She swallowed hard, fighting her revulsion.

"While you two go to the bank, I'm going to see an old

friend at the Department of Justice who might be able to help us," the colonel said, pulling several ten-dollar bills from his wallet and laying them down next to his empty plate. "Call me when you have the stocks," he ordered, looking at Danielle. "We'll coordinate a meeting place. Stay safe, both of you, and if you see anyone suspicious, call the police."

Call the police?

Was that guidance a criminal would advise? Was he just saying the words for effect? Nicole was confused—but then took a deep breath. *Just be aware*, she reminded herself.

They parted ways at the taxi stand outside baggage claim. As the colonel climbed into a cab and disappeared from sight, Nicole mused on the possibility that Rhyse Taylor could be telling the truth about everything. But if he were, then Kira was a liar. And she didn't want to even consider that as a possibility.

"Where to?" Danielle asked as they exited the airport. Nicole plugged the bank's address into the Garmin and Danielle let the computerized man's voice dictate when and where to turn. They didn't say a word to one another, and the atmosphere in the car grew increasingly strained with each passing mile. Nicole didn't have it in her to make polite conversation, at least not with a microphone strapped to her chest transmitting every remark she made, so she sat rigidly in her seat, loosely gripping the stun-pen her pocket.

"Do you think we might be friends when all this is over?"

Nicole looked over at Danielle. She was doing a good a job of acting the innocent. Far too good—was she that good an actress?

"Are you serious?" she asked, conscious of the wire taped to her chest. "You pretended to be my friend. Everything was a lie between us."

"Not everything," Danielle said quickly. Nicole knew she was referring to their brief kiss, and she felt a blush steal over her cheeks. "What if it was your mother, Nick? Wouldn't you have done the same if you were in my shoes?"

Nicole remembered what Kira had told her back in the restroom. If it was indeed true, right now Danielle believed her mother to be bound and gagged, sitting in the back of a car with two strange men. Something just didn't fit, and she couldn't figure it out. She longed to reach over, grab Danielle by the shoulder, and demand she come clean about everything—but the impulse remained nothing more than a fanciful whim. They were already at the bank.

"I'll wait here and keep a look-out," Danielle said, her voice unsteady as she parallel parked the Escape in an empty spot between two compacts. "Be careful. They might have been following us."

Nicole sighed heavily as she extricated herself from the air-conditioned interior of the SUV. Hopefully, Danielle was right. She cast an uneasy glance at the traffic zooming by. Where was Bogie?

The sidewalk was busy. A group of three young girls hurried past her, gripping grease-splattered paper bags from a fast-food restaurant, their faces glued to their phones. She looked around, trying not to appear too conspicuous. Were any of the pedestrians plants from the government, ready to pull a gun from some hidden holster at the slightest sign of threat?

Inside the bank, it was quiet and cool. A man in a suit and tie tried to make eye contact with her, but she made a beeline straight toward the garishly made-up woman who'd helped her yesterday. Once inside the vault and the safety-deposit box was open, Nicole quickly scooped up all the stock certificates and shoved them into her bag. She glanced at the bundles of cash and decided to leave them behind—no one had said anything about the cash, after all. Before returning the box to its slot, she looked over her shoulder to make sure no one was watching. Placing an index finger over the hole in her shirt where the camera lens was filming her every move, she folded the envelope with the incomprehensible gibberish printed on one side of paper and the names written on the other and stuffed it inside the cup of her bra.

On her way out, she grabbed the pen-shaped stun gun and tightly clutched it inside the folds of her fist.

"You have them? They were still there?" Danielle asked when Nicole returned to the car. The stun gun in Nicole's hand became hot and slippery as she reflexively clenched and unclenched her fingers around its slick metal. Sitting on the center console of the car was a leather pocketbook the color of warm paprika. It was wide open, as if recently rummaged through.

"Are you really going to do this?" Nicole questioned in a sad voice. She studied Danielle's face, paying close attention to her demeanor.

"Well, are you?" she repeated, trying to discern some little change in Danielle's expression that would confirm or deny her guilt. But there was no telltale bead of perspiration dripping from her hairline, no nervous shifting of the eyes.

"What are you talking about?" Danielle put the Escape in reverse, turning the wheel sharply to maneuver the front of the vehicle away from the curb. "Were the stocks still there or not?"

"I have them."

Their eyes met. In the depths of the hazel eyes looking back at her, Nicole saw nothing but honesty. And there was still that smidgeon of suspicion wedged somewhere in the back of her subconscious concerning Kira. How else could she explain the envelope stuffed inside her bra, the sharp corners of the stiff paper irritating the tender swell of her breast?

"Danielle, there's still time to get out of this. I'm not sure how your father is involved, but you don't have to take the fall with or for him. I'm positive they'll be lenient if you confess and help them with their investigation."

"Investigation?"

Nicole squirmed uncomfortably but said nothing. Had she just blown everything?

"Tell me what on earth you're talking about, Nicole." Danielle put the vehicle back in park. Her hands went to her lap and Nicole's eyes followed. Ensconced almost imperceptibly in the crevice between her two exposed thighs was what appeared to be the butt of a gun, its dull faux-wood grain a sharp contrast in texture to the smoothness of Danielle's tanned flesh. Nicole cast a nervous glance out the windshield. Where was the cavalry? Where was the SWAT team shouting for surrender from a megaphone? She fumbled with her shirt. Maybe when she'd stuffed the envelope inside her bra, a wire had come undone. She had to do something and quickly.

"Gun!" she shouted into the collar of her borrowed T-shirt.

Danielle's eyes were round with astonishment and incomprehension. The pen was still in Nicole's hand, but before she'd even contemplated exactly what she was going to do with it, a kaleidoscope of red and blue lights were flashing all about them. Someone flung the car door open, jerked her into the street and into the arms of a uniformed police officer. After regaining her balance, she turned back. A pair of ebony arms pulled Danielle roughly from the car. An object fell from her grip. Nicole watched it crash to the asphalt with disbelieving eyes. Not a gun, but a hairbrush.

CHAPTER TWENTY-THREE

People were shouting. Sirens were now wailing. Nicole felt as if she'd just stepped off a roller coaster. The presence of the police officer standing somewhere to her left was reassuring but it didn't stop the ground beneath her from shifting just a tad unevenly or the world all around her from beginning to spin wildly. A white Lexus emerged amidst the chaos and pulled up directly in front of her, its tires screeching as they came to a fast stop. The driver's side window was rolled down.

"I couldn't ride in on a white horse, but I found a white car." It was Stella. Nicole fought an irrational wave of disappointment that it wasn't Kira.

"Come, kiddo, get in," Stella fervently urged, reaching over in her seat and pushing the passenger door ajar with her right arm. "Everything's okay now."

She wanted to move but couldn't. Her legs had gone wooden. Okay, so it had been a hairbrush and not a gun, but her body needed more time to adjust to that reality. For a brief, blood-curdling moment, she'd been envisioning the muzzle of a gun pressed against her forehead.

Suddenly warm, strong hands gripped her shoulders from behind, steering her around the hood of the car, then positioning her suddenly limp body into the seat next to Stella. Delicately feminine fingers pulled the seat belt across her lap and shoulder, tugging at the harness to ensure it was secure before fastening it. It took a moment for Nicole to realize that it wasn't the police officer tending to her well-being. The shapely, manicured fingers belonged to the same determined hands that had pulled her from the Escape.

"Get her away from this madness," a woman's commanding voice dictated in a clipped tone. "I'll find you when I'm done here."

It was Kira. Nicole felt something tight inside her release. Stella was right. Everything was going to be okay.

"It was a hairbrush, not a gun," she managed to mutter through lips that felt a bit rubbery. Her breathing was growing slow and shallow. She had to fight to catch her breath.

"Nicole, you're going pale. Listen to me. Inhale. Deeply. Here, let's remove the camera and mic." With a quick, deliberate efficiency, Kira reached a hand down the front of her T-shirt and gently pulled the tapes and wire from her skin. The paper was still tucked into Nicole's bra. "Look at me, let me see your pupils." She searched Nicole's eyes. "Good. Breathe. Deeper this time, slowly." Kira took Nicole's wrist between two fingers while staring down at her watch. She was still in the same sexy business outfit she'd been wearing at the airport, although the carefully coiffed chignon at the nape of her neck had come a bit undone.

"For a moment I thought you might be going into shock, but your vital signs are normal."

"Your car. You found it," she said almost accusingly.

"Not *my* car, my uncle's. Your new friend at the truck stop was clocked doing almost ninety in it early this morning. Don't worry, no charges were pressed against her, but the local sheriff's office was very pleased because her *cooperation*," she stressed sardonically, "led to several other arrests involving the operation of an illegal chop shop and moonshine still. Now promise me, if you feel faint, you'll tell Shevchenko. I'd ride with you, Nicole, but I have to finish up here."

Bogie's deep, baritone voice echoed over the roof and into the interior of the car, a trace of disappointment in the pitch of his words. "Nothing else in the bag but the stocks."

"Go now, Shevchenko, but watch her color closely," Kira ordered before the car door was slammed shut and they sped away.

Nicole turned in her seat to cast a glance backward, looking for Kira's magnificent form amidst the growing swarm of humanity converging upon the frenetic scene, but she couldn't find it and soon all of it vanished as they turned onto Sixth Street. The lulling sounds of soft piano music playing on the car's stereo and the comforting coolness of the air conditioner gradually soothed her tattered nerve endings. A few blocks away, Stella looked over at her, a frown marring her dark brow. "You okay, kid?"

"Better now. Thanks, Stella. I don't know what happened. I almost lost it back there."

"Perfectly understandable. You've been under great strain."

Nicole reclined the seat a notch, closed her eyes, and did as Kira had advised, inhaling deep, calming breaths. Her body felt as if it had been zapped with a million volts of electricity. Her arms and legs were numb, her hands shaky as she grasped her head between them and squeezed, hoping the pressure would bring some relief. The headache that had been threatening all morning was coming back, knocking on the back of her head for entry. "This has got to be the craziest thing that has ever happened to anyone," she muttered tremulously. "I still think I might be hallucinating. Maybe I'm in a hospital in Kenya, delirious with that fever, and this is all a by-product of my imagination."

"I hope not," Stella said. "That means I won't be getting paid this week."

Nicole gave a weak smile. Her eyes were still closed and she replayed the entire scene back at the bank with Danielle and the hairbrush.

"Danielle is innocent," she said, lifting her head and opening her eyes. Stella turned sharply and Nicole repeated herself. "She's not involved. I mean, yeah, she is, but she was just trying to protect her father. She didn't know anything about my mother being kidnapped and used as ransom for the stocks."

"How can you be so sure?" Stella asked, uncertainty in her tone.

"I just do." The air conditioner was going full blast and now she was getting cold. Tiny goose bumps ran the length of her arms and she rubbed them vigorously for warmth. Seeing this, Stella turned a control on the dashboard and the temperature in the car immediately began to warm.

"What about Rhyse Taylor? Did you guys get him?"

"Who do you think was driving his taxi?" Stella volleyed back, her accent strong as a smile tugged the corners of her full lips.

"So where was he going? He told us he was on his way to Department of Justice."

"He'll end up there, one way or another." She smirked. "That is a very bad man." They were at a stoplight and Stella directed another glance her way. This one was inquisitive but not without a trace of humor. "You look tired. Maybe because you didn't get enough sleep last night?" Her voice was teasing. Nicole was certain her face was no longer pale, but a bright shade of red.

"I'd rather not talk about that," she admitted feebly, turning away from the Ukrainian's probing stare. The light changed and Nicole was grateful Stella's attention was pulled back to the traffic. "I'm glad to hear you're getting a paycheck for all this, Stella. But I'm just curious—who actually pays you?"

They were crossing over the Potomac, heading toward Arlington, the Pentagon visible in the distance.

"Your Uncle Sam, kiddo."

"And just how is it that someone from the Ukraine ends up working for the United States?"

"It's not a very exciting story, Nicole. When Chernobyl exploded, I was only eighteen. My brother and mother worked there." Hearing Nicole's horrified gasp she amended quickly, "Oh no, they weren't hurt, but I knew I didn't want to follow in their footsteps, stuck at that plant forever. Not a lot of people realize this, but the plant is still open. The reactors are of course not operating but my family still works there, maintaining the remains. They must work in shifts to minimize their exposure to radiation." She shrugged her shoulders, pushing a strand of long, black hair from her face. "That's where everyone in the town I grew up in went to work. There isn't much else. After the accident, I knew I had to go to school, study computers, learn DOS. It was my ticket out. And I get along much better with a keyboard than humans." She snorted, sharing a private joke with herself. "While in school, a professor from the great country of America came to teach one of our classes. He liked the programs I created, said they were complex but simple, whatever that meant. Next thing I know, he gets me a visa to do work here in DC. Some, how do you say, I forget all the American colloquialisms—bigwigs—they asked me to help with some of the Russian coding. They are very good at writing viruses. And they're great hackers too, always trying to break into everyone's systems and cause mayhem."

Nicole vaguely remembered Kira telling her that all the old mainframes in the Kenyan bunker had originally been programmed in Russian to disguise their country of origin. That would explain why they'd needed someone with Stella's expertise.

"I kept studying, staying very busy working and finally, I received security clearance. Eventually, I became an American citizen. And now, here I am. No Chernobyl, but sometimes, I think," she smirked again, "I would be safer back in a nuclear power plant."

Nicole smiled. After a long, quiet moment she gathered her courage. "There's no right way to ask this, so I'm just going to come right out with it. Have you and Kira," she hesitated and cringed in advance of the words, but her need to know outweighed her reluctance, "been romantic?"

A sharp, hysterical burst of laughter erupted from Stella. The Lexus swerved but was quickly reined back in.

"I'm sorry, little one. I didn't mean to laugh, but what you said was too funny. I don't want to say anything that might make you mad at me because I know you have feelings for Kira." Stella didn't look her way, but if she had, she would have only seen the top of Nicole's head because she suddenly found her seat belt fascinating. "But Kira and I, well, we are like a cat and dog that live in the same house. We respect each other's territory, but you cannot keep us in the same room together for very long. So no, Nicole, you don't have to worry. Kira has eyes only for you. But we'll talk more later, kid. We're here."

Nicole looked out the car window, disappointed to see a uniformed doorman rushing to open Stella's door, a jacketed valet at his heels. She'd wanted Stella to keep talking.

They were at the Ritz-Carlton, one of the most opulent hotels in the capital. Several National Guardsmen hovered about the polished entryway, their heavy camouflage dress and wool berets looking dreadfully uncomfortable in the heat of the late afternoon. As she and Stella entered the lobby, half a dozen tall, clean-cut men clad in dark, conservative suits wearing earpieces scrutinized her every move. The Secret Service?

"For some reason, I thought we were going to the Pentagon," Nicole whispered, feeling considerably underdressed in the Old Navy T-shirt and smudged linen pants she'd been wearing for two days in a row. "Isn't that where the Department of Defense is based?"

"We can't meet on government grounds since this mission is not only still active, but one that is—let me think of the words," she held up both hands and made quotation signs with her fingers, "hush hush. And the people Kira must meet with have a dinner here tonight."

They took the elevator to the eighteenth floor, emerging onto a carpeted hallway decorated in elegant tones of deep yellow and dark blue. Stella stopped at the second room on the left, inserting several different hotel key cards she'd pulled from her back pocket into the lock until finally a light within the door's mechanism turned green.

"Here, this is your key."

The hotel room was actually a two-room suite with a sitting area separate from the bedroom. It was so different than the motel room Nicole had slept a few hours in last night that it might have been on another planet. She rushed to the window, stared in amazement at the panoramic view of the skyline for all of ten seconds before feeling the stress and fatigue of the past twenty-four hours creep into her bones. She collapsed into a handsome, high-back armchair positioned directly across from a crisp blue and white striped sofa.

"You need a drink, little one. A real one. It will calm your nerves."

"You know, Stella, I have to confess. Up until the moment the police showed up at the bank, I wasn't sure that you, Kira, and Bogie weren't the real criminals."

"The three of us are an odd cast of characters," Stella said agreeably.

Nicole peered over her shoulder. Stella was at the mini-bar, pulling out a bottle of Perrier and a tiny bottle of clear liquid with a colorful label. "Stoli." She held it up for Nicole's inspection. "We Slavs know our vodka."

Nicole nodded, then turned back to stare out the window. She could hear a cap being unscrewed and bubbly liquid poured into a glass. She made to get up but Stella was already at her side. The mineral water with the vodka tasted like cold medicine, but it was cold and refreshing. She was thirsty and drank more.

"I must be so tired I'm seeing things. Is that my duffel bag on the bed?"

"Your clothes are in the bag. Drink. I'll come back for you in a few hours."

A wave of déjà vu came over Nicole, so strong she almost dropped the glass she was gripping onto the beige Berber carpeting. Her trip to Africa was repeating itself all over again: her luggage mysteriously appearing from out of nowhere and the same woman with a heavy accent insisting she stay hydrated.

"Wait, Stella, what happens next?" she asked, seeing that the Ukrainian was heading toward the door.

"We'll all meet up later. Now take a nap. At least try, okay? You've had a very long day."

"Will you tell me one thing before you leave?"

Her hand on the door handle, Stella turned, the slight inclination of her dark head indicating she would grant Nicole's request.

"When I was leaving Kenya, you wrote on my airplane ticket, *remember the tin man.* What did you mean?"

A gleam appeared in Stella's dark eyes. "If you remember the tale, the tin man searched the entire city of Oz for a heart, but one was inside him the whole time." She shot Nicole a penetrating look. "Think about it, kid."

"You mean you knew about my necklace?" She could hear a faint thread of hysteria in her own voice. Stella was referring to the engraving, wasn't she?

"While you were sick in Kenya, we saw the inscription on your necklace. Your father seemed to enjoy puzzles."

"Then why didn't you get the key to the safe deposit box yourselves? Why did you wait for me to figure it out?"

"We had no idea what that inscription meant. We had to be patient. We knew you would solve the riddle."

Well, that only leaves 410 questions that still need answering, Nicole thought, once she was alone.

She laid her head back against the chair, her fingers fiddling with the necklace, tracing the letters engraved into the silver. The hint of a grin touched her lips. It was almost amusing. Almost. She'd been wearing a key to a lost treasure around her neck for the past twelve years, taking it off only to shower or swim, never once thinking there could be a double meaning in the words inscribed into the metal. She recalled all the years that followed the day her father had given her the necklace, the hard ones; the times when she'd watch her mother deliberate thoughtfully about which meat to buy. Usually the choice was limited to ground beef or chicken cutlet. The widowed woman's decision always came down to which of the two proteins she could stretch into not one but two or three meals that her finicky daughters would hopefully eat with as much gusto the third night as the first. A teacher's salary paid the bills, but barely. True, no one in their house had ever gone hungry, nor had the electricity ever been threatened to be turned off, but two girls were a bit expensive to care for in the new millennium, especially when one of those demanding little brats was Liz and the area of Maryland they lived in was one of the more affluent. Being popular in their school required the right clothes, and the right clothes did not come cheap.

So had her father hidden away the stocks and cash simply to conceal his secret life from his family? If so, why hadn't he instructed Gavin Thomas to disclose the contents of the safe deposit box upon his death? Why all the mystery and intrigue? Perhaps, like Kira said, her father didn't think he would die. Perhaps no one does. *To some degree, we all feel we are immortal*, she mused, getting up and investigating the room. And her father most likely had anticipated the life insurance policy from the petroleum company would have been ample funds for his family to live on for years to come, never imagining his wife would listen to her financially imprudent brother's cockamamie advice to invest the bulk of the policy money in a dot-com company that went belly up ten months after it started.

The mini-bar called out to her, disrupting her thoughts. The only thing she'd eaten all day was a few bites of the cheeseburger and the piece of stale cake early that morning. With a fascinated trepidation she eyed the bountiful assortment of jarred nuts, cookies, and candy bars organized so appealingly on the shelves. The least expensive item most likely cost eight bucks. It didn't matter, she told herself. She deserved a treat.

After extracting a king-sized Snickers, a heavy glass

container of cashews some marketing major had labeled "fancy," and a can of Diet Coke from the tiny refrigerator, she crawled into the king-sized feather bed, promising herself that she would consume an extra serving of vegetables at dinner to make up for her unhealthy diet of late. She plopped a few nuts into her mouth, but her hunger wasn't such a priority as sleep suddenly was. Her eyelids were growing as heavy as cinder blocks, and she was having a very difficult time keeping them open.

CHAPTER TWENTY-FOUR

N icole woke, trying hard to make sense of the luxurious bed linens and button-tufted leather headboard. Since she'd slept in so many different places over the past two weeks, it took a moment for her memory to catch up with her life. Her head throbbed and a thick coating covered the inside of her mouth. She smacked her lips and swallowed, a piece of cashew making its presence known in the back of her throat. She'd fallen asleep, but for how long?

Flinging the lush bedspread aside, she reached for the unfinished can of Diet Coke on the nightstand, hoping to remove the awful residue from her tongue. She was terribly thirsty. The clock next to the can read 6:15. Surprisingly, the soda had already gone flat. In three hours? Fuzz like the cork of cotton in an aspirin bottle clogged her thinking.

What was wrong with her?

She felt—*weird.*

Sitting on the edge of the bed, she noticed her duffel bag had been moved to a luggage rack near the bathroom. Perched atop the blue nylon weave was her canvas handbag. The last time she'd seen the camel-colored sack, it had been nestled between her two sandaled feet on the floor mat in Danielle's Escape.

Someone had been in her room.

Ambling lethargically over to her handbag, she peeled open the flap. The stocks weren't there.

Her heart did a suspicious little flip inside her chest. She walked into the adjacent parlor, looking for signs of another's presence, but everything appeared exactly the same as it had a few hours ago.

Blood was beginning to pulse through the fogged circuits in her head. She hurried back to her bag, pulling out her cell phone. No need to hide from Bogie any longer. When at last it was able to connect with a signal, a tiny digital envelope appeared on the screen indicating she had a voicemail. She called and listened to the message.

"Nicole? Nicole, it's Mom. Where are you? Are you there?"

As if Nicole could hear her mother and respond.

"Okay, well, we're down here in the lobby. We'll wait for you a bit longer before we go to the dinner."

Nicole listened to the message again, this time not rushing past the date and time stamp. The voicemail had been left at 7:37 p.m.!

Last night!

Panic started to flood through her. Running to the window, she pulled apart the gossamer curtains. Could the pale gray sky really be the early haze of morning instead of twilight?

She hit the power button on the television remote and quickly scrolled through the channels, her mouth agape. The local DC news teams were all giving identical updates on Friday morning's weather and traffic before the networks took over at seven. She glanced once again at the digital numbers of the clock, the reality finally breaking through the nimbus of confusion muddying her head.

It's morning.

She'd slept for over twelve hours! Her eyes moved to her bag, still sitting where someone else had placed it.

Stella had drugged her.

The stocks were missing from her bag.

Danielle hadn't been holding a gun.

"Shit!" she cursed out loud.

The puzzle pieces started to fit. Her mother's teaching license had been mysteriously revoked. Stella was an expert computer hacker. It was all starting to make sense—too much sense. If Nicole called down to the front desk and asked to be connected to Kira Anthony's room, she was almost certain the hotel clerk's polite response would be, "I'm sorry, we don't have a guest here by that name."

But she didn't do it, couldn't yet. At this point, she wasn't ready to face that. And if it was true, it didn't matter—Kira would be long gone by now.

She stripped off her clothes on her way toward the bathroom, paying no heed to where they fell. She needed a hot shower more than anything. She felt dirty, and the heated water would her wake up and shake off whatever was left of the drug still clouding up her brain cells. Less than thirty minutes later, she was riding down in the elevator feeling decidedly better equipped to deal with whatever insanity this day would bring her way. She'd dressed in khaki capris, a cream-colored V-neck long sleeved T-shirt, and her sandals. Her casual attire suited her just fine—or so she thought until the elevator doors opened and she remembered she was not only at the Ritz-Carlton, but was five minutes from the Pentagon.

Despite the early hour, the lobby was already teeming with a loud, chatty crowd; all were clothed in either expensive business suits or in resplendently decorated military uniforms. But regardless of attire, all of them had *that* look of pompous self-importance that she'd grown accustomed to while going to school here. These were the movers and shakers: politicians, lobbyists, government officials, and their hangers-on.

"Is there a military conference here this morning?" she

asked the concierge politely, trying to keep her voice steady. But before the stout woman behind the desk could reply, a voice called out above the noisy din of human babble.

"Nicole, there you are! We were just about to go up to your room. We were beginning to get worried!"

Nicole spied her mother and sister strutting through the dignified mob. Her mother seemed to be perfectly at ease in the setting, dressed in an elegant blue skirt suit, her short brown hair shellacked into the shape of a helmet. Liz was dolled up to the nines as well in a gorgeous yellow dress. Her husband trudged along behind her, looking bored as usual.

Nicole had never been so glad to see her family as she was at that moment.

"You missed quite the dinner last night. Guess who sat just two tables away from us?" Her mother's heavily made-up face was alive with excitement. She didn't wait for Nicole to respond. "The secretary of state! Can you believe it? She's some smart cookie, I'll tell you that much. So well spoken and articulate," she gushed reverently. "It was a dinner given for the Women Officers Professional Association. After her speech, everyone gave her a standing ovation. Maybe someday Hillary will try running for president again. I bet she's still here at the hotel and you can introduce yourself. You never know, she might need an intern. That's how all these people get their swanky positions, hobnobbing with one another at places like this."

Nicole tried to take it all in, but she felt as if everything was happening in some other dimension and somehow she was stuck on the outside looking in. Her mother searched the lobby, as if Hillary Clinton would appear simply because she'd willed her to do so. Now was probably not the time to remind her mother she'd voted Republican in the past two elections.

Her mother's attention returned to Nicole. "Oh, my, Nicky, look at you. You're wasting away to nothing. And what on earth are you wearing?" Her wrinkled face grew dark with disapproval.

"Why didn't you put on the dress or the skirt I brought you? I was *afraid* you wouldn't look in the closet. All that ironing for naught," she bemoaned. "You know it's always better to be overdressed than underdressed. And why do you insist on lugging around that dirty backpack?"

"It's a shoulder bag, Mom. And it's not dirty, it's beige," she replied, looking back and forth from her mother to her sister. What were they doing here? *How* did they get here?

Where were the stocks?

"More like the color of mud," her mother replied through pursed lips.

"Get a load of the sexy blond heading our way," Liz whispered into her ear.

Nicole turned. She recognized the chiseled cheekbones and square jaw immediately. It was the helicopter pilot, Mike. He was wearing a suit and tie, his gold hair neatly combed to the side. The dark suit fit his frame perfectly, the white of his shirt matching his smile. What was *he* doing *here*?

But right behind walked a beautiful woman deeply engrossed in what appeared to be a very heated discussion with someone on the other end of a cell phone. Nicole felt the air leave her lungs in a single gasp.

Kira.

She hadn't run off.

But the momentary burst of joy inside her chest died almost as soon as it began. Kira *was* here, but with the pilot. Jealousy stabbed at her, like hot scissors held over a flame before being plunged into her heart.

And there was another feeling under the jealousy, ripping at the very fabric of her being, a pain unlike anything she'd ever experienced.

Their groups merged and all at once her mother was busy making conversation with Kira (who was no longer frowning into her phone) as if they were old acquaintances.

"Hello, Nicole," the pilot greeted her warmly. "Great to see you again."

Nicole couldn't find her voice. A surge of pugnacious adrenaline streamed down her arm and straight to her fist. She wanted to punch this guy, and here he was smiling genially at her, an engaging twinkle in his long-lashed eyes. If she couldn't punch him, she at least wanted to kick him. Hard.

She was faintly aware of her mother ogling their interaction, a hopeful anticipation oozing from her every pore. She could feel Liz studying her. And Kira too. She might as well have been on stage and charged them each admission.

"Did you know Mike's uncle is Senator Adams?" Her mother's penciled brows rose.

"Mike's a pilot but earns his living as an engineer," Kira said casually, moving to stand next to her. Nicole remained motionless, instantly aware of the heat she felt between them. "He runs his own aviation company. Although most of my brother's business is civilian and involves the manufacturing of copters and parts, occasionally we'll ask him to do some flying for us."

"Brother?" Nicole stiffened in shock.

Only now did she see the resemblance in their regal bone structure, the unusually light blue eyes, and their confident, poised posture. She sighed audibly. Mike and Kira were siblings. She said this inside her head and repeated it a few times so it could sink in.

And when it finally did, the dark emotions that had been strangling her ten seconds ago evaporated into thin air. It took her still another moment to digest the fact that the great Senator Adams was Kira's uncle. The man was a legend in Virginia, serving in the Senate for the last twenty years or so. He'd been a major force behind the movement to repeal the military's "Don't Ask, Don't Tell" policy.

"Yeah, but I think we can all agree Kira definitely didn't inherit my fabulous karaoke skills," Mike teased, grinning at his sister, who smiled back at him.

Everyone laughed, leaving Nicole feeling as if she'd walked into the theater twenty minutes late. Act one was already nearing the end.

Karaoke?

What had happened while she'd been in a drug-induced coma for twelve hours? Had everyone gotten drunk? She would've given her right arm to see Kira Anthony doing something as silly as singing up on a stage. *Definitely alcohol must have been involved,* she concluded. There was no way someone as tightly wound up as Kira Anthony would ever let loose that way while sober.

"As you all know," Kira said, her eyes coolly guarded when they met Nicole's, "I asked you to meet me down here this morning because we have some important business to discuss. If you'll come with me, there's a conference room reserved for our privacy. They'll have breakfast waiting for us as well."

They all followed Kira through the lavishly decorated hotel. Even now, with both her sister and mother walking next to her, Nicole could feel the sexual chemistry between them. It was like a living thing, tugging and pulling at her. How could something invisible be so intensely physical? Mindful of her sister's watchful gaze, Nicole attempted to steal a few inconspicuous glances.

Kira was wearing a simple vanilla-colored jacket with matching slacks. The melon-colored shirt she wore underneath the jacket gave her skin a flattering glow. Her hair was pulled back into a clip at the base of her head. Nicole looked away, only to find Liz staring at her. There was a knowing look in her eyes. Nicole blushed. She'd been caught.

"Mmm-hmm, I thought so," Liz said, her voice brimmed with a gloating satisfaction.

Kira showed them into a boardroom with a polished gold plaque at the door reading, *The Consulate Room.* An oval table monopolized the small space. On the other end of the wainscot-paneled room, two members of the hotel's catering department were busy fussing over several silver chafing dishes and coffee urns.

Nicole took a deep breath. The alluring aromas of coffee, bacon, and maple syrup made her stomach growl.

There was a balding man in his mid-forties already seated at the head of the table. He lifted a battered briefcase from the carpeted floor and placed it in front of him. He looked to Kira. She nodded her head slightly.

"Good morning, everyone." He pushed his chair back, stood, and held out his right hand to each of them. "My name is Jim Durcan. I'm a friend of Kira's. I'm with the Department of the Treasury, but I'm meeting with you in an unofficial capacity this morning."

Her mother had been stirring sugar into her coffee, but abruptly froze. Recalling the letter from the IRS hidden inside her desk, Nicole understood her mother's angst.

"Please grab some coffee and something to eat," he said, returning to his chair, "and then take a seat. Then I will explain why I'm here."

Kira took a stance in the back of the room. Her brother Mike was nowhere to be seen. At some point, he'd discreetly taken his leave.

"I'm here to share some wonderful news with all of you. Yesterday afternoon, Kira came to my office with an envelope. She asked me to assess a value to the certificates inside." He grew excited, for a few seconds looking more like a six-year-old than a forty-six-year-old. "For those of you not familiar with the term, bearer shares are simply paper certificates. Whoever holds the certificate owns the stock. Bearer stocks are no longer common and haven't been for many years. They were once popular in offshore jurisdictions for perceived confidentiality, but we're a global society nowadays and no one can hide from taxes anymore."

Nicole looked at her family's faces, seeing confusion and incomprehension. It was obvious Kira hadn't said anything to them about the stocks last night, and they were clearly wondering what he was talking about.

"The stocks inside that envelope had been issued for a company called Sinopia over a decade ago," he droned on, completely oblivious to his audience's bewilderment. Only Nicole understood what he was saying. She was listening attentively to his every word. "Back then, Sinopia was a fledgling petroleum company listed only in Hong Kong and London." He removed a set of horn-rimmed bifocals from his suit pocket and placed them over his ears. His hands shook slightly as he pulled a document from this briefcase. "Today, Sinopia ranks as the fifth largest oil company in the world. What I'm trying to tell you is," his voice quivered, "even in today's rough market, the conditions being what we all know they are, the certificates in that envelope are worth roughly two million nine thousand and eighty-six dollars."

CHAPTER TWENTY-FIVE

No freaking way." Nicole looked into Jim Durcan's nondescript features and saw confirmation of the outrageous fortune in his raised brows and expectant grin. Her initial disbelief evaporated. "Two million nine thousand and eighty-six dollars. No wonder everyone was chasing after those damned pieces of paper!"

A brilliant jubilance flowered inside her chest. Kira *was* one of the good guys. And her mother was rich. She slammed her hand down on the table, a giggle of delight erupting. She glanced quickly at Kira. Her expression was no longer indecipherable. She was smiling and her blue eyes were unnaturally bright.

"Mom, you're rich!" Nicole practically shrieked, a wide grin tearing at her cheeks. She jumped from her chair, elated. Her mother stared at Jim Durcan with baleful eyes, her lips pursed tight and her face drawn with disapproval as she shook her head.

"Is that what this is all about?" She pushed her cup of coffee from her and stood up. Looking at Nicole, she spoke in a choked voice. "I was wondering what had gotten into you. Africa for a week, then coming home and pulling apart everything in the attic. Is that what you were looking for?" She was looking at Jim Durcan's briefcase as if the stocks were inside the leather box. "Your father had the audacity to hide contraband in *my* house?"

Her bottom lip quivered. "That's blood money, and I want nothing to do with it."

She made to leave, but Kira stepped forward from the shadows. "Wait, Jane. Please. As I mentioned last night, this is important."

Nicole watched her mother reluctantly return to her seat. She fiddled with the spoon she'd used to stir sugar into her coffee cup, obviously uncomfortable. "I knew Luke was into something bad," she murmured quietly. "That last year of his life, he was secretive and jumpy. Now I finally know why. I spent the past ten years looking over my shoulder, worrying about you girls. Ten years none of us can ever get back," she said through gritted teeth.

"Would someone mind telling me what the hell is going on?" Liz asked, looking back and forth from Nicole to her mother.

"Your father was a thief," Jane Kennedy said, shame in her voice as she pulled her cup toward her then took a sip of coffee. "There. I finally admitted it out loud. I tried to keep it from you girls, but I knew one day the past was going to catch up with us."

"Your husband was no criminal, Jane," Kira said firmly. "Quite the contrary. Those stocks were rightfully his, and now they legally belong to you. While working for Davenport Petroleum as a geologist, Luke Kennedy was also working undercover for the Defense Intelligence Agency."

Nicole's jaw dropped. Just when had Kira been planning on sharing this piece of information with her?

"He was an IGO, which is short for Intelligence Gathering Officer. The Defense Intelligence Agency is a Department of Defense combat support agency. Luke's role, quite simply, was to collect information relevant to whatever case he was assigned. Traveling to Middle Eastern countries as an employee of Davenport provided an excellent cover. And at some point in his tenure, he wisely requested payment for his services in the form of those bearer stocks currently in a locked safe back in Jim's office. Your husband was a very smart, very brave man. He died serving his country."

Nicole watched her mother's entire demeanor slowly begin to lighten. She lifted her head and her brown eyes grew wide. "Is that true?"

Kira nodded. "It is. Not only did Luke do most of his traveling on Davenport's dime, ten years ago, Sinopia stock was worth pennies. His superiors at the agency most likely laughed behind his back, thinking they were getting the far better end of the bargain. But Luke was a geologist and, being on the ground and knowing many people in the oil industry, he was aware of facts few others were. Peers talk to one another. Luke must have heard about the team Sinopia was assembling—geologists from Amoco, Exxon, and investors from families in Kuwait and Saudi Arabia. I'm only guessing here, but I conjecture Luke must have determined the company would one day become quite successful. One of the first purchases Sinopia's board approved was a deal with the Republic of Guinea for oil exploration rights along the country's coast."

Nicole remembered Guinea was once a French colony. Many still spoke the language. Was that why her father had been practicing those Pimsleur tapes? Had he taken a trip to the country himself?

"The company didn't do much with those rights," Kira continued, "at least not until about two years ago when oil prices began skyrocketing and crude was in great demand. That's when someone from Sinopia's West African offshore drilling team hit the mother lode, a well with an estimated three million barrels of oil and twenty-three billion in gas. So you see, Jane, everything is legitimate." The room was quiet for almost a complete minute.

"I can hardly believe this." Nicole saw there were tears in her mother's eyes. "I've done a great dishonor to Luke's memory."

"And there's cash too," Nicole said. "Back at the bank, in his safe deposit box. Maybe another hundred grand."

One of the doors was suddenly thrust open, surprising them all with the force of the action.

It was Bogie. Cool and calm, he poked his bald head into the room, found Kira, nodded and said mysteriously, "They're ready for you."

Kira spoke directly to her mother. "Nicole has been instrumental in an investigation we've been working on. Very soon, we might be able to identify the individuals responsible for your husband's death and hold them accountable in a court of law. We still have quite a few loose ends to tie up, so if you'll please excuse us, both Nicole and I are needed at a debriefing being conducted here at the hotel this morning. Jim will explain everything to you about the stocks, as well as clear up some confusing issues pertaining to your taxes and other matters."

Everyone's attention shifted to Nicole.

Her mother, though still clearly baffled by the revelation of the stocks and their worth, and looking a bit peaked at the mention of taxes, was suddenly beaming at her proudly. She could tell that her sister could hardly wait to get her alone, no doubt to interrogate her about Kira. And for once, Liz's husband, Ted, no longer looked bored.

Nicole grabbed her bag up off the floor, then ran around the table and gave her mother a big hug. "I love you so much, Mom. Everything is going to be okay."

"Thanks to you. Oh, Nicole, I'm so proud of you," her mother gushed affectionately. "You saved me, saved our house." She looked toward the door pensively and Nicole followed her gaze. Kira was making a silent exit. "And it looks you're not done yet. You'd better go. You don't want to keep Hillary waiting!"

Out in the hallway, Nicole had to run to catch up to Kira. She was already halfway down the corridor, walking at a brisk pace in her heels.

"So when were you going to tell me that my father was working undercover?"

"I only just learned the full truth about that last night." Kira said this without even a sideways glance in Nicole's direction. She checked her watch but kept right on walking.

"Oh, while I was passed out unconscious?"

Kira said nothing.

"You're not even going to deny that you drugged me?"

"I had no idea Shevchenko was going to slip you one of her sleeping concoctions," Kira replied, almost apologetically. "She believed you needed to rest, thought you were too wired to do so without an artificial intervention. She thought she would give you a good two or three hours of sleep, not knock you out for the night. If it's any consolation, she's been disciplined and warned in writing never to do anything like that again. Know that she cares a great deal about you, Nicole, and never meant to harm you."

And what about you? Nicole longed to ask. *Do you care anything at all about me?* Instead she said, "And what are my sister and brother-in-law doing here?"

"I told you at the airport. We needed to ensure everyone was safe. We feared that if Rhyse Taylor's people couldn't get your mother, they'd simply abduct some other family member and use them for ransom. So we grabbed all three of them. You and your mother never have to work another day in your lives. You should be ecstatic, so why are you in such a bad mood? Have you eaten any breakfast?"

Nicole shook her head, realizing she'd missed yet another meal. Her stomach growled on cue. Loudly.

Kira rolled her eyes. They passed a conference room; its double doors were open wide to accommodate a large metal cart on wheels piled high with tables and chairs. Inside the room, a silver bowl filled with ripe bananas and green apples sat atop a table alongside trays of mugs and plates. A hotel employee was busy removing the tables, unfolding them and arranging them into a U-shape.

Kira grabbed one of the bananas, smiled, and asked the boy, "Would you mind?"

"Eat up." Kira handed it to Nicole. "Maybe you won't be so cranky with something in your belly." There was the ghost of a smile teasing the curve of her lips.

"Where are we going?" Nicole peeled the banana, breaking off a piece at a time and popping them into her mouth.

They reached the elevators. She dropped the banana peel into one of the polished brass waste bins. The lobby of the hotel was now practically empty. Music from the ceiling speakers, softly muted, could be heard above the hushed voices of the three women manning the front desk. "A room on the second floor." Kira sighed, a forlorn sound in the awkward quiet between them. "A debriefing with my superiors. I usually hate these meetings." She smoothed an invisible wrinkle in her slacks. "But I have hope today's will be different."

Kira stepped inside the elevator. Nicole wavered for a fraction of a second.

"Whoa!" She jumped in just before the doors slid shut. A shiny, smudgeless reflection of herself stared back at her from the gleaming elevator doors, reminding her just how inappropriately she was dressed. She looked down at her sandals, then at the fuzzy image of Kira's pressed suit mirrored in the metal. Turning, she was about to beg for a moment to run back to her room and change when she realized Kira had taken a step toward her.

"I have something to tell you." Kira's voice was husky and warm. Nicole's heart did a somersault inside her chest. Kira took another step closer, and it was suddenly difficult for Nicole to breathe. The smell of Kira, that distinct sweet jasmine and baby powder scent made her insides melt. Kira leaned in. "I need to—"

And then there was an electronic chime and the elevator doors opened. Kira retreated backward, her face showing her annoyance. "I need to tell you something before we go into that room." Her voice wasn't as steady as it normally was. "Stuart's going to ask you to join our team."

Nicole was forced to corral her thoughts and her weak-kneed legs.

"I don't understand." And she didn't. She was confused and disappointed. She'd misread Kira's intention. Again. She thought for sure Kira had not only been about to kiss her, but to say something far more poignant and personal.

"He's going to offer you a job, Nicole." Kira was back in control of herself, and reached out a hand to prevent the elevator doors from closing. "Stuart observed how you handled this situation with Rhyse Taylor and was extremely impressed. Bogie and Shevchenko think you'd make a great addition as well. But I doubt you'd be interested. Teaching is your calling, right?"

Nicole was speechless

"C'mon, we're down the hall, on the left," Kira urged.

There was really no need for the direction. Bogie was standing outside a closed door, making their destination rather obvious. A big grin splintered the serious set of his face when he saw her, his tawny eyes filled with a secret excitement.

Could it be true? Might there be a job offer waiting for her on the other side of the door? And what exactly would she be doing?

She had absolutely no skills and still had another semester of school and a thesis to finish. The few pieces of banana she'd eaten felt like cement blocks in her stomach.

CHAPTER TWENTY-SIX

B ogie brushed the back of his knuckles against the panel of the door three times before a voice on the other side beckoned entry. When it opened, Nicole saw three men sitting around a large mahogany table, papers and files scattered all about its surface. The other side of the room contained a wet bar stocked with a bucket of ice, glassware, and bottles of water. Next to it was a sofa and two reading chairs with a glass table. The men all looked at her, curiosity in their gazes.

"Well, well, well," one of the three said in a booming Texas drawl, rising to his feet. "Is this the sassy little sprite I've been hearing so much about?"

Everyone else was in business attire, but he was dressed in a pale blue chambray shirt, jeans, and black Frye cowboy boots. For a moment, Nicole didn't feel so self-conscious about her own outfit. She turned toward Kira. There was a persuasive glimmer now emanating from her blue eyes, a gentle reassurance in them (*It's all right, I promise*, they seemed to say). She would have much preferred a soft touch or a light squeeze to her shoulder. But Bogie gave her an enthusiastic thumbs-up before closing the door behind him, and that was enough to make her feel better.

"Nicole, this is Judge Jay Carper," Kira said, her manner formal despite Judge Jay's goofy smile and plastic mobility. He was tall, thin, and lanky, reaching out to her, energetically pumping her hand with both of his before pulling her into the room and closer to the morning light spilling though the room's only window.

"Let me have a better look at you, little girl," he said, grinning. He was around fifty, his gray hair receding at the temples and his face drawn with lines of wear from the sun and age. When he opened his mouth, two rubber bands on both sides of his jaw stretched tautly between a netting of wires encasing the upper and bottom rows of his teeth. It took a second for Nicole to realize he was wearing braces.

"Luke Kennedy's daughter, that she is, eh, fellas? Not in the looks department, little lady, lucky you, not that Luke wasn't a handsome buck, but in spirit, you two are one and the same, that's for dang sure." He seemed about ready to slap her on the back in hearty acknowledgment but stopped himself, grabbed two folders from the pile on the table, and tucked them under his left armpit. His Texan charm seemed to turn everything he said and did into a compliment.

"You knew my father?"

Jay Carper shrugged. "Only met him about an hour ago. Pictures and archived computer files. But I could tell we were lucky to have him on our side. By the way," he turned toward Kira, "what's this I'm hearing, Anthony? Stuart said you don't want this pretty little filly on the team."

The judge's remark was aimed at Kira, but his eyes were on Nicole, gauging her reaction to his words. Nicole did her best to hide her response, but the comment stung. Because she knew it was probably true. Maybe that was what Nicole had been about to tell her back in the elevator: *"Stuart will offer you a job, but I don't want you to even consider accepting it."*

"Don't you have some place you need to be, Carper?" one of the two men at the table asked dismissively, tossing a pad of yellow legal paper with a bunch of doodles drawn on it down on the table. He had an exaggerated New York accent and a head of wiry black hair. His eyeglasses were thick and black-framed. Fine dark hairs grew from his bulbous nose, his ears, and all along the back of his neck. Even his fingers were hairy. After straightening his red tie, he took a swig of water from a glass.

"Yup, you're right. Gotta get back to the dog-and-pony show," the judge said, a twinkle in his eyes. "The circus needs their clowns. Pleasure finally meeting you, Nicole. Maybe I'll see ya 'round." He winked at her and this time he did pat her on the back, but his touch was light and not in any way offensive.

"Good God, that buffoon will drive me crazy," the New Yorker complained after the judge left the room. "I apologize, Nicole." He massaged his forehead with two fingers. "That's terribly unprofessional of me to say. Judge Carper is chief judge on the FIS court and is an indispensable member of our team."

"He's still an asshole, though," the silver-haired army man seated next him said in a quiet but gruff aside.

"FIS?" she asked timidly.

"FIS is yet another lovely acronym. Washington does like using them." Kira walked over to where Nicole stood and set an empty glass and a bottle of water down for her in front of a vacant chair. "Foreign Intelligence Surveillance. Jay Carper is one of eleven judges on the FIS court who determines whether or not we have enough cause to monitor individuals we suspect, either here in the States or abroad, of terrorism or espionage."

"Basically, the court grants us permission to spy on Americans," the man in the uniform stated candidly.

"Not how I would choose to word it, but that's how we were able to place listening devices in your house and your apartment," Kira admitted.

Nicole felt her face blanch. She sank into the proffered seat, offended by the fact she'd been a suspect, and a bit scared.

"We were following ghosts," the military man interrupted, steepling his hands over his belly and reclining in his chair. His faded blue eyes considered Nicole thoughtfully. "Dormant for a decade, but come back to haunt and torment us." He glanced at the Kira. "Never would have suspected Kohl," he muttered, shaking his head in disappointment and disbelief.

Kohl? Nicole couldn't recollect where she'd heard the name or why it was so significant. "Before we get completely off track, let's finish the introductions," Kira said, taking control of the room. "Nicole, this is Lieutenant General Joe O'Keefe of the United States Army." She turned to the New Yorker with the red tie and all of the curly hair. "And Stuart Lee. He heads up our team." The two men stood, reached across the table, and shook Nicole's hand.

Again, she eyed her sandals and capri pants dismally. She heard her mother's voice inside her head repeat, *"Better to be overdressed than underdressed."*

She would remember her mother's advice as long as she lived.

"I don't want you any more confused than I'm sure you already are, Nicole," Stuart Lee said kindly, smiling. "We're damned good at doing that. So I'll tell you everything that we now know. Feel free to stop me with questions at any time." He pulled open one of the folders sitting on the table. Nicole could see there was a photo of her father inside of it stapled to a sheaf of papers. "In the late eighties, your father, Luke Kennedy, was recruited to work for what was then a clandestine division of the CIA. The entire department has since been assimilated into what we now know as the Defense Intelligence Agency. Luke worked as a civilian undercover for almost twelve years until he was killed while on assignment in Yemen."

"But back in Kenya," Nicole looked questioningly at Kira, "you said my father might have been involved in something criminal with Rhyse Taylor."

Kira unscrewed the cap from a bottle of water and took a small sip.

"We only just found out about your father's employ with the DIA," Stuart answered. "Someone purged all his records from our databases. Only last night were Shevchenko and an IT team finally able to retrieve some of those documents. But others are lost to us forever. Rhyse Taylor made it look like Luke Kennedy's murder was the act of some random anti-American religious group. With his personnel file and any reports he submitted deleted, Luke Kennedy became just another American citizen in the wrong place at the wrong time." Stuart pushed himself from his chair and shuffled his weight toward the door. He stood to the side of it and jammed his hands into his slacks. "Except they didn't delete everything. There was one handwritten report. Most likely, some type-A administrative bee found it at the bottom of a file cabinet and scanned it into our hard drive back in," he waddled back to the table, lifted one of the papers in the folder up to his face, and squinted, "late 2005. Your father had been dead for five years at that point. Unfortunately, that report wasn't very detailed. It simply linked your father's name to Major Rhyse Taylor of the U.S. Army. There was a blurb in it about the suspected sale of military weapons but not much else. But that one file was all we needed."

"As I already explained to you, Nicole," Kira found her voice, "I was researching past car bombs for a link to bin Laden. When I began looking into the bomb that killed your father, I entered his name into our system, and it was that one handwritten file that popped up, triggering the start of this entire investigation."

"Someone had to have a pretty high security clearance to delete all my father's files, right?"

A look passed between Kira, Stuart, and the general.

"Cassandra Kohl." The general said the name as if it was a curse. "She was your father's go-to at the agency. Unbelievable. She's worked for us for thirty years."

Stuart was still standing. He fumbled through the stack of files until he found the one he'd been searching for. He opened it, pulled out a photo, and pushed it across the table. Nicole picked it up and examined the woman in the photograph. The picture had obviously been taken for a badge of some sort, and looked to be fairly recent. Cassandra Kohl was an elegant woman in her early sixties. Her strawberry blond hair was cut into a fashionable bob and her green eyes looked sharp. Yet as Nicole stared at the picture, the grandmotherly features began taking on a more sinister look. Now she remembered the name. *Kohl*. She'd seen it scrawled upon the back of the computer paper she'd found inside the safe deposit box at the bank.

"This is the woman who killed my father?"

"Rhyse Taylor was the one who planted the car bomb but it was Kohl who ordered it," Kira confirmed. "Back in the day, when Kohl believed herself untouchable, she had her team of IGOs doing her dirty work, searching out Sunni extremists willing to pay large sums of cash for weapons. She and Taylor were quite the team. Kohl drummed up customers and Taylor shipped the weapons he'd been skimming from the military's surplus inventory through an intricate system of shell companies they'd set up. Your father Luke must have figured out their scheme."

"But we know all this *now*," Stuart said. "When we first came upon that lone PDF file, we had no idea the can of worms we were about to open." He pushed his heavy glasses up over the bridge of his nose. "We set Shevchenko up with access to the mainframes at the Pentagon to see what she could find out about Luke Kennedy. Who was he? Was he a chance victim? A whistleblower? Then we had Bogie look into what Rhyse Taylor was up to these days. You can imagine our shock when Shevchenko informed us Kohl had been using her security clearance to conduct searches for bank accounts in your father's name and Bogie told us that Rhyse Taylor's daughter had just moved into an apartment with you."

"They were both looking for the stocks," Nicole deduced out loud. "But why now? Ten years after they killed my father?"

Stuart paced the room. "Sinopia only recently became a name in the news when they hit that well off the coast of Guinea. Almost overnight the company became the sensation of the stock market. Their stocks went from three dollars a share to sixty-five dollars. I'm sure it was quite a memorable event for Kohl when one of her IGOs asked to be compensated in the form of a bearer stock. The name Sinopia must have stayed with her all these years. As his immediate superior, I can only surmise she had somewhat of a close relationship with your father and knew he was hoarding the stocks in a safe place. But ten years later, she probably had no idea if those stocks were still out there, sitting somewhere waiting to be discovered or if your mother knew of their existence and had already cashed them in. But Kohl was determined to find out. She most likely understood if they were still floating around, they were now worth millions. And she knew your father was clever. The stocks could be anywhere. So the first thing she did was rekindle her relationship with Rhyse Taylor. Together, they used his daughter Danielle to do their dirty work."

Nicole flinched. She'd completely forgotten about Danielle. What had happened to her?

"When they came up empty-handed, they went to Plan B. The threatening letters your mother received back in the spring from the IRS, her mortgage company, even the school district, looked authentic because they were." Stuart opened another folder. "These are mug shots of all the hackers Kohl and Taylor bribed or hired. Some of these morons actually had fairly decent jobs with the treasury department or school district. Benefits and 401(k)s. Idiots." He closed the folder, a look of disgust pinching his brows together. "Kohl figured if mounting financial pressure didn't force your mother to cash in the stocks, she was throwing in the towel. And that's what happened. When money didn't magically appear in your mother's bank account to cover all the bills that began arriving at her house, Kohl wiped her hands of it. Told Taylor she was done. That was about two months ago. Taylor too had given up the chase. But again, we didn't know any of this. We only knew you and Danielle had been living together. And suddenly you're booking a flight to Nairobi. We were confused. Maybe the wiretaps hadn't picked up all your conversations."

"I didn't know about Danielle. And I really did go to Kenya to teach."

"We know that now, Nicole," Stuart replied pleasantly. "Coincidence can be fate working in mysterious ways."

"Remember in Nairobi when you were stuck sitting on the bus, waiting for the driver?" Kira asked Nicole. She nodded, slowly recalling the oppressive heat and her fatigue.

"You were actually waiting for me. I was in the ticket office on a conference call with Stuart and General O'Keefe and a few other fun-loving bureaucrats. We were delayed, waiting for one of the higher-ups to approve our method of interrogating you. I knew you wouldn't sit on that bus much longer, so I hung up and took the risk."

Nicole raised her brows. Red tape wasn't easy to navigate around in any organization, never mind one involving an agency of the United States government. If things had not worked out as they had, Kira Anthony would have been the fall guy in all of this.

"There's one thing I don't understand," Nicole said, frowning. "When I met Rhyse Taylor at the airport, he seemed almost too eager to implicate Kohl in all of this. At the time, I thought he was referring to Kira. He even went so far as to tell me my father had been working undercover."

"You called Danielle." Stuart heaved his body into a chair and dabbed at his unibrow with the tip of his tie. "You told her you'd been kidnapped by someone from the government. Taylor thought Kohl was double-crossing him. I'm sure he was in a rage when his flight landed?"

"Now that you mention it, yeah, he was."

"But now he knew where the stocks were. He was determined to get them before Kohl. He hired three goons to kidnap your mother, then run you and Danielle off the road. And now here we are."

The room was oddly quiet. "So that's it?" she asked warily. "Kohl and Taylor are in jail?"

"Yeah, for about three minutes," Stuart replied. "Taylor's already got himself a date with a judge this afternoon requesting bond. Kohl might be in the clinker till Monday, but she'll be out."

"But they're murderers!" Nicole was aghast.

"And traitors," the general chimed in, rocking back in his chair.

Kira took a sip of water, then said dejectedly, "We're charging them both with murder and treason, but we've got zip to go to trial with. We've no evidence, physical or circumstantial, tying either one of them to the car bomb that took your father's life. Shevchenko and her IT guys had little luck resurrecting deleted files. They found a few, but none supplying us with anything to substantiate our claims. In the span of ten years, the mainframes' operating systems have been updated about four times and cleaned and purged about three million."

"And there's a bunch of crooks still out there," the general carped, leaning forward and impaling Nicole with a piercing blue stare. "Kohl and Taylor didn't manage the arms deals by themselves. They needed a team of insiders to move the shipments, fabricate inventories, et cetera, et cetera. The nameless scumbags are probably sitting back collecting a pension and veteran benefits or, for all I know, maybe they're still serving. Hell, I probably placed a few medals on their lapels. Or maybe they pinned a few on mine."

Nicole's mind raced. She recalled Kira's constant questioning about the contents inside the safe deposit box. Only now did Nicole understand it hadn't been the stocks she'd been seeking. In her mind's eye, she saw the names written in her father's familiar scribble. *Kohl and Taylor.* She was having difficulty drawing air into her lungs as the realization of what she possessed slowly dawned upon her.

CHAPTER TWENTY-SEVEN

I think I have something that may help prove Kohl and Taylor's guilt." Nicole made to stand, but her feet had become entangled with the strap of her shoulder bag. Frustrated, she wrestled it off, watching it land inches from the general's glossy black dress shoes. "In the safe deposit box, there was an envelope with my name on it. Inside was a sheet of paper with a bunch of jumbled letters. It made no sense to me at the time."

Kira's face was instantly alight with hope, her voice eager. "My God, Nicole, please tell me you still have this paper?"

"I'll go get it!"

Kira pulled out her phone. "Shevchenko, meet us in the debriefing room. Bring your laptop. Hurry!"

Nicole ran for the elevator, her heart pounding in her chest. She prayed housekeeping hadn't cleaned her room yet. The envelope had been inside her bra. She hadn't paid any attention to where it had fallen when she'd undressed this morning.

The elevators seemed to move in slow motion, but finally she was at her room ramming the keycard into the designated slot. When at last the little light above the handle glowed a bright lime green, she flung open the door and rushed inside. Her heart, which had been hammering wildly, slowed to a dull thud. All of her clothes had been picked up off the floor and were now folded neatly, stacked on the edge of the made bed in a nice square stack.

Normally, she would have felt a moment's discomfort for having left her things for someone else to tidy, but she had one thing on her mind—finding that envelope.

Frantic, she tore through the clothes then peeked under the bed. Nothing. The wastebaskets were empty too. She cast an anxious glance back toward her clothing, which were now strewn around the room haphazardly. Maybe it had become stuck in the folds of one of her garments. Once more, this time slower and with more consideration, she carefully picked through her pants, her bra, her shirt, and her underwear. No luck.

Hands on her hips, she stood in the center of the hotel room scanning every inch of the recently vacuumed carpet but in her mind she knew exactly what had become of the envelope. She could see the crumpled paper clearly, wet with crud, stained and now most likely unreadable, sitting at the bottom of an industrial-sized garbage bag in the hotel's Dumpster.

Stuart said Colonel Taylor's appearance in court was sometime this afternoon. How long would it take to sift through all the morning's trash? She glanced to the digital clock on the nightstand. It was already a few minutes after ten. That left less than two hours to find the envelope. She did a double take. There, next to the pen and pad of paper with the Ritz-Carlton's fancy letterhead…a scrunched-up accordion of white paper. Could it be her father's envelope? It was. She closed her eyes and breathed a long sigh of relief. There was a strong temptation to shove the paper back into her bra for safekeeping, but instead she hugged it to her chest and raced back to the second floor, promising the universe she would reward the housekeeper with a few of the seven hundred bucks remaining in her bank account. When she got to the meeting room, breathless and winded, Stella was just powering her laptop. Everyone stopped and stared at her, identical looks of anxious expectation stamped across their faces.

"Found it!" she exclaimed excitedly, waving the envelope over her head. With a clumsy lack of finesse, she pulled the computer paper from the creased packet and handed it to Kira.

Kira spread the sheet of incoherent letters out on the table for everyone to view. The general was the only one who didn't get up. He did, however, finally lift his eyes from his BlackBerry for all of thirty seconds to determine if there was anything developing worthy of his consideration, but grew bored and returned to his e-mail.

"Looks like your father used a method called crypto source coding to encrypt his communication." Stuart studied the letters for a long moment. "It was quite a popular tool IGOs used out in the field during the eighties and nineties to communicate with one another. Simple but effective. They'd all agree on a series of numbers and use it to decode their messages. Change it up every week or so. But even if he used something more complex, Stella has every cryptography program ever created."

"Mono-alphabetic substitution," Stella concluded with the same scientific certainty a gemologist might identify a natural diamond amidst a pile of man-made clones. She grabbed the document from the table, sank her long, slinky body back into a chair, then slowly typed each letter into data entry fields that were similar to the squares on a crossword puzzle. When she was done, she turned to Nicole. "What's the key, little one?"

"Key?" Nicole repeated, having difficulty keeping up with their job-related vernacular.

"The numbers to decipher your father's encryption. What are they?"

"Oh my God, are you serious?" Nicole looked to Kira, panic coming over her. "I have no idea!"

"Yes, you do," Kira insisted calmly, picking up the computer paper. "Your father wrote your name on the envelope this was in. He intended for *you* to find it. No one else. So think, Nicole. What numbers would have been significant between the two of you?"

Nicole squeezed her eyes shut. She could feel everyone watching her, waiting for her to hurry up and figure it out. *No pressure here, folks. The show will be over soon when my brain explodes. Get ready, because it's going to blow. You may want to back up. Three, two, one...* She put her hands over her ears and leaned forward, supporting her head with her elbows on her knees.

"Concentrate!" she silently implored, squeezing her temples harder. What numbers were important to her dad? Their old phone number? Their address? But then she heard Stuart's voice coming from faraway as a visual of an old photograph of her and her father taken on her seventh birthday in front of their newly planted willow tree slowly appeared before her eyes: *"Coincidence can be fate working in mysterious ways."*

"It might be 423," she mumbled hesitantly, lifting her head up. And then, recalling her recent encounters with the three digits—her flight number to Kenya, the safe deposit box, and the motel key—she said the number again, but more firmly and with confidence. "Yes, try 423. It has to be!"

"April twenty-third, your birthday," Kira breathed softly. "That makes perfect sense."

For one brief moment, it was as if it was just the two of them all alone in the room. Kira's blue eyes were bright with suppressed emotion, but there seemed to be a deeper significance to the visual interchange. It felt like an invisible current of energy was passing back and forth between them, and if Nicole allowed it, the force could easily overtake her entire being and she'd happily shatter into a million fragments of pure white light.

"Okay, 423. I'll try every fourth letter, second and third," Stella said, breaking the spell. "Not sure if the algorithm will be based on letters across, down, or vertical, and in the order of 423, but I'll take a shot."

As the morning aged, the sun had grown stronger and the small room even stuffier. When Stuart Lee wasn't tinkering with the thermostat's controls, he was pacing back and forth, occasionally hunching over Stella's shoulder, pushing his glasses up and squinting at the laptop screen. After about five minutes, which felt more like sixty to Nicole, Stella pushed the computer away from her and shook her loose, dark hair side to side. "No, that cannot be. It cannot."

"What?" everyone demanded simultaneously.

"You're not going to believe this." She turned the laptop around so that they could see the word that kept repeating itself across the screen: "Home."

"That's impossible." Kira frowned, a divot forming between her eyebrows. "That house has been searched more times than Scotland's Loch Ness, by us as well as Danielle Taylor."

"I know where he hid it." Nicole reached for her shoulder bag where it still lay strewn at the general's polished feet. After unzipping the inside pouch, she pulled the tiny Chinese fortune from it and placed it on the table. "This was in the safe deposit box, on top of the envelope."

Kira picked it up and read it out loud. "Your best friend is often in the mirror." She shrugged her shoulders. "I don't get it. Chinese fortune cookie wisdom?"

"In my mother's house, at the end of the stairway, there's an old gold mirror. It's as ugly as sin—been there for as long as I can remember. It's heavy too. We tried to take it down once to paint the hallway. We ended up painting around it. I think we inherited it from my grandparents."

The general spoke but his eyes remained glued to his BlackBerry. "There's an extra mirror. The backing's a dummy. If you remove it, you'll find nothing. But between the two pieces of glass, if there's anything worth hiding, that's where it'll be."

Stuart checked his watch. "We need to move quickly. The judicial task force will want to look at whatever we find before court at three. Bethesda, right?" He asked Nicole. "That's where your mother's house is?"

Nicole nodded. "Yes!"

"We can send a few military cops over." He was thinking out loud now, his actions pensive. "Or call the locals."

"Hell no!" the general barked, for the first time that morning becoming fully engaged in the proceedings. He shoved his phone into his trousers, jerked erect, and marched around the table, slamming the flat soles of his dress shoes against the carpet like they were boots and he'd just been given orders to attack. "At this point, I don't trust anyone. I'll go there myself."

"We don't have time," Stuart complained, running meaty fingers through his black curls. "With traffic, it'll take over an hour."

"Who said anything about driving?" The general seemed almost merry. "Kira, your brother's meeting with the Coast Guard this morning, showing them his latest bird, isn't that so?"

Kira looked suspicious. "Yes, he's bidding for the new contract."

"Give 'em a call and tell 'em I need a lift. Pronto."

"I'll come too," Stella said, closing her laptop. "I know the kid's house better than anyone else." With a sly wink aimed at Nicole, she explained, "I'm the one who bugged it."

Kira and the general moved back to the table to work out the details of the helicopter ride. They had Kira's brother Mike on speakerphone. Stuart was shouting into his cell phone too and the room became a noisy cacophony of voices talking over one another.

"Hey, kiddo. Sorry about yesterday. I didn't mean to knock you out." Stella pulled Nicole into a corner furnished with a fake ficus tree. Her big black eyes were sheepish. "Just so you know, I didn't give you anything illegal. Just half a dose of over-the-counter sleeping medication. Fifteen milligrams of diphenhydramine. Kira thinks it's my own proprietary sleeping potion and I let her think that. Makes me more valuable to her. But I only thought it would help you relax."

"No worries, Stella. I really did need the sleep. I was running on dead batteries. Here," she said, digging through her bag and handing her house keys to Stella. "This way you don't have to kick my mother's door down. Do you want me to hold your laptop until you come back?"

"Oh no, little one. I never go anywhere without my baby."

She patted the hard black plastic fondly, then grew serious. "Do you remember yesterday when you asked me about what I wrote down on your ticket before you left Kenya?"

"Remember the tin man. You said it was a clue to help me find the heart in the tree."

As if to ensure no one else was listening to their conversation, Stella cast a quick glance around the room. They were standing so close to one another, Nicole could make out a thin vein through her thick, black bangs. Its slightly bulging length ran from her hairline down to her temple.

"Yeah, kid, and maybe now that you found your secret heart, you can help someone else find hers." Her dark, heavy-lidded eyes strayed significantly from Nicole's brown ones over to where Kira was talking to the general and settled there. "Sadly, it's been lost far too long. I probably shouldn't tell you this—no, I know I shouldn't." She looked conflicted. "I'm breaking Kira's trust, but I want her to be happy. I thought you might find it interesting to know that when we first put you under surveillance, I would find her spending an unwarranted amount of time watching you, listening to your conversations, tracking your movements. I'd often tease her, say that she had a crush on you. Of course, she denied this. But when I saw how she took care of you when you became ill, I never teased her again. And then, when I found her chained to the table yesterday morning, I was certain. Kira Anthony has never let her guard down. Ever."

Nicole felt herself turn red. "I sort of imagined she had a girl in every port, so to speak."

"C'mon, Stella, we're moving out!" the general growled eagerly as he rocketed past them. "We've got a helicopter to catch."

Seeing the sudden commotion, Stuart quickly finished the conversation he was having and closed his phone. "Wait a second, you two! We've got a few details to coordinate!"

But the general was already through the door and Stella was running after him. Stuart was about to give chase but stopped short when his eyes met Nicole's. Kira remained by the door, holding it open for him.

"When we have a chance to have a normal conversation, Kira and I have something very important to ask you." His eyes darted nervously from Nicole to Kira, then back to her again. Beads of perspiration dotted his forehead. He rubbed at the moisture with the back of his hand. "I wish we had time right now," he took in a gigantic breath of air, "but I think you understand the time constraints we're under. Maybe over dinner tonight?"

Nicole nodded agreeably, then Stuart took off as fast as his excess flesh would allow, hollering down the hallway, "Wait up!"

CHAPTER TWENTY-EIGHT

So, would you accept Stuart's job offer of a job?" Kira moved from the doorway over to the window. She stood quietly, staring out into the bright morning sunshine without comment. Beyond her, the second-floor window framed a pale blue sky dotted with white puffy clouds. Whatever else might happen, at least Mike's helicopter would not be delayed by foul weather. Nicole's eyes returned to Kira. She noticed how tired and thin she suddenly looked. The tendons of her neck stood out prominently and the graceful curve of her face appeared even more fragile. Why had she not noticed this before?

Four, maybe five feet of carpeted flooring separated them, but Nicole knew it could easily be a million miles. She thought about what Stella had said before running off with the general. Help Kira find her heart, she'd encouraged. How was Nicole supposed to accomplish such a colossal feat? The woman was a complete mystery. For Nicole to even attempt to solve the enigma of Kira Anthony, she'd need time, eons of it. A magic potion wouldn't hurt either. She smiled inwardly, shoving her hands into her pockets as she cast a besotted gaze upon the woman she'd fallen for. If only she had that time, maybe she could break through those walls, navigate through the invisible barbed wire and dance around the land mines to get to her heart, but time was something she simply didn't have. Once the helicopter returned with whatever information her father had stashed away behind the mirror, Kira's work here would be done and she'd be gone from Nicole's life for good. Unless…

"C'mon, Kira, give me some credit for not being a completely gullible dolt. As much as I'd love to believe that Stuart finds me worthy of such a spectacular consideration, I can't help but think you're having an incredible laugh at my expense. The little I know about al-Qaeda, I learned from Wikipedia."

"We need someone who can read Arabic," Kira replied in her typical nonchalant manner. She stepped away from the window toward the couch and, after a quick peek at her watch, decided to make use of its comfort, but not before removing her jacket and tossing it across the back of a cushion. Nicole stayed where she was by the door, leaning her weight against the wall, but her eyes followed hungrily.

"All right, I'll bite." She knew she probably sounded like an idiot, giving the outlandishly improbable proposition merit. "What would I need to do? Enroll in some sort of specialized training program after I finished school?"

"You'd fly to Paris with us next week and begin on-the-job training immediately." She unclipped her hair, then combed her hands through the silky strands. Nicole couldn't help but admire the taut definition of her arm muscles. The woman had no body fat.

"I should warn you, Stuart will try to make this position sound much more cloak and dagger than it really is. Although we travel extensively, our work can still be rather mundane. Long hours in front of a computer and lots and lots of rules and regulations. The tasks you'll initially be assigned will be mostly administrative. If you've had any dealings with the government, then you know there's a ton of paperwork associated with every simple operation."

"So I'll be your secretary?"

"That's an interesting premise." An amorous glow brightened her eyes. "The idea of you bring me coffee in the morning calls to mind all sorts of entertaining scenarios," Kira said in a low voice overflowing with sexual innuendo.

Nicole tried to quell her growing excitement. The prospect of spending every day at Kira's side suddenly seemed very viable. She had to remind herself it was never going to happen.

Fantastic things like this happened to other people, not her. Yes, life had taken an odd turn about fourteen days back, but it was just a matter of time before the universe corrected itself and her world returned to its dull but stable rhythm. Still, she indulged that part of her mind's penchant to believe fairy tales could actually come true. A position on their team not only sounded like a dream come true, but it would give her the time she so desperately needed to win Kira's heart. When she spoke, she couldn't quite keep the helix of hopeful elation from bursting to life inside her and inflecting the tone of her words.

"But what would I do about school? I have one more semester and my thesis to finish."

"Stuart would mostly likely see to it that the work you performed in the field substituted for the dissertation you're required to write in order to graduate. They have various ways of making things work to their benefit, so you needn't be concerned. Once the agency decides they want you, they'll do pretty much anything to ensure your recruitment goes smoothly. And they do want you, Nicole."

"But you don't, do you?" Nicole had sensed Kira's reluctance but had hesitated to give voice to it. "Want me, I mean. Judge Carper said as much."

"Oh, I do want you," Kira admitted huskily. "I don't think I can deny that any longer. But not on my team," she added firmly, crossing her arms. "The first argument I've ever had with Stuart. He and I got into it pretty bad this morning."

Nicole's spirit had been soaring but now it plummeted like a flaming ball of hot metal submerged into cold liquid. She'd anticipated rejection, but to hear it come from Kira's perfect lips so matter-of-factly hurt like hell.

"Does he know about us?"

"Us?" Kira questioned, slipping her shoes from her feet and stretching her long legs out in front of the couch.

"You know," Nicole flushed, her voice almost inaudible. "About what happened between us the other night."

"I didn't *out* you to Stuart, if that's what you're asking. I simply explained to him that my," she paused to consider her words, "*feelings* for you might not be entirely professional and it would be best for all parties involved if he were to place you somewhere else within the agency. Forcing us to work closely together on a daily basis might prove to be detrimental to the harmony of the team. But he's a stubborn New Yorker." Kira laid her head back and sighed wearily. "Obviously determined to have things his way."

Nicole fought the impulse to ask just what kind of *feelings* Kira had for her. "Would working with me really be so bad?" She walked into the room then cautiously took a seat at the other end of the couch. "You make it sound like a punishment."

"Are you serious?" Kira stared at Nicole, eyes wide with incredulity. "I almost sent an innocent girl to jail. Danielle had absolutely no knowledge whatsoever of her father's criminal exploits. I was jealous. So jealous it skewed my perception, something that's never happened in my career. I had that poor girl tried and convicted before she'd even been charged." A possessive gleam emanated from the depths of her clear blue eyes. "God, I can't think straight," she shook her head, "I can't concentrate when you're around. Even right now, with the threat of someone walking in unexpectedly, I want to push you down into the couch and ravish you with my hands and mouth."

Nicole's heart quickened its beat. At last, something encouraging.

"That sounds like a good thing."

Kira lowered her head and sighed again. "Nicole, I've devoted every minute of every day since my parents were killed pursuing the cowards responsible for their murders."

Running, she's always running.

Those were the words that popped into Nicole's mind. She remembered Kira had admitted as much that night of the storm, before they'd made love.

Kira lifted her head, and Nicole saw so much suffering in her features. This woman had been prepared to forfeit living a full life to avenge the murder of her parents. Why? Did she somehow feel guilty for being alive when her parents were dead? Was this what kept her from letting anyone in? She longed to reach out, take Kira in her arms and comfort her, hold her, love her but feared the results might be cataclysmic. Time, she reminded herself. Time and patience.

"I've worked very hard to avoid emotional entanglements, and for the most part, I've been successful keeping distractions to a minimum. This," she touched her chest with a manicured finger, "is all new to me and I'm not really sure how we proceed here. Just for the record, I've never before mixed business with pleasure."

Nicole had no clue how to respond. Should she be flattered or was she being told to take a hike and not let the door hit her in the behind on the way out?

"You never know, Kira." Nicole swallowed hard, gathering her waning courage. "Now that we're not adversaries wary of one another's motives, we might actually work well together." She turned slightly, sliding her hand tentatively across the cushion, the effect imbuing her overture with a guileless sincerity. "Let me help you," she whispered.

Kira lowered her eyes. "Why would you want to do that, Nicole?"

"Because I love you," she yearned to say, but the words echoed inside her head unspoken. It would be a long, long time before she could give voice to such sentiments—weeks, months, maybe even years. To do so too soon would be like trying to throw a saddle on a wild horse the day after capture. Her hand

MISSION OF DESIRE

remained where it was, outstretched, waiting for reciprocation. Kira looked into Nicole's eyes, then down at her hand.

A cell phone rang, startling them both. Nicole withdrew her hand.

"It's Stella," Kira informed her excitedly after grabbing her phone from her jacket's pocket. As Kira listened, Nicole watched a smile light up her face and thought how amazing it would be to see her do that more often.

"You were right!" She held the phone to the side of her mouth so that she could share every word of Stella's conversation. "They found five data-filled CDs taped between the two mirrors in your mother's stairway!" She held up a finger to indicate Stella was talking. "Stella said they're just getting back onto the helicopter, so she won't be able to talk, but they loaded the CDs onto her laptop." She returned to listening mode, her trance-like gaze staring off into space, but she reached across and grabbed Nicole's hand where it lay in her lap. Their fingers meshed, entwined, squeezed. The significance of the gesture was not lost upon Nicole. They fit perfectly, like pieces of a puzzle.

"Apparently, the evidence is better than we could have hoped for," Kira said breathlessly, closing her phone. "Your father actually captured Kohl on film in the act. There are pictures of her meeting with several suspected terrorists, as well as bank statements from three overseas accounts with a detailed list of deposits and wire transfers."

"That's awesome!" Nicole faltered mid-syllable, uncertain her exultation was appropriate considering what they were discussing.

"It is awesome," Kira softly assured her, staring hard into her eyes. Nicole wanted to look away but she couldn't. Their hands were still clasped tightly together. She was appalled to feel the tingling awareness between her legs pulse and surge to life. Now was definitely not the time to be thinking about sex, yet it was as if her body was operating separately from her head.

She gazed longingly at Kira's mouth, remembering the taste and feel of her lips, the light pressure of her hands, the coaxing encouragements.

Kira suddenly closed the distance between them, pulling Nicole across the couch and into her arms. "If you look at me like that while we're working together, Bogie and Shevchenko are going to get quite an eyeful." She cradled Nicole's face in her hands and slowly kissed her. After a few minutes, she raised her mouth, her breathing ragged, face flushed with want. "Are you sure you want to work with me, Nicole?"

Kira was watching her, appraising her, her blue eyes filled with emotion. There was another meaning entirely in her softly spoken words.

Shock deprived Nicole of the ability to speak. When she did finally find her voice, her words emerged as little more than a whisper. "I've never been more sure of anything in my entire life."

About the Author

Terri Richards lives in Tampa, Florida, and loves the outdoors, international travel, eating organic, and keeping fit.

Books Available From Bold Strokes Books

Dark Wings Descending by Lesley Davis. What if the demons you face in life are real? Chicago detective Rafe Douglas is about to find out. (978-1-60282-660-1)

sunfall by Nell Stark and Trinity Tam. The final installment of the everafter series. Valentine Darrow and Alexa Newland work to rebuild their relationship even as they find themselves at the heart of the struggle that will determine a new world order for vampires and wereshifters. (978-1-60282-661-8)

Mission of Desire by Terri Richards. Nicole Kennedy finds herself in Africa at the center of an international conspiracy and is rescued by the beautiful but arrogant government agent Kira Anthony—but can Nicole trust Kira, or is she blinded by desire? (978-1-60282-662-5)

Boys of Summer, edited by Steve Berman. Stories of young love and adventure, when the sky's ceiling is a bright blue marvel, when another boy's laughter at the beach can distract from dull summer jobs. (978-1-60282-663-2)

The Locket and the Flintlock by Rebecca S. Buck. When Regency gentlewoman Lucia Foxe is robbed on the highway, will the masked outlaw who stole Lucia's precious locket also claim her heart? (978-1-60282-664-9)

Calendar Boys by Zachary Logan. A man a month will keep you excited year-round. (978-1-60282-665-6)

Burgundy Betrayal by Sheri Lewis Wohl. Park Ranger Kara Lynch has no idea she's a witch until dead bodies begin to pile up in her park, forcing her to turn to beautiful and sexy shape-shifter Camille Black Wolf for help in stopping a rogue werewolf. (978-1-60282-654-0)

LoveLife by Rachel Spangler. When Joey Lang unintentionally becomes a client of life coach Elaine Raitt, the relationship becomes complicated as they develop feelings that make them question their purpose in love and life. (978-1-60282-655-7)

The Fling by Rebekah Weatherspoon. When the ultimate fantasy of a one-night stand with her trainer, Oksana Gorinkov, suddenly turns into more, reality show producer Annie Collins opens her life to a new type of love she's never imagined. (978-1-60282-656-4)

Ill Will by J.M. Redmann. New Orleans PI Micky Knight must untangle a twisted web of healthcare fraud that leads to murder—and puts those closest to her most at risk. (978-1-60282-657-1)

Buccaneer Island by J.P. Beausejour. In the rough world of Caribbean piracy, a man is what he makes of himself—or what a stronger man makes of him. (978-1-60282-658-8)

Twelve O'Clock Tales by Felice Picano. The fourth collection of short fiction by legendary novelist and memoirist Felice Picano. Thirteen dark tales that will thrill and disturb, discomfort and titillate, enthrall and leave you wondering. (978-1-60282-659-5)

Words to Die By by William Holden. Sixteen answers to the question: What causes a mind to curdle? (978-1-60282-653-3)

Tyger, Tyger, Burning Bright by Justine Saracen. Love does not conquer all, but when all of Europe is on fire, it's better than going to hell alone. (978-1-60282-652-6)

Night Hunt by L.L. Raand. When dormant powers ignite, the wolf Were pack is thrown into violent upheaval, and Sylvan's pregnant mate is at the center of the turmoil. A Midnight Hunters novel. (978-1-60282-647-2)

Demons are Forever by Kim Baldwin and Xenia Alexiou. Elite Operative Landis "Chase" Coolidge enlists the help of high-class call girl Heather Snyder to track down a kidnapped colleague embroiled in a global black market organ-harvesting ring. (978-1-60282-648-9)

Runaway by Anne Laughlin. When Jan Roberts is hired to find a teenager who has run away to live with a group of antigovernment survivalists, she's forced to return to the life she escaped when she was a teenager herself. (978-1-60282-649-6)

Street Dreams by Tama Wise. Tyson Rua has more than his fair share of problems growing up in New Zealand—he's gay, he's falling in love, and he's run afoul of the local hip-hop crew leader just as he's trying to make it as a graffiti artist. (978-1-60282-650-2)

Women of the Dark Streets: Lesbian Paranormal by Radclyffe and Stacia Seaman, eds. Erotic tales of the supernatural—a world of vampires, werewolves, witches, ghosts, and demons—by the authors of Bold Strokes Books. (978-1-60282-651-9)

Derrick Steele: Private Dick—The Case of the Hollywood Hustlers by Zavo. Derrick Steele, a hard-drinking, lusty private detective, is being framed for the murder of a hustler in downtown Los Angeles. When his brother's friend Daniel McAllister joins the investigation, their growing attraction might prove to be more explosive than the case. (978-1-60282-596-3)

Nice Butt: Gay Anal Eroticism edited by Shane Allison. From toys to teasing, spanking to sporting, some of the best gay erotic scribes celebrate the hottest and most creative in new erotica. (978-1-60282-635-9)

Murder in the Irish Channel by Greg Herren. Chanse MacLeod investigates the disappearance of a female activist fighting the Archdiocese of New Orleans and a powerful real estate syndicate. (978-1-60282-584-0)

Initiation by Desire by MJ Williamz. Jaded Sue and innocent Tulley find forbidden love and passion within the inhibiting confines of a sorority house filled with nosy sisters. (978-1-60282-590-1)

Toughskins by William Masswa. John and Bret are two twenty-something athletes who find that love can begin in the most unlikely of places, including a "mom-and-pop shop" wrestling league. (978-1-60282-591-8)

me@you.com by KE Payne. Is it possible to fall in love with someone you've never met? Imogen Summers thinks so because it's happened to her. (978-1-60282-592-5)

Bloody Claws by Winter Pennington. In the midst of aiding the police, Preternatural Private Investigator Kassandra Lyall finally finds herself at serious odds with Sheila Morris, the local werewolf pack's Alpha female, when Sheila abuses someone Kassandra has sworn to protect. (978-1-60282-588-8)

Awake Unto Me by Kathleen Knowles. In turn of the century San Francisco, two young women fight for love in a world where women are often invisible and passion is the privilege of the powerful. (978-1-60282-589-5)